DOUBLE SHADOW

Also by Andrew Ludington

Splinter Effect

DOUBLE SHADOW

A Splinter Effect Novel

ANDREW LUDINGTON

MINOTAUR BOOKS
NEW YORK

This is a work of fiction. All of the names, characters, organizations, places, and events portrayed in this work are either products of the author's imagination or used fictitiously.

First published in the United States by Minotaur Books, an imprint of St. Martin's Publishing Group

EU Representative: Macmillan Publishers Ireland Ltd, 1st Floor, The Liffey Trust Centre, 117–126 Sheriff Street Upper, Dublin 1, D01 YC43

 Printed in the United States of America. For information, address St. Martin's Publishing Group, 120 Broadway, New York, NY 10271.

www.minotaurbooks.com

Designed by Meryl Sussman Levavi

The Library of Congress Cataloging-in-Publication Data is available upon request.

ISBN 978-1-250-34933-0 (hardcover)
ISBN 978-1-250-34934-7 (ebook)

First Edition: 2026

10 9 8 7 6 5 4 3 2 1

To my parents, biological and otherwise, present and departed, for never talking me out of being crazy

DOUBLE SHADOW

ROME

64 CE

If Rabbit Ward could have foreseen the series of events he was about to set into motion, he might have done things differently. He might not have stayed for the last act of the bawdy farce being performed at the Theatre of Marcellus to a tepid audience. He might have tried to steal the scrolls earlier from the Porticus Octaviae. He certainly wouldn't have followed the screams. But that's history for you. Woulda, coulda, shoulda.

The Great Fire of Rome, the one Nero supposedly fiddled through? It had kindled to life about an hour ago and was presently consuming the north side of the Aventine Hill. The city was in a mad panic, which was precisely why Rabbit had traveled back to this time.

Breathing through a wet cloth against the smoke, he climbed out of the deep hole at the foot of the Domus Tiberiana, on the northwestern corner of the Palatine, where he had just buried a thick-walled lead box. From the ashes of the fire, Nero would initiate a program of civic reconstruction, including a pedestrian bridge over the shops of the Vicus Tuscus connecting the Palace to the Forum. With a little luck, Rabbit's box would be protected under the bridge support for a few thousand years, safe and sound and ready for excavation when he got home.

The quarry this time was a collection of scrolls written by the former Emperor Claudius, most notably his Etruscan dictionary, which promised to illuminate present-day scholars about that confounding early Italian language. It was a good grab.

Since the practical application of time travel began in the late 1990s, Rabbit had been the Smithsonian's senior chrono-archaeologist for the ancient and classical Mediterranean. The rules of engagement were simple. Steal the treasure. Hide the treasure. Get back to the exact spot where you entered the time-space twenty days earlier to go home. Don't change anything.

Rabbit was very good at his job.

He dusted himself off as he hopped down from the terrace. Time to go home.

He had left a horse stabled outside the Porta Aurelia, the closest exit from the walled city, due west across the Tiber. Hundred-foot columns of flame were dancing over the shoulders of the Circus Maximus as they consumed the rickety insulae on the Aventine, but Rabbit's path would be clear and easy until the wind shifted north. He had plenty of time.

Feeling happy about a job well done, he set off at an easy jog for the river, passing furtive knots of criminals looting everything that wasn't nailed down from the quaint little stores.

In a few minutes, he was passing through the Forum Boarium, the downtown cattle market. No one had cleared out the calves from their pens, and the poor things were bellowing in terror as black smoke choked out the sun. The din was unnerving. Rabbit had to fight the urge to release them. He tried to close his ears as he ran between two wharf warehouses.

Rabbit skidded to a stop, every nerve lit up.

That was a scream.

It wasn't the full-throated scream of terror. This was the voice of pain, scraping through a clenched windpipe. And it was close by. The sound rocked him so strongly that its absence left a hollow in the pit of his stomach. He stood rooted to the spot. Just when he thought he might have imagined it, a second scream followed the first. *Leave it,* he commanded himself. *You can't change the past and shouldn't even if you could.* But another voice whispered to him, too. *You already planted the box. Who cares if you splinter time now? You'll still get your scrolls. At least the poor man will live in someone's history.*

Another scream.

He swore under his breath and veered toward the warehouse door.

The darkness in the warehouse was disorienting. Rabbit felt his way forward in halting steps. What the hell was someone doing in here, anyway? Taking refuge from the fire? That would be a huge mistake; the building was made entirely of timber and housed god knew what flammable goods.

"Hey! Call out if you can hear me!" Rabbit yelled in Latin.

A sharp cry answered and was cut short.

He turned toward the noise and immediately barked his shin on something hard. Stifling a curse, he felt a long stone object on the ground. Fluted sides. Cool to the touch. A column. He used it as a guide, following the stone all the way to its Corinthian top. Probably looted from some Greek temple.

At the end of the column was an open space. Rabbit blinked hard, trying to clear a flickering illusion from his vision. Only it wasn't an illusion. There was candlelight in the distance, dancing through a chink in the wall ahead. He groped his way to the small gap in the boards and put his eye to it, but he could discern nothing.

He followed the wall to the right, running his hands over the rough wood. The terrified lowing of the cattle in the distance was his alarm clock. If they stopped, he would know the flames had reached their pens and he would have to get out of the building immediately. For now, their piteous cries still echoed through the cavernous warehouse.

At last, he found an open doorway and passed through it. The man's screams had stopped. He was probably unconscious. This was stupid. In all this blackness, it would be too easy to take a wrong turn and trip downstairs or pull something down on himself. Rabbit knew he should turn back. Instead, he crept through the menacingly human shapes of statuary toward the flame, regretting every step but unable to curb his concern.

Finally, he picked out the actual source of the illumination. An olive oil lamp flickering from a high shelf. Rabbit rounded the last obstacle and gasped.

A young man was splayed on the floor, his wrists and ankles tied to spikes set in the wood. His stomach was open, his entrails arranged around him like the petals of some grotesque flower. Rabbit rushed to his side. There was something about the face that looked familiar, but Rabbit couldn't place where he'd seen it before. He reached to close the wide, staring eyes and jumped when they blinked.

"Help me," the man pleaded. Rabbit could see the bottom of the man's lungs contract.

He looked over the ruined body helplessly. "I'm sorry." His hands were shaking. There was no way the young man could survive this. It would be a mercy to end his suffering.

And then the most important question hit him.

Where was the person who did this?

Rabbit whipped around in a burst of panic. A monster was rushing toward him, swinging something. Rabbit raised his arms in self-defense, and the something hit his elbow with a crack that knocked him sideways. He rolled with the force of the blow and tried to push up to his feet, but his hands slipped in the blood, and he went back down, the bludgeon hissing through the space where his head had just been. Crabbing madly backward, he found dry boards and gathered his legs under him. The monster loomed, raising the club high.

No, not a monster. It was a man wearing a grotesque theater mask with an oversized nose. Rabbit threw his weight backward onto his left hand, swept a leg at the man's ankle, but the bastard just leaped over it and countered with an almost balletic kick of his own that caught Rabbit squarely between the legs. His guts recoiled in an explosion of pain. A stomp to the thigh turned his right leg to clay. Defenseless, Rabbit waited for the killing blow to land. When a heartbeat passed in silence, he opened his eyes and saw the clown mask considering him, head cocked to one side like a curious dog. The club slowly bounced in his hand.

In the distance, there was a change in the soundscape. The terror of the calves was changing to something else. Rabbit smelled cooking beef in the air.

The masked man turned his ear toward the sound, too, but never took his shadowed eyes off Rabbit. He sniffed the air theatrically and sighed. Raising the club over his head, he spoke.

"Well, isn't it your lucky day?"

In English.

The club fell.

ROME, ITALY

2019 CE

Buongiorno, signore!" chirped a peppy voice. Window blinds clattered up and sunlight speared Rabbit's eyes. He peeled his gluey lids open. A nurse in pink scrubs was bustling around the room. His room. He was reclining in a hospital bed. His right arm was in an air cast. He didn't remember being admitted.

The light from the burning roof of the warehouse had roused him to consciousness. He had stumbled out of the building shortly before it collapsed in on itself. A cloud of flame had licked at him as he half ran, half stumbled for the river. After that, his memories were fragmented and incomplete, as though revealed by a strobe light. Vomiting over the rail of the Aemilian Bridge. Slumping in his horse's saddle, clinging to its mane. Collapsing at the decay point.

The insulated plastic cup at his bedside read *Ospedale San Camillo Forlanini*. So, he had made it back.

"Scusi," he started and regretted it instantly. His throat was raw and swollen. Smoke inhalation.

"Si, signore?" the nurse called while wheeling over a little stainless steel instrument cart. Her ID badge said her name was Val. She had bright blue hair.

Rabbit swallowed, trying to lubricate the Hamburger Helper in his gullet. "Da quanto tempo sono qui?" How long have I been here?

"Sei stato ammesso ieri sera." You were admitted last night. "Sei Americano, si?"

"Si."

"We can talk in English if you like." She unrolled a blood pressure cuff and wrapped it around his left arm. "A man and a woman brought you in. They are family?"

That had to be PJ and Ian, his boss from the Smithsonian and the lead time dilation tech. Rabbit shook his head and regretted that, too. It felt like his brain was too big for his skull. "Coworkers."

"Oh? What do you do for a living?" As the cuff inflated, she slipped a plastic sleeve onto a thermometer.

He didn't feel like explaining. "What was I treated for?"

She slipped the thermometer under his tongue. "Concussion, smoke inhalation, some burns, and a hairline fracture of the elbow."

"But other than that, Mrs. Lincoln, how did you like the play?"

She smiled politely. "Your blood pressure and temperature are normal, Signore Ward." Discharging the plastic thermometer shield into the garbage with a click, she asked, "What happened to you?"

He took a long sip from the plastic water cup, which felt amazing on his raw throat. "Workplace accident. When can I leave?"

"A doctor will let you know this morning. Also, the police want to speak with you."

"Police? Why?" Rabbit's stomach lurched. He had been in enough sticky situations with foreign authorities to avoid them whenever he could. The image of the tortured man in Rome came racing back to him. Of course, they couldn't know anything about that, but he still had the unsettling fear of being blamed for the crime.

She shrugged. "I'm sure it's just routine." She rolled up the blood pressure cuff and reassembled her cart. "Rest now."

He interrupted her retreat. "Did I have anything with me when I was admitted?"

She pointed to a duffel sitting on the visitor's chair. It was his usual kit bag with his street clothes and personal effects. "Do you need something?" she asked.

He shook his head no, and she left.

The moment the door closed, he swung his legs over the side of the bed and pulled the chair to him. Found the burns, he thought. The backs of his calves were bandaged and painful where his tunic had ended.

On top of the duffel were his singed and torn tunic and sandals. No wonder the nurse had asked about his profession. He had been dressed for 64 CE when he was admitted; that must have been quite a sight. Under the tattered costume were the jeans and button-down shirt he'd been wearing when he made the jump. His phone was in his jeans pocket, powered off before he left. No reason to burn down the battery for twenty days. Now he thumbed it on and waited while the device booted up. He was impatient to talk to PJ and didn't want to wait for visiting hours.

The screen lit up with alerts.

Voicemail full.

Voicemail full? Rabbit had never had more than one or two when he returned from a mission. He didn't even know how many it would take to fill the box.

The phone rang before he could play any of them, and he was greeted by PJ's Bit-O-Honey Tennessee accent.

"You're up!"

"Hey, PJ."

"I'm glad I caught you—"

"Hold on," Rabbit said.

A doctor knocked and entered without waiting. A gaggle of young people in scrubs flocked after him like ducklings. They began talking to Rabbit and each other, ignoring the phone in his hand.

"Buongiorno. Se non ti dispiace, ho con me alcuni studenti di medicina."

"Ian and I are on the way, but we're stuck in traffic," PJ said in his ear.

Ian's voice, muffled: "That side street looks open."

"I don't think he speaks English, honey."

Farther away, a driver: "English yes."

"We're in a taxi," PJ explained.

"You don't say," replied Rabbit.

The doctors approached the bedside. "Come ti senti stamattina?" the senior physician asked, pulling up Rabbit's eyelid and shining a light in it.

"What's going on over there?" PJ again.

"Ahhhhh," the doctor instructed.

"Doctors. Ahhhhh." Rabbit opened his mouth and extended his tongue.

"Il danno alla gola è spesso indicativo di danni ai polmoni," the doctor explained to the med students, a little louder than strictly necessary.

Ian again: "How's he doing? Tell him I'm itching to spar next week so he has to get better."

Everyone took turns looking down Rabbit's throat. Nodding, murmuring.

"Are you still there?" PJ again. "Listen, I'm sure you've checked your voicemail by now. I tried to keep you out of it . . ."

"Ow uh uht?" Rabbit asked, his mouth still gaping.

"Per favore, signore," the senior doctor said, indicating the phone.

"I have to go, Peej. I think they might be discharging me," Rabbit said.

"That's terrific, honey, but before you go, I have to . . ."

"Signore," repeated the doctor firmly.

"Talk later," Rabbit said and hung up.

For the next few minutes, the physicians continued their inspections. They seemed most interested in the sound of his breathing and in the state of his concussion. Through it all, he heard his phone vibrating on the rolling table next to the bed.

Finally, the attending doc told him he was free to go. Rabbit changed into his street clothes and tried PJ back, but it went straight to voicemail.

At the nurse's station his signal went out while he completed his paperwork. The administrator told him apologetically that the whole interior of the building had a poor signal due to the thick stone and plaster of the old construction.

He was looking down at his phone again as he walked through the sliding glass doors of the exit, so he heard them before he saw them. A dozen or so people with massive cameras snapping pictures and shouting questions in Italian and English.

"Any comment on Misherenko, Dr. Ward?"

"Dottore!"

They crowded in close, shoving microphones in his face. A security guard waded in among them trying to shoo them away, but they were like water. Push back one side and more rushed in to fill the gap.

"Are you meeting any of these people on your job?"

"Rabbit!"

"Are international authorities prepared to . . ."

"Rabbit!"

Through the melee, Rabbit spotted PJ shouting and waving to him from the open door of a compact white Fiat.

Rabbit pushed through the reporters with his good arm until he reached the waiting taxi. Ian dragged him into the back seat and slammed the door, muffling the sound of the reporters' shouting.

"Hotel Artemide," PJ instructed the driver as the taxi lurched into motion. A photographer jumped out of the way, narrowly avoiding being flattened by the accelerating car.

Rabbit stared over his shoulder at the paparazzi receding in the distance. "What the hell was that all about?"

ROME, ITALY

2019 CE

The story broke about a week ago," PJ said, craning around from the front passenger seat. "Ever heard of Alexi Misherenko?" The taxi darted through the streets like they were in a Steve McQueen movie, forcing PJ to cling to the dashboard to steady herself.

"No," Rabbit replied, gripping the side door handle. Ian held up his phone with a picture of a round-faced man in his thirties aboard a yacht surrounded by disturbingly young-looking girls in bikinis.

"Rich playboy with more money than sense. His family are oligarchs." She dragged out the final *A* like molasses. "Heaven knows how, but he got his hands on a dilator and was setting up time travel tours for a million euros a pop."

"Please tell me he's not calling it Time X."

"That's exactly the joke the press made," Ian said delightedly.

"It's on every station and social media feed," PJ explained. "They've been having a field day with it."

"He got caught?" Rabbit was intrigued.

She nodded. "Interpol set him up. One of his 'friends' tattled on him in exchange for clemency. Now he's in prison awaiting trial."

"Hence the paparazzi."

PJ nodded again. "They're trying to dig up anything they can to keep the story alive. Someone must have leaked that you were in the country on a job. The hotel or the hospital, who knows. People get paid good money for these tips."

"Why me? Why not hound the Natalis?" he asked, referring to the time-traveling brothers who worked for the Vatican Apostolic Archive.

"No one is safe, honey. The Natalis, Alfonse Damiano, they'll suck up quotes from anyone that will let them print a new headline."

"What did you tell them?"

Ian shook his head subtly, shooting Rabbit a warning look that said it all. They hadn't asked PJ, and she felt slighted.

"Or did you just tell them off?" Rabbit continued without missing a beat.

She puffed up like a hen. "I wouldn't give them the satisfaction."

Ian nodded at him and mouthed, *Smooth*. As though she heard it, PJ looked back from the front seat and glanced between them.

"What happened to you, anyway?" Ian asked, trying to avoid PJ's gaze. "I know I always say it but this time you really do look terrible."

"I got the scrolls," Rabbit replied.

"That's the one thing you did tell us before you passed out," PJ said. "The authorities have already blocked off the site. We'll check out the dig this afternoon."

"Let me clarify. I meant who kicked your ass?" said Ian.

Rabbit grunted and explained the last violent hours of his mission. They were back at the hotel checking out by the time he finished.

"I need a coffee," he said to their ashen faces in the lobby.

"The nurse said you were supposed to drink lots of water . . ." Ian said.

"I. Need. A. Coffee," Rabbit repeated.

Moments later, they sat in a little café on the corner staring into their steaming cappuccinos.

"Are you sure it was English?" Ian ventured carefully.

"I know what you're thinking," Rabbit said.

"It's just that the shock of what you saw . . ." PJ began.

"It was English. American Deep South accent, mostly trained

out but still there in the lack of rhoticity." He sighed. "I'll have to report the murder, I guess, but I don't know what the authorities can do about it. Adams-Cortez outlaws unsanctioned time travel, but it doesn't say anything about what you do once you get there."

"Do you think you would know his voice if you heard it again?" PJ asked.

Rabbit saw the leering clown mask in his mind's eye. Heard the words again. *Well, isn't it your lucky day?* He took a long sip of his coffee. "I'd know it."

An hour later, they reviewed the dig site with an archaeological team from Rome. It was a solid group with members from the Universities of Cambria, Michigan, Northwestern, and Stanford under the auspices of the Sovrintendenza Capitolina ai Beni Culturali. Unlike most of Rabbit's missions, this one had been funded by the consortium of universities, not by a private sponsor. The group would treat the site as they would any high-value dig, working their way slowly and meticulously down through the layers of soil, cataloging any finds along the way to the lead case. It would take time, but they'd get there.

"Do you know what generation of copy the writing was?" asked Dr. Nicolas Terrento from the U of M Kelsey Museum in Ann Arbor. Terrento was wearing cargo shorts and a baggy golf shirt, the most American thing he could possibly have donned for the job.

"The librarian from the Porticus Octaviae claimed they were the originals. In Claudius' own hand."

The archaeologist pursed his lips slightly. Rabbit didn't fault him for being dubious. What Rabbit did for a living required a great many skills, but it wasn't archaeology.

"The man seemed awfully sure of himself," Rabbit said, realizing how dumb that sounded.

Terrento shrugged. "Well, it's the content that matters. Copies of copies inevitably introduce mistakes. Any chance you were able to get a comparative sample of Claudius' handwriting for corroboration? No? Pity."

The man turned back to his work without another word. Rabbit took a deep breath and let it out slowly. He didn't need the appreciation of this smug prick, but the dismissal was irritating, nonetheless. "Real" academics seemed to fall into three camps with respect to Rabbit's profession. The first regarded time travelers as privileged practitioners in the history community. The second viewed them as a completely different, and often enviable, profession, something akin to sports stars. The third, and it seemed Terrento fell into this category, looked down on the chrono-archaeologists as a less serious discipline, the same way that some mathematicians felt about sociologists. Rabbit wouldn't have admitted it to anyone, but it still stung a little when he encountered this variety.

Rabbit had struggled in his PhD program at Stanford, not because he lacked acuity or work ethic, but because his interests were too wide and varied to fit the modern mold of the profession. The broad strokes of history were well documented already. Modern historians were hyper-specific in their studies, digging deeply into increasingly narrower fields. Whereas Rabbit was enchanted with the entire sweep of the classical Mediterranean and struggled to find the focus he needed to be successful in contemporary academia. Writing his dissertation years ago had made him question everything he'd worked for. He'd rushed the work, and privately suspected that his paper had only been approved because he had been offered the first chrono archaeology position at the Smithsonian two days before his defense. The review board seemed to regard him as a curious new species. And in a way, he was.

Rabbit awkwardly backed away from the archaeologist and inspected the site, feeling more like a tourist than part of the team.

"We have tickets home tonight," PJ said behind him, her business concluded with the site supervisor. "How are you feeling? Do you need somewhere to rest until we go to the airport?"

"Can't. The police want to talk to me before we go."

"About what?" she asked.

Two serious-looking men were approaching them, their eyes fixed on Rabbit.

"Ask them if you want."

Half an hour later, Rabbit was sitting in an interrogation room in the headquarters of the Italian Polizia di Stato, sipping tepid water from a tiny, crinkly plastic bottle.

"How did you get hurt?" asked the younger of the two detectives in excellent English as they waited for his partner to return. It was just small talk; the tone was offhand.

"I stumbled onto a murder scene and got jumped by the killer."

The cop's mouth dropped open. "Dici sul serio?"

Rabbit nodded.

"Where did this happen?" He pulled out a notebook.

"By the Forum Boarium."

"When? You should have contacted . . ."

"64 CE."

The cop stopped writing mid-sentence. He looked at Rabbit with the rueful amusement of someone who just realized the joke was on them. "64."

Rabbit nodded. "CE."

The cop stowed the pen behind his ear.

"Not that this matters," Rabbit said, "but the killer is from here. From 2019, I mean."

"How do you know that?" The man sounded only mildly curious.

"He spoke English."

"Uh-huh. So, someone went back to ancient times to kill you?"

"Me? No, I just got in the way." Rabbit pictured the broken young man from the temple complex staring up at him. *Help me*. Once again, he was struck by the feeling that he had seen that face before. "Excuse me?"

"I asked, could you pick the killer out of a lineup?" His pen was still behind his ear.

"He was wearing a mask. Anyway, it doesn't matter, does it? The statute of limitations is somewhat expired."

The cop didn't get his joke or didn't respond to it if he did.

Rabbit explained. "There are no laws to prosecute it, are there? Adams-Cortez only cares if you travel without a license, not what you do once you get there."

"Italy follows . . ."

"The EU TTP. Yeah, I know. Does it cover cases like this?"

The cop looked a little embarrassed. "No."

"That's why I wasn't in a rush to report it."

"Signore Ward," said the older of the two cops as he entered the room with a manila folder. "Did Detective Camarano say why we want talk to you? No? So, we know you are back in Rome only yesterday. But you have heard of the Misherenko trial, yes? Yes. So, Misherenko named fourteen his customers." He looked to his partner.

"To plea down his sentence," the younger cop said.

"To plea down." The older cop laid the folder on the table. "You also do time travel."

"Legally," Rabbit clarified.

The older cop nodded. "We want to know. Have you seen any of these people?" He tapped the folder with a thick index finger.

"In the past?" A week ago, Rabbit would have said that it was impossible for him to have coincided with someone across all of history by accident. That was before he was almost killed by one of them. "Let's see."

The cop pulled out a mug shot of Misherenko dressed in clothes that spoke of a late-night party interrupted.

"Misherenko," Rabbit confirmed. "But I never heard of him before today."

"Si. Now his people." One by one, the cop laid out pictures of the Time X customers. Some were mug shots, a few looked like informal paparazzi grabs. The tenth was an actor's headshot.

"No kidding," Rabbit said.

The cop shook his head sadly. "I like his films, too." The picture was of Ethan Davies, a young movie star with curly blond hair.

"I met him. At the Kennedy Center last year. Said he wanted to make a movie about time travel. That's a shame. He seemed like a good kid."

The cop turned over two more pictures. Neither of them looked familiar.

The police didn't seem concerned about sharing information about Misherenko's clients. The accused were uniformly wealthy, but the similarity ended there. They hailed from nine different countries. Some were self-made, others inherited their wealth. None of them had any significant criminal history. They were distinguished by their ability to afford the price of admission and the confidence to assume they could get away with it. In the current climate of uneven wealth distribution, it was no wonder this story had exploded in the news.

Something occurred to Rabbit as the stack of pictures thinned. "Are any of these guys originally from the American South?" The cops gave him a blank look. "Alabama, Georgia, Mississippi?"

Young cop glanced at old cop. "Why do you ask?"

"The murder I told you about, in the past. I swear the killer had a trace of an American Southern accent."

"We look into it," the older cop said. "It is not strong, but maybe something."

"Shall we continue?" the younger cop asked and turned over the thirteenth picture.

Rabbit felt his stomach drop.

It was Helen.

"This is the only woman accused. Do you know her?"

The picture was taken from a distance with a long lens. She was looking over her shoulder in the direction of the photographer, about to enter a glass-fronted building. Turkish writing above the entry. Summoning his training, Rabbit looked up casually and shook his head. "Never seen her before."

ROME, ITALY

2019 CE

Rabbit gripped the sink in the police station bathroom, his heart racing. *Breathe.* He forced himself to release his clenched muscles.

He had made it through the last picture without giving himself away. Excused himself to the restroom. Forced himself to walk as though nothing were wrong.

Helen.

How had she gotten mixed up in this? Surely, she was too shrewd to have involved herself with these amateurs. Someone might have sacrificed her to save themselves, but they would at least have needed to know who she was. Rabbit had never so much as seen her face in the present. She was too careful to let this happen.

Rabbit exhaled for a five-count to drain the shock from his system.

. . . three, two, one.

Okay. So . . .

Helen was on the hook with the rest of these rich dilettantes. If she had been arrested, they would have shown him a mug shot, not that . . . what was that? It looked like a surveillance photo, like something a private investigator or cops on a stakeout would take. Her hair was longer in the picture than he had ever seen it, so it wasn't recent. They knew who she was, but they didn't have her. The question was, what was Rabbit going to do about it? Admitting he knew Helen could only hurt her—and him. *No, officer, I don't believe this woman would be involved with these idiots. She's a highly skilled, professional thief. How do I know that? Well, you see, I have been aiding and abetting her criminal activity for over a year.*

At the moment, he was merely an expert witness on time travel. He didn't particularly want to be promoted to accomplice. What help would he be to her then?

That thought surprised him, but he knew it was true. He would help her. Of course, he would. He knew Helen. Knew she would never mix herself up with these people. She might be a thief but, hell, wasn't he, too? The only difference between them was that he had a license and a key to the Smithsonian archives. It was no different than a skilled but unlicensed driver getting behind the wheel. Technically criminal but not morally so.

Right?

The rest of the interview was uneventful. The Interpol investigators would stay in touch if they had any questions for him but, no, he wasn't required to stay in the country. Rabbit left the station and was at Leonardo da Vinci Airport in plenty of time for his flight.

He spotted the team from a distance. PJ, Ian, and the two junior technicians, Claire and Trey, were hovering around a single chair and a pile of carry-on luggage like a quirky family on vacation. Rabbit felt a warm rush of comfort at the sight of them.

"You take the chair, Rabbit," offered Claire, popping up as he approached.

He shook his head. "You better stay in it, or some sweet little Italian granny will swipe it." She started to protest. "I'll get more sitting than I want on the flight."

"You want anything? Coffee?" offered Ian.

"Guys," said Rabbit. "I'm okay." He wasn't, really. His lungs hurt, his calves hurt, his shoulder was aching from being immobilized in the sling.

"What did the police want?" PJ asked. She knew better than to offer Rabbit assistance when he was feeling independent. He was a product of the Midwest. Part of that was the insistence on being "fine" no matter the circumstances. PJ had once declared that Rabbit would decline a glass of water if his hair was on fire.

"To see if I could identify any of Misherenko's accused clients. I couldn't," he said, responding to her questioning look. The lie hurt more than his throat.

The gate attendant's voice struggled against the noise of the crowd. "Il volo 102 per Washington DC inizierà l'imbarco tra quindici minuti."

"Fifteen minutes to boarding," Rabbit translated.

Like Pavlov's dogs, his colleagues whipped out their phones at the threat of their removal.

Freed from social interaction, Rabbit resumed what he had been pondering before he arrived. How could he help Helen? Did she even know she was being pursued? She hadn't shown up for the Claudian scrolls job as she had for every other expedition since Aaron's rescue. Rabbit had been disappointed by her absence. The two of them had been more efficient working together instead of competing. That, he told himself, was as far as his feelings for Helen extended.

Rabbit glanced at Ian and briefly considered calling his friend's slimy ex, Devon. The little creep had been using Ian to collect and sell the team's information to Helen's organization all last year. Devon might still know how to contact them. But Rabbit dismissed the thought just as quickly as it had formed. He had strong-armed the jerk into breaking it off with Ian. Devon had no incentive to help Rabbit and, besides, his link to Helen's organization would have been cut the moment he was of no value to it.

So how would he contact her? Helen's life outside of work was a complete mystery.

Sighing, Rabbit imitated his companions and pulled out his phone. Might as well use the time to purge all the junk he had received while he was out. Before looking at any of it, he put in a reminder to change his number.

He started in on the drift of text messages. Most of them were listed by phone number. He deleted these as quickly as his finger could swipe. About halfway down he hit one from Sarah Kahan, mother of his former mentee, Aaron, whose loss and eventual rescue had played such an outsize role in his life last year.

Like many people of her generation, Sarah tended to format text messages like emails, which is to say, like letters.

Dear Rabbit. I wonder if you might have some time to talk this week. I'm worried about Aaron and thought you might have some ideas. Thanks, Sarah.

He made a mental note to contact her when he got home, feeling a twinge of worry for Aaron. No, not *for* Aaron. About Aaron. That didn't feel great.

More junk. Junk, junk, a picture from his dad of the new dock, junk.

He was halfway to deleting the next anonymous message when the first two words caught his eye. He opened it with a thrill of recognition.

H1 H4nds0me. H3lp pl33z. V+T's KQ 3.3.68. *Find Einar Eshek. FAST.*

He read it three times, his heart beating fast. It was from Helen.

"Somebody die?" Ian intruded on his thoughts.

Rabbit rammed the phone into his pocket. "What?"

MALIBU, CALIFORNIA, USA

2019 CE

Rabbit stared at Helen's encoded text message for the hundredth time. "Hi handsome" identified its sender; no one else had ever called him that. The 3.3.68 had to be March 3, 68 CE; the V+T would be the Roman general Vespasian and his son, Titus. The date and people narrowed the KQ down to Khirbet Qumran in first-century Judea. Helen was asking him to go there and find someone named Einar Eshek. Rabbit had written back asking for more information before the flight left Rome. The space under his reply was still blank when he powered up his phone on the DC airport runway.

Her request left him with a new problem. Traveling to the past wasn't like catching a bus. First of all, it was expensive. Rabbit would need sponsorship for the expedition from someone rich enough to pay for it, and no one was going to fund a mission to rescue an international criminal. He needed a juicy grab in 68 CE Judea to entice a sponsor, and no one had justified a trip to that time-space in years.

Put simply, Rabbit had to lie.

He texted Sarah Kahan later that day from his kitchen counter. *I bought the earliest ticket I could. It's for next Thursday.*

She replied quickly. *That's very thoughtful, but isn't that inconvenient for you? A phone call would suffice. Thanks, Sarah.*

I'd like to see Aaron in person. Plus, there is something else I'd like to discuss with you while I'm there. It's time sensitive.

Why didn't you say so? Cancel your flight. I'll send the plane.

He had demurred at the offer, but she wore him down. Which is how he ended up on a private jet to LAX at eight the next morning sitting uncomfortably in a very comfortable seat. Rabbit was staunchly against private travel. It was ruining the environment, it wasted money. He didn't even own a car. On the other hand, Helen needed his help now, and this shaved days off his timeline. So, he stewed in his mixed feelings and enjoyed the excellent coffee and continental breakfast. The Danish was delicious.

Sarah and David Kahan owned homes across the world, but Sarah, who was a California native, spent most of her time in Malibu. The house had apparently been designed to look as though it had sprung organically from the cliffs overlooking the ocean. Rabbit thought the architect had misread "organic" as "geometric." The house was a sprawling striation of white stucco and glass with a jade green yard designed by a master gardener from Japan.

A courteous staff member led Rabbit through the house and deposited him on a white leather couch in the shade by the pool. The day was warm and dry and the breeze off the ocean was perfect. He sipped his orange juice and admired the view until the glass door slid open behind him with a whisper.

"Thank you for coming, young man!" Sarah was dressed in something white with entirely too many overlapping parts. She was in her early seventies, animated and lively as always, her glasses pushed up to hold back her thick mane of silver hair.

Rabbit rose and accepted her embrace. Sarah didn't mess around. It was a full bear hug. While he wasn't much of a hugger himself, after twenty years of guilt and recrimination associated with the Kahan family, Rabbit appreciated every one now that they were reconciled.

"What did you do to your arm?" Sarah strolled into the sun and Rabbit followed.

"Occupational hazard. It's just a hairline fracture."

"Well, don't be in too much of a hurry to use it like David did. Remember that? He rushed back onto the tennis court and only made it worse."

Rabbit had no idea what she was referring to, but that seemed par for the course with Sarah these days. Rabbit was happy to have renewed his relationship with the Kahans, but Sarah, it seemed, was choosing to pretend there had never been a rift. From the day Rabbit had rescued Aaron, the Kahan clan had resumed friendly relations as though nothing had ever happened. Well, that's how some people dealt with an uncomfortable past, he supposed.

"What's going on, Sarah? You sounded worried."

By way of reply, she led Rabbit wordlessly away from the house. They followed a winding slate path through a carefully raked sand garden that echoed the wave patterns of the sea at the base of the cliffs.

"He's different, since you brought him back," she said, gazing out at the ocean.

"Are you sure it's him? Maybe it's all of us who've changed." The world had aged two decades in Aaron's absence, but he came back the same twenty-year-old kid Rabbit had taken to Rome. Well, not the same, exactly. No one could experience what Aaron had and be unchanged by it.

Judging from the way Sarah was watching the water, the lone swimmer in the shallow bay must have been her son. He was gliding steadily through the waves parallel to the beach about fifty yards from shore. Not wanting to sound dismissive, Rabbit adopted a softer tone. "Aaron had a traumatic experience. Does he ever talk about it?"

"Never."

"What's the change you're seeing? Is he depressed?"

She shook her head. "No, not depressed. More like . . . agitated? Hunted. That's the word. He's hunted. It's as though he's late for something all the time but can't remember what he's late for."

"White Rabbit," he said.

Sarah smiled ruefully.

Rabbit continued. "The mission changed his mind about his calling. Maybe he just needs to find his direction."

"Maybe. I don't know; he won't talk to us about it. He spends all his time on his computer or on the phone with people all over the world."

Rabbit had seen what Aaron was capable of under the wrong circumstances. Eighty years in the ancient world had molded him into a megalomaniac, a mass murderer. Rabbit had saved the young man from himself. The idea that Aaron saw him as an inspirational role model made Rabbit distinctly uncomfortable.

He had told no one about Aaron's master plan for the ancient world. Even he and Helen avoided the topic once they started working together on missions. The memory of what became of Aaron haunted him but, if he was honest with himself, seeing young Aaron after he'd rescued him from that fate troubled him more. Since witnessing the fruit of true evil in his ancient mentee, Rabbit kept searching for the seeds in the younger version. How much of one's character was molded as a reaction to one's environment and how much was innate?

Sarah broke Rabbit out of his reverie. "I thought he might open up to you about what he's struggling with. He admires you so much."

Twenty minutes later, Aaron crested the hill, tapping the side of his head against his palm to clear water from his ear.

"Rabbit?!" The athletic young man rushed over to his old mentor and pumped his hand. "What are you doing here?"

"I was in the neighborhood; thought I'd stop by."

Aaron grinned mischievously, and Rabbit could see hints of the wrinkled, bearded face of the old man from Constantinople. "My mother asked you to come check in on me."

Rabbit shrugged.

Aaron wagged a finger at him and walked over to an outdoor shower set discreetly in the corner of the overhanging balcony floor. Water fell from unseen ports like a perfect cube of monsoon rain. He soaped away the sea salt, spluttering through the water as he talked. "She's worried about me. They both are. I get it. But I'm fine."

"Are you?" Rabbit asked, leaning back on the leather couch and looking out at the ocean.

"Why wouldn't I be? I'm alive, aren't I?" He turned off the water. "Thanks to you." Aaron pulled a fluffy white towel from an inset shelf and scrubbed himself, stepping out of the shade into the warm sun. "Don't get me wrong, it's been weird as hell. My college and prep school friends are all middle-aged with careers and kids. I make them uncomfortable. It's been isolating, you know? But I can deal with that. It's this world that gets me. Have you seen *The Matrix*? Of course, you have. Everyone saw it but me. I can't believe it came out the month after we left for Rome. That's what it feels like all the time here. Internet on your phone, self-driving cars, politics has gone completely off the rails, and the entire world is making porn. I feel like I took the red pill."

"I imagine it must be overwhelming," Rabbit said.

"Are you kidding? It's outstanding! When I left, everything felt like it was carved out of stone. Like nothing of any real substance would ever change. Now it's been totally destabilized. I mean, at this rate, America won't even exist in twenty years!"

Aaron was pacing the edge of the pool, energy radiating from him.

"Is that a good thing?" Rabbit understood why Sarah was worried.

Aaron stopped and fixed Rabbit with his burning eyes. Reacting to something he saw in his mentor's face, the young man's whole demeanor changed. He seemed to shrink, the energy retreating and condensing inside him again. When he spoke next, his voice was casually polite. The transformation was chilling.

"Of course not. It's just fascinating to see how much things have changed while I was away. How are you doing on that OJ?"

"Your mother said you have been spending a lot of time on the internet. What are you looking for?"

Aaron stared out at the ocean. He held and released a long breath. When he finally spoke, he sounded far older than he was.

"Purpose."

For the rest of the afternoon, Aaron was charming and civil. Rabbit never saw the fire burning behind his eyes again, but sensed it just beneath the surface. Hiding.

As he observed his former mentee, he plied Sarah with his ulterior motive. He invented an obscure source pointing to newly suspected artifacts at one of the best excavated sites in the Holy Land. Qumran. Would the Kahans be willing to fund an expedition to the site to secure the finds? During dessert, she said yes.

WASHINGTON, DC, USA

2019 CE

You've got to be joking." PJ was hovering over Rabbit as he packed his go bag. "Your doctor didn't even want you to fly to California and you want to do another mission?"

"How did you know about my doctor?" He paused, a pair of shoes in hand.

"I didn't but thank you for confirming it."

Rabbit rolled his eyes and continued packing. "I'll take it easy."

"Your arm is in a sling," she protested.

"They had slings in the first century."

"You're acting like a crazy person. Where are you even going?"

"Israel, March of 68."

"You're going to"—she made finger quotes—"'take it easy' during the First Jewish-Roman War?"

He dismissed that with a wave of his hand. "Vespasian won't leave Galilee until late spring. I'll be fine."

"And what, pray tell, are you supposed to be after?"

He purposefully avoided making eye contact as he mumbled, "Dead Sea Scrolls."

"Dead . . ." she sputtered and had to start again. "Rabbit Ward is going after the Dead Sea Scrolls. I forget, what is it you always call Qumran?" She glared at him with pursed lips, demanding his answer.

He mumbled his reply. "The time travelers'—"

"The time travelers' tourist trap!" she completed. "That place is picked clean, what makes you think there is anything left to find?"

"New information . . ." he started.

"Oh, new information? Tell me about the new information. I'm entranced."

He zipped the bag closed aggressively. "I'm going, PJ."

"Not if you don't get medical clearance."

It was a threat. One he'd prepared for. "If you try to stop me, I'll go to the Israeli Agency."

"You'd need the secretary's authorization to make an international agreement."

"I called yesterday. They said they'd be happy to have me."

She blinked at him in disbelief. "You'd be in breach of your contract if you go with them."

"I know."

"The Institution turned a blind eye last year to your blatantly illegal actions because you got Aaron back, but they'd fire you for this."

"I know."

Her anger melted away into worry again. "What are you doing?"

He couldn't meet her eyes. "I have to, PJ. Can't you just trust me enough to accept that?"

"Can't you trust me enough to tell me why?" She strode over and took hold of his shoulders, forcing him to stop moving.

They stared at each other for a long moment. Rabbit wanted desperately to explain but he couldn't. If he told her what he was doing and anyone ever found out, she would be complicit in fleecing a sponsor. It would ruin her. Rabbit shook his head. "I'm sorry."

The pain and concern etched across her face slowly cooled into the professional mask of courtesy he had seen her wear so many times with strangers. From the genteel Southerner, that was worse than any tirade. It broke his heart.

"I'll get the paperwork in order."

"PJ," he started.

She cut him off, smiling politely. "I'll see you on the flight."

From Reagan National to Tel Aviv, no one spoke. PJ acted as though Rabbit didn't exist. The rest of the team side-eyed each other the way that kids do when they know mom and dad are fighting. Thankfully they weren't seated together on either of the connecting flights.

Rabbit had forced her hand. PJ had talked the Smithsonian secretary into authorizing the trip to keep him from defecting. He had no idea what that conversation had been like but was sure he had burned all his political capital with his boss's boss. That didn't worry him nearly as much as the injury to his friendship with PJ. She'd been angry with him before but never cold. *This had better be worth it, Helen.*

Truth was, although he had managed to scrape together an expedition in record time, he had no plan. He had lied to PJ and Sarah about artifacts for which he had no evidence as a pretense to find this Einar Eshek. Throughout the flight, he pondered his first moves, while also dwelling on the last line of her text. *FAST*. He couldn't afford to be gone for twenty days this time. Which is why he followed Ian into the bathroom during their layover in Vienna.

"I need to ask you a favor." Rabbit was waiting at the row of sinks when Ian exited the stall.

"Oh, great," said his friend and coworker, washing his hands. "We're going to make this weirder."

"Ian . . ."

"What is going on between you and PJ? And why are you going on a job when you still look like something I scraped off my shoe?"

A man in a rumpled suit exited one of the stalls, considered the two of them, and left without washing his hands. Ian's face twisted with disgust as he methodically scrubbed each of his soapy fingers.

"Ian, listen. I know you always bring me back twenty days after I leave, but do you have to?"

"No, I could leave you there. And right now—"

"Could you bring me back earlier?"

Ian furrowed his brow. "You want a shorter trip?"

"No, I want the same amount of time in the past, but I want to come back sooner."

Ian rolled his eyes. "You'd be twenty days older than when you left."

"I know. Can you do it?"

"I *can* do it. Why the fuck *should* I do it?"

"I can't tell you that."

"Great. Then I won't do it." Ian punched the air dryer to life with his elbow and rubbed his hands furiously in the hot airstream. "Do you know how many rules you are asking me to break? I would be double-dipping in the national electric grid for one. They frown on that!"

"I'll take the blame."

The air stopped. Ian glared at him. "Why?" he demanded.

Rabbit was stuck and he knew it. With PJ, he had held the cards. Ian had flipped the table on him. He took a deep breath and swallowed his medicine.

"You remember the stringer who robbed me a few times last year?"

He nodded, his lips a thin line.

A father and his young son entered the bathroom wheeling suitcases. Rabbit lowered his volume. "I've been, sort of, seeing her."

"You're dating?" Ian practically squealed. He couldn't help himself. Angry as he was, Ian loved love.

"No! I mean we've been running into each other in the past. On missions."

"Oh, Rabbit."

"I know, I know. I haven't said anything to the authorities, which probably makes me an accessory."

"It definitely makes you an accessory."

"That's not the worst thing."

Ian glanced at the father and son standing at the urinals and leaned closer to hear Rabbit's confession.

"She's on the list. Misherenko's list."

Ian's hand flew to his mouth. "Oh, fuck me."

"I don't know what the accusation is, only that she's a suspect. I can't believe . . ."

He cut himself off as the man and boy flushed and washed their hands. The father raised his eyebrows at the clandestine conversation but said nothing to them. He ushered his son out.

"I can't believe she would have anything to do with these joyriders. She's a . . ."

"A criminal?" Ian offered.

"A professional," Rabbit finished.

"And what does this have to do with you?"

"She asked for my help."

Ian stared at him.

"And she needs help fast."

His friend's glare didn't waver. Rabbit knew what he was asking. Ian would have to figure out a way to make this work. He'd have to do it after Rabbit departed. He was leaving Ian to deal with PJ and the Israeli Energy Authority all for someone Ian didn't even know.

"Do you have feelings for this woman?" The way Ian said it made it clear this was the crucial point.

"We've helped each other out on—"

"Do you have feelings for her?"

Rabbit hesitated. It was the question he had been unwilling to ask himself. He was terrified the answer was yes. "I don't know."

Ian slapped both very clean hands down on Rabbit's shoulders. "Forget about it. Let the authorities deal with it. If she's innocent, she'll be fine."

Ian released him and started to go. "There is one other thing," Rabbit said.

Ian stopped, eyeing Rabbit grimly.

"The illegal jump I did last year. The one that cleared your name? She made that possible."

Ian glared at him. "I hate you," he declared. "How much time do you need?"

Twenty-four uncomfortably quiet hours later, Rabbit stood on the platform of the Israeli Historical Authority's time dilator. The facility was located a mile east of an industrial park on the outskirts of Jerusalem. Despite being so close to the old city, the arid valley that housed it was and always had been remote and uninhabited, which made it an ideal spot for jumping into the past unnoticed. The morning was cool, dry, and sunny. Rabbit hoped it would be the same when he arrived.

Deep within the fortified cement building, he was wearing a short-sleeved, calf-length jacket of coarse linen, a leather belt, sandals, and a long wool tunic with tassels tied at the four corners. As usual, the team from the Institution had done a bang-up job making the kit look and feel legitimate and lived in. Rabbit would fit right in. His purse was full of Judean shekels and Roman aureus coins; enough money to buy a farm where he was going. A short, functional knife rested on his hip beside it.

Rabbit turned off his phone and put it in his duffel bag. By their own personal ritual, PJ always accepted his duffel from him and wished him "good hunting" as their last interaction in the present. Today she accepted the bag without a word.

I'll make it up to you, PJ.

He glanced at Ian, who was frowning at his controls like he wanted to kill them. The tech made the last adjustments and began his count down. "Spinning up in three . . . two . . ."

I'll make it up to you, too, pal.

". . . one . . . jump."

JUDEA

68 CE

Rabbit had squeezed his eyes shut in anticipation of the bright desert landscape he had left. Instead, he found himself in the dappled shade of a walnut tree. Rabbit had been to Galilee and Joppa at various points in history, but this particular time-space was new to him. The controversial historian Flavius Josephus had described Judea as lush with all kinds of fruit and nut trees. He hadn't exaggerated. Even here on the edge of the desert between Jerusalem and the Dead Sea, there were scattered trees in the valley and dotting the hillside. Modern observers often wondered at how so many large and powerful early civilizations had sprung from desert regions. The answer, of course, was that they weren't always deserts. Climate change had birthed and felled many a people over the centuries.

Rabbit carefully marked the location of his decay point with a cairn of stones. This five-foot circle of land would become the most important location in Rabbit's world twenty days from now, as it was the only place from which he could return to the present.

"Well," he said out loud, habitually switching to Greek, "now what?"

Find Einar Eshek. And then what? Helen hadn't said. All he had was a time period, a location, and a name. Qumran only contained a hundred or so people, but that was still a lot of interrogating. If his quarry had any skill at staying hidden, this would be tricky.

He took a deep breath and hoped that his purpose would become clear once he found his mark. Tightening his sandals, he headed through the lonely canyon that led to the main road between Jerusalem and the Dead Sea.

The valley floor made an easy walking path, but there were no wheel ruts or hoofprints in the sandy soil. Feeling safely isolated, he let his mind wander, ticking off what he knew about the era. He had reread Josephus, Cohen, and Mason the whole way to Israel, a crash course to prepare him for his destination. As a historian, Josephus was spotty at best, but he was the only contemporary to write about the period. The late Yeshua Nazarian from the Israel Museum had spent some time in the region documenting the facts of the war, but he had mostly covered the siege of Jerusalem, which wouldn't begin for a year.

Thirteen months ago, the Roman general Vespasian landed at Ptolemais on the northern coast of Galilee in what some marked as the start of the First Jewish-Roman War. In truth, his arrival was a response to the violence that had already been racking the country for a year before that.

One version of the story, which was too entertaining to be likely, was that some Greeks had pissed off the Jewish priestly class of Caesarea (now Tel Aviv) by sacrificing birds on sanctified ground. In retaliation, the priests had stopped offering prayers for Emperor Nero. The local Roman procurator, Gessius Florus, had responded by confiscating seventeen talents of gold from the Temple "for the emperor." It was such an obvious act of self-enrichment that it inspired a parody campaign across the region. In Jewish cities from Arabia to Anatolia, people made a public show of passing around a basket to collect money for "poor" Florus as if he were a pitiful beggar. Ego bruised, Gessius Florus wasted no time in arresting, flogging, and crucifying a bunch of notable Jerusalemites outside the city walls. The butchery sparked an uprising. Jewish militias slaughtered the Roman garrison in Jerusalem, as well as the ill-fated legion from Syria who arrived to restore order.

Unfortunately, the revolt only escalated tensions between the priestly and working-class Judeans. Numerous factions sprung up across the region with vying opinions of how to handle the inevitable Roman retaliation. Two years from now, Vespasian's son Titus would destroy the Great Temple in Jerusalem and ship its riches back to Rome, including the menorah Rabbit had secured last year. But before then, the Jews would do more harm than good to their own cause through infighting between the factions.

For now, however, the Romans were still occupied in Galilee. This eastern trade road from Jerusalem to the Dead Sea should be off the radar, giving Rabbit safe passage.

Or so he was thinking when a stone smacked the rocks he was passing. He flinched as a chip flew off the hurled missile, biting his arm.

A figure was standing halfway up the slope to his right, already spinning a second stone in the sling.

His assailant's head was covered as was traditional for all Jewish men. Rabbit himself was wearing a cloth over his head, held in place with a braid of leather. But the slinger's face was covered with a drape as well, almost like a Bedouin, and that was unusual. For a man.

Simple answer. It wasn't a man.

"Take another step and the next stone meets your head," the masked woman called out in a clear voice.

A familiar voice.

Rabbit raised his hands in surrender.

His heart skipped a beat. It was just one sentence in a bouncy desert canyon. He could be wrong, but he knew he wasn't when she spoke again.

"What are you smiling about?"

Rabbit almost laughed with relief.

It was Helen.

JUDEA

68 CE

Instinct stopped him from calling her name. Or at least what people call instinct. In truth, his brain had performed a rapid set of probability calculations to come up with that conclusion. It wouldn't be surprising for Helen to scare him with a slung stone. She was prone to recklessness and loved a joke. But the tone of the threat was too menacing. No, not menacing. Scared. He had only known her to be scared once before, and that was in the middle of bloody carnage. The woman on the ridge still hadn't revealed her face either. And Helen surely would have done so if she was playing with him. That left two options. One, it wasn't Helen, but someone who sounded like her. Unlikely. Two, for whatever reason, she didn't recognize him, and that opened up a whole string of questions.

She was approaching slowly, her eyes unwavering above the rough cloth veil.

Why didn't she know him? Amnesia? No, that only happened in movies.

She switched to English. "You just came from the Israeli Commission time dilator, right?"

He nodded.

"Then I've got one more question for you. I'll know if you're lying." Another spin of the sling. "Are you Einar Eshek?"

Rabbit stared at her, blinking dumbly. He shook his head. "My name is Ward. Rabbit Ward."

"What kind of sadistic mother names her kid Rabbit?"

He ignored the jab. "I work for the Smithsonian."

"Congratulations." Her snark didn't hide her hesitancy. She didn't seem to know what to do with him. Again, very unlike Helen.

"I'm here on business." He pointed to her spinning weapon. "Can I put my hands down?"

The sling dropped to her side. She kept the stone swinging in its pouch like a pendulum, however, ready to fire if need be. With her other hand, she pushed a lock of hair away from her eyes, but it just bowed out of the space above her veil. In irritation, she tore loose the cloth from her face and it fell across her shoulder.

It was Helen, all right. But there was something different about her. Freed from the veil, the lock of hair fell all the way to her abdomen. Ever since he had known her, she wore it just below the collarbones. It was long now. It looked like the picture the police had shown him.

Then it clicked. This Helen didn't recognize him because she hadn't met him yet. He was talking to a younger version of Helen than the one he first met in Alexandria over a year ago.

"Who's the secretary?" she demanded.

"Excuse me?"

"You said you're here on business from the Smithsonian." She dripped the name with disdain. "So, who's the secretary of the goddamn Institute?"

"Institution," he corrected her and winced inwardly.

She rolled her eyes and corrected herself. "The goddamn *Institution?*"

He was stuck. Martin Friedman had been secretary since 2012. Before that was Jean Welles. What year was Helen from? Could she be seven years younger than the version he knew? Her face didn't look that different. Rabbit rolled the dice. "Marty Friedman."

Her dismissive shrug told him he'd rolled a seven. "What are you here for?" she asked.

Rabbit repeated the lie he had invented for Sarah Kahan.

"Somebody thinks they found evidence of the Book of Esther at Qumran. I'm supposed to find it." It was paper-thin. There had been plenty of supposition about "the Megillah" being among the Dead Sea Scrolls in Qumran's caves, but no one had proven it. There wasn't even enough evidence to justify the expense of a mission to find out.

It didn't seem to faze her. "So, you're going to Qumran?"

"That's the plan."

She glanced eastward and fell silent for a moment.

"Who's Einar Eshek?" he ventured.

She snapped her eyes back toward him.

"That's the name you said, right? Is he your partner or something?"

"No. Just some fucking guy I'm supposed to find." She didn't sound very convincing.

"And you thought you might catch him coming through the Israeli time dilator?"

She didn't answer, but her clenched jaw answered for her. Seven again.

"Is he official?" Rabbit asked. "Does he work for one of the state-sponsored agencies? I mean, he's not going to come through an official dilator if he's a stringer."

"A what?"

"Stringer. It's what we call unlicensed time travelers."

She sighed. "He's . . . he's not official."

"How long have you been staked out here?"

"A while."

Rabbit waited, staring at her.

"Three days," she admitted through tight lips.

Clever Helen. It was no mistake they had run into each other here. This was part of her past. All she had to do was direct him to this valley at the right time to ensure they met. She was offering herself, her past self, as a partner. Of course, it was up to Rabbit to close the deal.

"Three days, huh? Well, however he got here, he's not likely to hang out in this barren valley. I hate to say it, but I think you missed him. You want my advice, I'd say your best bet is to home in on his target.

He's bound to show up there and reveal himself. Do you know where he's headed?"

She grimaced. "Qumran."

Thank you, Helen. "Well, then. Might as well travel together, at least until we get there. Safety in numbers."

"I don't need some state-sponsored Boy Scout on my trail."

Shit. Played it too eager. He shrugged. "Suit yourself. Enjoy the walk." Without another look, Rabbit breezed by her and continued east along the valley floor. In a quarter mile, he would cut north and pick up the main road. Qumran was only ten miles away. If he was lucky, he'd make it there before dark.

This younger Helen was obviously new to this. Her classical Greek was impeccable, but she lacked the confidence, the swagger, of the woman he knew. Three days of waiting? Rabbit's Helen would be long gone by now, hot on Eshek's trail.

Rabbit was just heading up the north cut in the hills when he heard her trot up from behind and fall in beside him. He grinned.

"This is just until we reach Qumran," she said.

"Understood."

She side-eyed him for a few hundred yards before curiosity got the better of her. "Why do you have a sling as part of your costume?" She was referring to his injured arm, of course, not the weapon.

"Kit."

"What?" she asked.

"Everything you bring back with you, we refer to it as a 'kit,' not a costume."

"Why?"

"It sounds cooler."

She nodded. "Why do you have a sling as part of your kit?"

"It's real. I hurt my elbow before I jumped."

"And they made you go anyway? Hello, corporate overlords."

"That was me. I insisted." He felt a twinge of guilt about PJ.

"How'd you do it?" she asked.

"Long story."

"We have time."

"Story I'm not ready to tell you."

She shrugged. "Suit yourself."

The arid desert hills creeped by as they walked.

"I never was, you know."

She looked at him blankly.

"A Scout," he said. "Couldn't abide the uniforms."

They walked in silence until they got to the main road, ten miles of packed dirt trail that threaded its way through the hilly Judean desert between Jerusalem and the Dead Sea.

Rabbit watched Helen out of the corner of his eye. At first, he thought she was nervous, the way she kept scanning the rocky escarpments flanking the road. But as they continued east, he started seeing her distinctive dimples, which always looked to Rabbit like parentheses around her wide smile. She might have started out nervous, but she hadn't remained so.

He broke the silence. "Pretty amazing, isn't it?"

She nodded. "How often do you do this?"

"Expeditions? Three or four times a year. It was slowest during the 2008 recession. Why? How many times a year do you jump?"

She blushed and looked toward the hills. "This is my first one."

"What do you think so far?"

"It's surreal . . . I was just on this road yesterday. It was paved. The mountains look the same though. What's so damn funny?"

"Nothing. Seriously. I envy you. That sense of wonder will make the job a hell of a lot more fun."

Helen shook her head. "This is it for me. One and done. Find this Eshek guy, bring him back, and I can forget all about this shit."

"Doesn't sound like this trip was your idea. Who roped you into it if you don't mind my asking?"

"I don't mind your asking if you don't mind not getting an answer."

"Fair enough."

A mile later, Helen stopped.

"What is it?" he asked.

She pointed at her ear, while her eyes slowly scanned the surroundings.

"Water," she said.

He concentrated and picked up the burbling sound of a stream tumbling over rocks. "There must be a spring nearby," he said. "Come on. Let's check it out."

They picked their way up a narrow, crooked valley. Sure enough, around a bend in the wash was a little patch of green shrubs. Helen pulled out her water bottle, a leather pouch with a copper mouthpiece.

"What?" She had picked up the look on his face.

"Nothing."

"You were smirking."

"Your waterskin. The materials are right, but it was made by machines in a factory." He pulled out his own. The leather was unevenly blackened from years of skin oil, the copper hammered by hand and showing green an inch down from the mouthpiece. "Nobody beats the museum at the details." Rabbit was remembering the one time he had traveled with Helen's people. He'd been humbled by their speed, efficiency, and, yes, money. The craftsmanship of the museum artisans had been the only thing that allowed him to feel superior.

She stared at him, rolled her eyes, and pushed through the shrubs.

"Taste it before you fill your flask. It might be brackish." He followed her.

The water had cut deeply into the stone over millennia, creating uneven steps down the sides of the narrow stream. He hopped down the easiest path he could find to the water's edge, squatted, and dipped a finger. It tasted fresh enough, so he lowered his flask into the stream.

"Look at that," she said, holding up her full leather bladder. "I guess those blue-collar factory workers make something functional after all." She was smiling, but there was no mirth in it.

"I didn't say it wouldn't hold water."

"Right. Just that the house elves at the Institution"—she stressed the last syllable—"do superior work. I'm sure it helps to have an army of minions at your beck and call."

"Who said anything about minions?"

"Not everybody has access to your pseudo-academic industrial complex."

"All I was saying was you stringers may have more money . . ."

He trailed off. Helen started to reply, but he raised a hand to silence her.

He felt it rather than heard it. A low rumble in the pit of his stomach that made every hair stand on end.

Rabbit launched himself at Helen. Drove his shoulder into hers and rolled them both ass over elbows across the rock ledge. Something brushed past him, clipped his shoulder as it passed overhead. It landed with a scrape of claws on the other side of the tiny stream, then spun to face them, crouching for another pounce. Scraggly black and tan mane, mouth hanging open, eyes black and huge. Rabbit swore he could feel its breath across the gap.

Lion.

Its tail bobbed back and forth like a hypnotist's watch above a maw full of yellow teeth. Bobbing tail meant it felt threatened, right? Hadn't he read that? Why didn't he know how to handle lions?

He jerked a dead shrub out of the rocks and waved it at the animal. Disrupt its view. Confuse it.

"Hey!" he shouted.

In response, the lion roared. Rabbit felt his legs go weak as the sound seemed to physically penetrate him. *Don't run. Don't run.*

"Heeeey!" He stepped toward it, shaking the dead shrub.

"Get down!" Helen's voice, behind him.

He dropped to a crouch. Heard a hiss overhead and a whack ahead of him.

The lion jerked back, shaking its mane.

The sling. Helen had scored a direct hit. Rabbit scooped up a handful of pebbles and flung it at the beast's face as another stone whispered by overhead. This one bounced off its flank.

The beast roared again, but this one sounded less menacing, more aggrieved. It coiled itself and bounded over the spring to disappear between the boulders.

Rabbit stared at the gap in the rocks where it had vanished. He realized he was holding his dagger in his shaking left hand. It looked smaller than one of the lion's teeth. *Got to get a better weapon.*

"Do you think it'll come back?" she asked from behind him. The sling was tracing lazy circles in her hand.

"I doubt it. That first shot was a beauty." The chorus of bugs and breeze and shifting stone that had sounded so peaceful a moment ago now seemed full of menace. "Still, let's not hang around to find out."

They backed up to the road, shaking, eyes darting. A few minutes later, as the anesthetic effect of adrenaline left his system, electric jolts started zapping his right elbow. He nestled the arm back into its sling.

It was another mile before Rabbit stopped looking behind them at every sound.

"Where'd you learn to sling a stone like that?" he finally asked her. "I've never gotten the hang of it."

She glanced at the weapon she was still carrying at the ready. A thin, braided fiber rope about the diameter of a climbing line with a pouch in the middle to cradle a stone the size of an egg. Preferably, the stone would be pointed at two ends to give it the ballistics of a bullet, but Helen's was loaded with something basically round. A properly slung stone was deadly, even to fully armored soldiers. Slingers would be a mainstay of battlefields well after the militarization of the bow.

"I made my first one out of string when I was a kid after I read the David and Goliath story. I used to chuck pebbles with it." Her eyes took on a faraway look. "My dad, when he saw it, he marched me up to the house. I figured I was going to get my ass chewed out. You know, 'you're going to break somebody's window.' That sort of thing. He was an old-fashioned guy, my dad. Very big on civics. Instead, he sits me down at the kitchen table, looks me right in the eye across the Formica, and says, 'I thought I taught you better. Cotton is too elastic for a proper sling.'"

Rabbit laughed.

"So, he taught me how to make one right—out of hemp or sisal. He set up a target stand in the backyard so I could practice. I haven't used one in a long time," she said, giving it a twirl, "but it's just like riding a bike."

"Was your dad a survivalist or something?"

She chuckled and shook her head. "Historian."

"Really, where?"

Rabbit knew so little about Helen in present day. Oh, he often knew how she might react to a situation or how she might feel about it. But he knew nothing about her life. Her stories. Funny how much of getting to know someone was about learning their past, no matter how little relation it had to their present.

She looked at him out of the corner of her eye. "Uh-uh. This isn't interrogate-me time. Fair trade. Story for a story."

Now there was the Helen he knew.

"How did you get into this weird fucking business?" she continued.

"Interrogating? Me? I haven't even asked your name."

"No dodge. Smithsonian. Go."

"I was ABD at Stanford. 'All but dissertation,'" he explained.

"I know what it means."

"I was preparing for my defense when it hit the news that the government budget omnibus included a big new pile of money for the Smithsonian. If it was supposed to be a secret, they did a crap job of keeping it. Everybody started writing articles speculating that the government was building a time travel program."

"Sure," she said. "It was like the space race."

"Exactly. And I really wanted the job. So, I got on a plane. I went to DC, snuck into the secretary's locked office, and addressed her in Latin and Greek when she came in for work the next morning."

"Holy shit. Go, Boy Scout. Was she impressed?"

"She spilled her coffee on an antique Persian rug and had me arrested."

"No."

He nodded. "I spent two days in a cell before someone came to let me know the charges had been dropped and they wanted to interview me."

"And you got the job, of course."

"Good thing, too. I think it's the only reason Stanford gave me the degree."

"Not a model student?"

"Profoundly average."

She chuckled again. They walked on in comfortable silence for a few minutes. She was looking up at the cliffs when she said offhandedly, "It's Helen, by the way." She had stopped on the road, her eyes fixed on the rocks.

"What is it?" he asked quietly, slipping his dagger from its sheath.

She shook her head. "Dunno. We might have picked up that raggedy-assed lion again."

They stared at the same spot in the rocks for a long moment. Then, with a noise of shifting pebbles that carried clearly down from the hills, a man stepped out into view.

For a fleeting moment, Rabbit fancied he was looking at one of the gods.

Low sun reflected off the young man's gleaming bronze muscle cuirass, the type movies had long associated with the Roman legions but which, in truth, was an outdated relic of the Greek hoplites. His sandy blond hair was clipped short over a tan, handsome, slightly boyish face. He waved his javelin at them in salutation and descended the hill gracefully in their direction.

Rabbit and Helen exchanged a look of shared uncertainty. The man didn't appear threatening. He skipped out onto the road.

"Greetings, friends! Leocharis. I apologize for my stealth, one can never be too careful on the road, eh? Your woman has good ears."

Rabbit took in the whole package now. Greek cuirass, Roman leather pteruges hanging from his waist, indeterminate sandals, short sword at his belt. He spoke in lightly accented Latin.

"Are you Roman?" Rabbit asked.

Again, the man flashed his relaxed grin and shook his head. "Macedonian. I did serve in the Fifth for a while, no offense to you fine folk."

Rabbit noted that Leocharis had stopped within spear range but beyond the reach of Rabbit's dagger.

"You sure you're not with them still? The Fifth is north of here with Titus. That javelin's a legionary pilum, isn't it?"

Leocharis glanced at the weapon and shrugged. "My centurion didn't object to my keeping it." He grinned again. His teeth gleamed white. "What you're really wondering is if I'm a spy."

"Well, are you?" Rabbit asked.

"I'd be a poor one, dressed like this with a mouth full of the father tongue, wouldn't I? Do you think the empire fields bad spies?"

"An outrider, then, reconnoitering the countryside around Jerusalem," Rabbit said.

"If I'm a rider, where's my horse?"

"You may have lost it to bandits or lions."

The young man planted the sharp butt of the javelin in the dirt. "There is a more parsimonious explanation. What looks like a soldier and talks like a soldier but isn't a soldier?"

"A deserter," Rabbit concluded.

The young man grinned. "I decided the war and I weren't comfortable bedfellows after all."

"I thought the legions looked down on such partings."

He shrugged. "Well, why should divorce be the sole providence of domestic life? We weren't a happy match, that's all. The Fifth had too many arbitrary rules for me and I had too many ideas for her. After the sting fades, we'll both be the better for the parting."

Helen snorted.

"Aha, you both speak my language. What a pleasure for my tongue. And tell me, how ever did such a distinguished couple end up on the road alone?"

"I'll ask the questions," Rabbit replied.

Leocharis fired off a legionary salute but lost none of his mischievous grin.

"Where are you going?" Rabbit pressed.

"I joined the army to see the world. It gamely got me across the wine-dark sea, for which I thank it. Now I plan to continue east to make my fortune across the desert."

"Syria, then?"

"Syria, Parthia, Hodu. Perhaps I'll retrace Alexander's footsteps." He knocked on his bronze chest plate. "I'm clad for it."

A Macedonian mercenary who quotes Homer. With antique armor and perfect teeth. Rabbit was used to forming opinions about people quickly enough, that were right enough, to help him navigate unfamiliar worlds. Leocharis made no sense to him, which made Rabbit simultaneously nervous and excited.

"We're heading to Qumran today. Would you like to accompany us?" He felt Helen tighten beside him.

The young soldier shook his head. "Where?"

It was a clumsy trick on Rabbit's part. The name Qumran wouldn't come into use for many years. Recognition on the soldier's part would have identified him as a fellow time traveler.

"A religious retreat for Essenes."

"Oh, Secacah," Leocharis said, using the era-appropriate name. "Sounds miserable. I'd love to."

Half an hour later, the trio was well on their way to the desert oasis. Helen and Rabbit had fallen back to trail the mercenary.

"What are we doing?" she whispered. "I don't trust this guy."

"Me neither. But he's just off enough to make me wonder if he might be your mark. Let's see if he gives anything away."

"Eshek," Helen blurted, loudly enough that it should have reached those Macedonian ears. The soldier made no sign of recognition.

Rabbit stared at her.

"What? It was worth a try."

The sun was below the horizon when they spotted points of light across a gently inclined plain. The mineral tang of the Dead Sea rode on the breeze.

"That's it," said Rabbit, pointing at the distant building outlined against the darkening eastern sky.

A sudden wave of sound rolled out of the silent village. Shouts. The clatter of metal. The three of them had their hands on their weapons, but before they could draw them, silence fell again, leaving nothing but the breeze in their ears.

They stood rooted to the spot.

"What was that?" Helen whispered.

"Carefully" was all Rabbit said in response, and they continued toward the village.

QUMRAN

68 CE

The lights were farther away than they looked. Several more times in their approach the auditory pattern repeated itself. A sudden burst of noise followed by eerie silence.

The top windows of the building complex flickered with candlelight. That would be members of the brotherhood who lived here studying and scribing, which they did in shifts twenty-four hours a day. Rabbit had expected that. What surprised him was the dancing glow of a bonfire outside illuminating the two-story walls of the compound. Firewood in the desert was a luxury item, what was the occasion?

Elongated shadows stretched up the walls of the building like ghosts. A crowd was gathered around the fire, hidden behind a tall ring of thorny brush surrounding a tent village occupying the flat ground west of the buildings.

As the trio approached, they made out the shuffling of many feet and a single sonorous voice reciting verse.

Whatever was happening, it didn't appear to be violent.

They quietly rounded the brush wall.

"Bring forth the villain!" chimed the voice. He was speaking Aramaic, the most popular local language of the region. "For his errors we drive him from our sight!"

The cacophonous response made Rabbit jump.

Voices, lots of voices, erupted in howling recriminations. Like a stampeding herd of cattle, they poured around the brush wall, chasing a man running with his wrists tied together. The people in front lashed the poor guy with switches, shouting and swearing. He ran, tripped, fell in the dust, struggled to his feet under the snap of the lashes, and ran again.

As the man disappeared into the night, the crowd's angry shouts dissolved into laughter and conversation. They didn't pursue him beyond the tent village. A hundred yards away, the exile's run slowed to a trot, then to a stumble. With backward glances, he slunk away into the gathering darkness.

Helen mouthed at Rabbit in English, *What the fuck?*

Rabbit sheathed his knife and indicated to Helen she should do the same. Leocharis could hardly sheathe his javelin, opting to lean on it like a walking stick with surprisingly convincing ease.

"Oh, hello!" someone said, finally noticing them. The stranger staggered forward from the noisy crowd, hugged Rabbit, bowed his head to Helen, and regarded the mercenary with bemusement. "Are you visitors? Avraham, guests! You need wine!"

As he gesticulated for them to follow, Rabbit leaned close to Helen and whispered, "Holy shit. The noisemakers, the scapegoat, the wine. This is some kind of proto-Purim celebration."

Their host led them to a long table near the fire where casks of wine flanked platters of food. Joints of meat were being carved and served up to the crowd, as well as piles of roasted vegetables, fruit of all kinds, stuffed breads, and cakes. Ceramic plates and cups were pressed into their hands and loaded up from the feast table.

Everyone appeared to be tipsy on the way to drunk, and the wine kept flowing. There were toasts and songs. A few of the men broke out instruments and began to play little flutes, drums, and lyres. The music sounded Greek. No surprise. Alexander the Great's legacy was still strong in Judea hundreds of years after his death.

Leocharis joined the celebration with gusto, slaking his thirst with wine and accompanying the musicians on a little set of pipes he produced from his traveling pack.

Rabbit and Helen found a place to sit on some stones near the edge of the festivities.

"Wow," Rabbit said through a bite of raisin cake, "I didn't expect to eat so well."

"Do you want this?" Helen held up a piece of meat.

Rabbit took it. "Never pass up a meal." He took a bite of the lamb. It was smoky and tender and spiced with what might be sumac.

She shrugged. "I don't like lamb."

Rabbit shook his head in wonderment, watching the crowd. "Purim. What are the odds?"

"Not everybody is having a good ti-ime," she sang, pointing up at the lit window of the complex. A man was glaring down at the partyers, dourly shaking his head.

"Huh." Rabbit popped a dried fig in his mouth. "Maybe the Essenes who live here aren't on board. There are some theorists who think Purim started as a co-opted Persian or Babylonian festival that later got associated with the Book of Esther. Maybe we're seeing the transitional phase."

"Then the book really is here."

"It seems that way." Rabbit was shocked, too. Of all the things he thought he'd find in the compound, the last thing he expected was the very artifact he'd claimed to be here for.

He realized she was staring at him.

"What?"

"I mean, don't you want to go get it?"

"And fight the crowd for it? No thanks. The way this party is going, no one is going to be sober enough to miss it in a few hours. In the meantime . . ." He gestured with his head. She followed his gaze to a box and stool under the feast table. "I know right where it is."

"Well, shit. Looks like it's going to be an easy job for you," she said.

Rabbit grinned. She didn't know how right she was. Sure, he'd have to pilfer the thing without being seen and hide it in a place where it could rest safely until 2019. But at least it was here.

Helen studied the faces of the revelers, drinking, eating, telling jokes, singing songs. Her jaw was clenched, the muscles bunched up. Rabbit followed her eyes and read her thoughts. Eshek could be any one of them. Or none of them. This was her first mission. She probably didn't even know where to begin. Which, he admitted to himself with some shame, would make it easier when it came time to steal Eshek out from under her.

"Want help?"

She eyed him suspiciously.

He shrugged. "Like you said, I'm one step away from getting what I need. My trip won't decay for nineteen days. Why not?"

"I thought you Boy Scouts were too pure to hang around with nefarious types like me."

"I hope this won't offend you, but you don't seem all that nefarious," he said.

"You don't even know why I'm after this asshole. What if I'm an assassin?"

"Are you?"

"Would I admit it if I was?"

Rabbit shrugged. "The offer stands. What am I going to do, sit in the valley for three weeks waiting for my jump?"

She gazed out over the crowd of young men. Sighed. "Okay, I'll take some advice. Where would you start?"

Rabbit rubbed his hands together.

"Our Macedonian friend is suspicious, but don't let that bias you against other potential suspects." He settled in, pleased to have permission to be pedantic. "This compound is owned by an apocalyptic sect of the Essenes who call themselves the Yahad brotherhood. Very into religious purity and cleanliness, the Yahad. Those guys up in the window"—he inclined his head toward the compound—"they're the brothers. We can rule them out; they've all been here for years." He looked around the party. "Now these guys are initiates. They're required to put in two years' labor before they're inducted into the cult. They live in that tent city behind us and spend basically every waking hour in each other's company."

"And the brothers live in the buildings?"

"No, they live in the caves that surround the place. The compound is more of a community center. It houses the library, kitchens, offices, workshops, and of course the ritual baths the place is famous for. The point is, if anybody here is new, they'll all know it. It's just a matter of finding the right way to ask them who turned up in the last twenty days. They'll help us narrow down the suspects."

"Why two years' labor?"

Rabbit shrugged. "Cults. I guess if you make it hard to become a member, people value it more. See, the Yahad think the final fight between good and evil is coming, and they will be the deciding factor in that fight. They want to make sure they have total commitment from these kids. Did nobody brief you on what you were getting into before you jumped?"

"I barely had time to brush up on my languages."

Rabbit flashed back to his own experience with Helen's organization. When he needed their help, they had shipped him back to Rome with the same alacrity. Present-day Helen seemed to be a major player in this enterprise, but this younger version obviously wasn't yet. Rabbit was dying to ask more questions, but caution told him to play it cool. It would come out with time. "If you ever do this again, and I'm not saying you intend to, the more you can figure out about the time period, the better."

"I was never the historian in the family."

"But you speak ancient Greek and Aramaic."

"Latin, too." She shrugged. "You couldn't grow up with my dad and not learn dead languages." Helen glanced around the crowd. "Shiiiiiit." The word came out like a sigh. "All right, you say mingle, I'll mingle. What's our NOC?"

"Our what?"

"Our cover story. Why are we here? What's our relationship?"

"Married couple, Rachel and Joseph. Refugees from Galilee. Avoid saying a city unless somebody really presses you."

She nodded. "You could end up talking to somebody who's really from there."

"Exactly. But if you're pressed, say we're from Tiberias. It surrendered to the Romans without a fight so there shouldn't be too many refugees around. Plus, it's big enough to provide plausible anonymity if you do meet someone from there. If you're asked, say we left because we didn't want to be Roman subjects. That ought to play well with these guys."

"What's the worst-case scenario?" she asked.

Rabbit shrugged. "They think we're Roman spies and kill us?"

"Not great," she mused. "Okay, if it comes to that and we need to get out, where do we rendezvous?"

"There's a natural spring a mile or two south of the compound called Ein Feshkha. Just follow that split in the hills."

She nodded, a curt little bob of the chin that made him smile.

"What?" she asked.

"Nothing," he said. "You just seem remarkably calm about all this."

"Good," she said, rising. "That's how I want to seem."

He rose with her.

"What are you doing?" she asked.

"It's going to look pretty suspicious if I just sit here while you mingle. Why don't we both make the rounds? We can cover more ground that way. I'll tell you if I find anybody new to the party."

As the Purim revelers got progressively looser on wine, Rabbit and Helen separated and mingled among them. Rabbit followed a joke as it passed around the crowd, each person elaborating on the basic structure until it was almost unrecognizable. The initiates acknowledged him vaguely but were too focused on their own celebration to question the newcomer in their midst. As he passed through, he caught a snippet of conversation between two young men that pulled at his attention.

"No, this is the first time. Last year the brothers forbade it. Isaac especially. He said we couldn't afford to let our vigilance wane, even for a night and certainly not for 'some Babylonian debauchery dressed up as prayer.'" The initiate who was speaking had a thin beard and bright blue eyes.

"Everybody in Jerusalem celebrates it now. Even the priests. I'm sorry I missed the story." The second speaker looked to be in his early- to mid-twenties with all the marks of an urban visitor, not a member. Well-trimmed red beard and hair. Clothes that looked more fashionably colorful than the simple white and tan robes of the initiates. He looked more clear-eyed than the initiates, too. Visitor, Rabbit would bet money on it. The young man clocked Rabbit's attention and opened the circle to admit him into the conversation.

"Good feast day to you," the urbane young man said with a nod of his head that suggested a bow.

"And to you," Rabbit replied. He pretended to swig from his cup and allowed a droopy-lidded smile to creep onto his face. Sober people always felt superior to drunk people. "Joseph," he said, touching his chest.

"Tuvia ben Antipas," he replied. "From Jerusalem."

Rabbit wished he had enough experience in this time-space to judge if "Tuvia's" accent was legit. His Aramaic sounded grammatically flawless.

"This is quite a feast," Rabbit lightly slurred. "I didn't anticipate such largesse here in the desert, but I appreciate it," Rabbit said, turning his attention to the blue-eyed initiate.

"We eat well at Secacah. Meat every Sabbath." The initiate turned his head and burped.

Tuvia ben Antipas eyed Rabbit. "You're not a brother, then. What's your story?"

"My wife and I fled the Romans in the North."

"Why would you come here?" Tuvia said, painting the last word with distaste.

"Just stopping off for the night. We're headed for Ein Gedi."

The visitor scowled. "Then go no further."

The initiate nodded sadly. "Ein Gedi is gone. Burned by the Sicarii, the dagger men. They took everything of value and burned the rest."

Rabbit knew that story but pretended he didn't. "They attacked their own countrymen? Why?"

Tuvia snarled his answer. "Pillaged to fund their mad cause. The men were impressed into service. The women and children they had no use for."

"They abandoned them?"

"They slaughtered them." His voice dripped venom.

Rabbit tried to read Tuvia's face. His anger looked real. If it was, then Tuvia was likely a Sadducee or a Pharisee, the upper classes of Jerusalem who wanted to make peace with the Romans and spare the South of Judea from Galilee's fate. They had little love for the resistance who wanted to fight. If the expression was an act, it was a good one. Then again, every time traveler Rabbit knew was a master liar. Came with the territory.

"Why didn't you go to Jerusalem like everyone else?" Tuvia continued. "The city is overrun with refugees."

"Zealots?" Rabbit asked. He knew that the militias from the North had fled to the city when Galilee had fallen.

"Factions, yes. But also farmers, tradespeople, even foolish foreigners who failed to heed the warnings of the last year."

Rabbit nodded. "We thought that might be so. And surely the Romans will strike the city soon. My wife and I thought it would be safer to make our way down the Salt Sea. Maybe even flee to Idumea, where she has family."

Tuvia nodded. His face softened. "You may be the wise ones after all."

"What brings you to Secacah?" Rabbit asked.

At once, the young man's expression sharpened again. "My business with the Yahad is my own."

Rabbit raised his hands in supplication. "I meant no offense."

The man scanned Rabbit from head to toe as though he expected violence. Finally, he sighed, relaxed somewhat. "Offense is the new coin of the realm." He offered Rabbit and the initiate a curt nod and stalked away.

The blue-eyed initiate watched Tuvia carefully until he was sure he was out of earshot, then turned excitedly to Rabbit.

"He arrived this evening, too, demanding an audience with the brothers. They told him he would have to wait until after morning prayers."

"Is that wise? He seems like a powerful young man."

The initiate puffed up. "The Yahad aren't intimidated by the Sadducees."

"So, he's a Sadducee?"

"He talks like he's highly connected, but I've never heard of him."

"What do you think he wants?" Rabbit asked.

"For the Yahad to join the war effort, of course."

"Did he say that?" Rabbit pressed. The priestly upper classes didn't want war. If Tuvia was singing a different song, that might give him away.

"No, but it's obvious," the initiate said, puffing up his chest.

"Do you want to go to Jerusalem?" Rabbit asked, responding to the young man's bravado.

"It's not a matter of wanting. This is the end of times. The Yahad will be there, and we will defeat this evil that besets the people."

No, young man. Jerusalem will fall within the year and the brotherhood will never be heard from again.

Rabbit changed the subject. "How long have you been with the Yahad?"

"Almost two turns of season. I'll be initiated in the summer if we don't march first."

"Do you have specific responsibilities with the newer members?"

He stood up a little straighter. "Of course. When a hopeful joins, they need guidance, someone to introduce them to their new brothers, show them around, you know. Hopefuls are assigned to more experienced men to guide them."

"Sort of a big brother, little brother arrangement?"

"Exactly."

"I bet you've had a lot of people join recently, what with the unrest in the city."

He shook his head. "Not in months. All we've seen is refugees, mostly passing through on their way south like you. And only women and children. Some of them stayed. They keep to themselves in the residential caves facing the sea. The men have all joined the militias." He gave Rabbit a judgmental look.

"Enoch!" called a drunken voice from the crowd, and the initiate swiveled. A group of young men was beckoning him to join their dance.

"Excuse me," he said. "Enjoy the rest of the feast." Then he danced into the embrace of his brothers.

Rabbit scanned the faces for Helen. If no other men had come to Qumran in months, that limited the additional suspects to one.

"Tuvia ben Antipas," Rabbit said to Helen, inclining his head toward the young man from Jerusalem. The Sadducee was standing by the banquet table, glancing up at the second-story windows of the compound. "Apparently, he's the only male newcomer."

"What's his story?"

"Unclear. Might be recruiting, but that's just speculation. He gave me the brush-off when I asked. The name Antipas pops up a lot in the priesthood of the era, so that checks out. What do you know about Eshek that would help confirm or deny it? I take it you never saw a picture."

"No, all the bitch gave me was 'slim build, good-looking.'"

Rabbit suspected he knew who "the bitch" was. The woman with the glasses who ran Helen's jump last year certainly qualified for the epithet in Rabbit's opinion. *Put a pin in that.*

"Is he good-looking?" Tuvia was slim. Regular features, maybe a little on the sharp side. Rabbit had never been good at figuring out what women found attractive in a man.

"He's all right."

"What about him?" Rabbit inclined his head toward Leocharis, who had joined the ring of initiates dancing.

"I mean, only if you have eyes."

Rabbit studied the Macedonian. Leocharis had removed his antique breastplate and was stomping among the initiates, hands overhead. Lean, well-muscled. Graceful, too. The young man made the unfamiliar dance look effortless. If they filmed this, Ethan Davies, the Hollywood actor implicated by Misherenko, might play him in the movie. Fine. Slim and good-looking—check.

"Well, that's two suspects, anyway. What did you find out?"

"Oh, you know that kid they ran off right when we came in? The scapegoat?"

"Is he new?" Rabbit asked.

She waved that away. "Not new enough, he joined a few months ago. No, my point was he's a ben Antipas, too."

"Hnh, what was he being punished for?"

She rolled her eyes and placed finger quotes around the word as she said it: "'Onanism.'"

"They exiled him for that?"

"It seems like it's mostly for show. He can come back tomorrow. Still, how fucking stupid is that?"

"Well, even if he was new, that would rule him out."

"Why?"

"Believe me, when you're on the clock for twenty days, nobody has time for . . ."

She watched him squirm, a little smile forming on her face. "Masturbation?"

"Right."

"You mean you never, in all the twenty-day missions you've had, you've never gotten yourself off?"

Rabbit felt heat creeping up his cheeks and was embarrassed by it, which only magnified the reaction. "I've got other things to focus on."

She whistled through her teeth. "No wonder you're wound so tight."

"I think we ought to—"

"You should. It clears the mind, relaxes the body. It's good for you. There have been studies."

"Could we stick to the task at hand?"

She laughed, then caught herself when he didn't join in. "Oh, you're serious. I thought that was a pun. Okay, sorry. Go ahead."

Rabbit barreled on. "It's not conclusive, but we have two people who could be Eshek. It would be awfully helpful to know what he came here to get."

She looked away.

"Do you know what he's here for?" Rabbit pressed.

Helen was silent for a moment, then finally admitted, "He's here for the Copper Scroll."

Rabbit thought about that and shook his head. "Not the scroll."

"That's what they told me."

Rabbit looked through the crowd toward Tuvia-maybe-Eshek. The young man was nibbling some food while talking to a couple initiates. "I mean, he's not here for the scroll itself. The Copper Scroll was found in 1952 by archaeologists excavating the caves surrounding the compound. It's on display in the Jordan Museum; I've seen it. A single sheet of rolled copper stamped with the locations of multiple caches of treasure hidden across the Holy Land. If he's here for anything, it's the treasure the scroll purports to point to."

"What kind of treasure?"

"Gold, silver, religious artifacts. If it's real, it would almost have to be the treasury of Herod's Temple. In our time it would be worth billions of dollars."

She stared at him. "Billions with a *B*?"

He nodded. "Thing is, no one has ever found any of the treasures it points to. People have debated for years whether the whole thing was just some kind of ancient hoax. Then again, why go to all the trouble of making such an elaborate, expensive map if it isn't real?"

"Maybe someone got to the treasures first. Two thousand years is a lot of time for treasure hunting."

"That's possible. But if someone used the scroll to find the treasures, they would have taken the scroll itself, and it was still safe and sound in the cave waiting to be discovered."

"I just know when he gets back from his mission, Einar Eshek will steal what he was sent back for. I assumed it was the scroll but you're probably right that it was something the scroll points to."

"And your bosses want him found."

Their eyes flicked between the raucous Leocharis and the imperious Tuvia.

She nodded. "Very badly."

QUMRAN

68 CE

The next morning, Rabbit was awakened by the shuffling feet and painful groans of those initiates who had taken seriously the guidance to drink until you couldn't tell the difference between "Blessed is Mordechai" and "Cursed is Haman." He and Helen had slept on borrowed bedrolls between two initiates' tents. The night had been cold and the ground hard. Rabbit felt like his body was one big knot. The years were creeping up on him.

He started into his cycle of stretches that were the oilcan to his morning Tin Man joints.

The initiates oozed out of their tents in various states of fragility. Chimes rang from the compound just as the sun peeked above the mountains.

Helen sat up and looked around, seemingly surprised by her surroundings.

"How'd you sleep?" he asked.

"What do you mean?" She pointed at the bedrolls. "Do you think we should leave these here, or . . ."

"I assume so. What do you mean, what do I mean?"

"Like you want a description? I closed my eyes; I opened my eyes. I slept. I don't know. A-plus?"

"You don't wake up at all in the night?"

"Do you?"

He grunted, grabbed his possessions from the ground, then

followed the queasy line of initiates through last night's dance floor to the entrance of the compound.

Although Secacah was technically made up of several buildings, they had been constructed in such close contact that it seemed more like one flowing structure. A defensive wall molded into a tower molded into several interconnected buildings with windows set high on their walls. Over it all was a sparkling white mineral skin that rounded the corners and edges like New Mexico adobe. Deep green leaves of date palms poked up over the walls of a courtyard on the southwest corner, making the salt skin seem even brighter by contrast. Behind it, the land dropped away in a long slope to the vivid blue of the Dead Sea.

"The Emerald City," Helen said, interrupting his thoughts. "Remember that? From *The Wizard of Oz*? On a smaller scale, but that's what it reminds me of."

He studied it, too. Shook his head. "*Fight Club*."

She looked at him in confusion.

"The feel, I mean. Not the look." He glanced pointedly at the line of initiates shuffling through the gate. "A bunch of disaffected young guys from Jerusalem trying to prove their commitment to a doomsday cult."

She followed his gaze. Hesitated. "I guess there's always been a market for a sense of purpose and a simple, communal life."

"Simple, maybe, but not poor. The last thing all these guys do before becoming a brother is give all their worldly possessions to the Yahad. There's a lot of money in these caves."

"Not the kind of money we're after," Helen said.

"True."

For a moment, Rabbit was on the California seaside and Aaron was stretching in the sun. "Purpose," he had said. *Oh Aaron, I hope you're careful about who you expose that need to.*

Helen nudged him. The initiates and brothers were queueing up at a ceramic basin in the picturesque courtyard. Would it be offensive for strangers to join? To not join? They silently agreed to give it a try and queued up at the back of the line. After a moment, however, one of the brothers approached them.

"You are guests of the Yahad. Come." He led them forward in the queue and inserted them between the last brother and the first initiate. You could tell the two apart by the vivid blue braid around the head coverings of the full brothers.

The water in the basin was still relatively clean when Rabbit dipped his hands in it and rubbed them together. A brother stood by with a damp cloth to dry their hands. Rabbit had heard the quiet prayers uttered by the men ahead of him but couldn't make out the words. He aimed for a close approximation of the length and cadence in a whisper so soft he couldn't hear it himself.

When the last member of the community had dried their hands, the assembly stood with heads bowed. A prayer leader intoned a series of blessings that both brothers and initiates softly echoed.

The initiates immediately fell into another line that passed through a gatehouse between the outer wall surrounding the garden and the inner courtyard of the compound.

The same brother who had reordered their position in line now gestured for them to follow. "The Yahad are eager to hear your news of the world."

As they followed him, Rabbit leaned close to Helen and whispered, "We should have rehearsed our story better."

"Next time."

Next time. Despite himself, Rabbit smiled.

The inner courtyard was wide enough for the passage of a wagon, with a clean-swept buff brick floor. On the left rose the blocky three-story watchtower, attached to a long, two-story building into which the brothers were disappearing. To its right was a zigzagging wall topped with a reed-thatched roof. Those would be the mikvot, the famous ritual baths, of Qumran.

Goats bleated somewhere in the distance, and Rabbit was pretty sure he heard horses, too.

Joining the agrarian noises was a sound he didn't expect to hear.

Children. A small group of women shepherded a herd of chirpy kids into the dining hall at the far end of the inner courtyard. Must be the refugees the initiate, Enoch, had talked about.

The Yahad brother escorted Rabbit and Helen into a building that housed what looked like a classroom in its ground floor. Two-person wood tables were arrayed in a neat grid facing the narrow end of the rectangular room. Its walls and low ceiling were plastered white like the outer skin of the building and unmarked by any ornamentation.

The room was packed with cultists. Some sat at the tables, but most were on their feet. Dressed in their identical off-white robes and blue headbands, they reminded Rabbit of a restless flock of desert birds. Leocharis stood at the head of the classroom. He must have already reported his news to the assembly, because he was ushered out as Rabbit and Helen were ushered in. He grinned at them, looking none the worse for yesterday's wine. Probably didn't have to stretch when he woke up either, Rabbit thought, a little jealous of the dancer-like grace with which the young man moved.

"Quiet," one of them said, waving his hands for order. "Quiet down." One by one, the brothers settled into silence.

"We understand you have come from the North," the man said. He was tall, with a deeply creased face behind his bushy salt-and-pepper beard. Despite the wear and tear, he probably wasn't older than forty. The desert climate was hard on its inhabitants.

Rabbit nodded. "From Tiberias." He was racking his brain for whatever dregs of information he could come up with about the city.

"Has it fallen?"

"The whole of Galilee has fallen. Tiberias surrendered without a fight. So did Sepphoris."

The Yahad brother sneered.

Getting into his role, Rabbit felt a little indignant at the brother's attitude. "They were spared the fate of Gamla and Gischala. The Romans razed those cities after resistance broke."

"Where are the Romans now?"

"Vespasian is at Caesarea with the bulk of his force. He's securing the sea trade lines to Egypt. He won't stay there long, though."

"Where will he go next?"

"How should I know? Jerusalem, I suppose. They might cut it off from the countryside first. I don't know."

"Why are you here?"

"My wife and I escaped Tiberias just ahead of the incursion. After we heard of the capitulation, I didn't want to go back. We were ashamed."

The man chewed the inside of his cheek, his eyes unfocused for a long moment. Finally, he pronounced, "Tiberias was corrupted by impurity and worldliness. The welcome into the Roman fold is a curse, not a blessing. Soon it will wish it met the fate of Gischala." There were murmurs throughout the room. He continued, in rising tones. "We should march for Jerusalem now. That is where the final battle will come between light and darkness."

Another brother raised his hands for quiet. He was short and stocky, with a furrowed brow over his black eyes. "Yes, Isaac. Yes, a battle is coming. But is it our battle?"

Isaac jabbed him with a horny finger. "You don't want the fight, Malachai. We all know it."

"I am ready to lay down my life on a mountain of my enemies' corpses. But will I do so at the word of this Tiberian? If that's what he is."

"And what do you propose he is instead?"

"He could be a spy, sent to sway us."

Rabbit tried not to roll his eyes. *Sway you? The Roman army doesn't give a shit about this flyspeck cult.* Their decision wouldn't make a difference in the outcome of the war, no matter what they did.

"I didn't ask to address this room," Rabbit reminded the stocky man.

"Why did you come, then?"

"All my wife and I wanted was a respite from the road. Perhaps to be cleansed in the mikvot. The Yahad are famous for their hospitality."

Hospitality was a cornerstone of many world cultures, including classical Judaism. To imply a lack of welcome was a low blow.

Isaac and Malachai glanced at each other. The shorter man spoke. "These are uncommon times, Joseph, with uncommon problems. But that should not make us less than we are. You and your wife are welcome to the hospitality of the brotherhood. Break your fast. We still have much to discuss among ourselves. Can you find the dining hall?"

Rabbit nodded. "We saw it when we came in."

Expressing their gratitude, Rabbit and Helen left the building the way they had entered. As they rounded the corner of the courtyard, they almost collided with a Yahad initiate leading Tuvia ben Antipas. The initiate apologized while the haughty young Sadducee glared at them. The moment they were out of earshot, Rabbit caught Helen's sleeve. "Can you cover for me? I'm going to see if I can find out if"—he enclosed the name in finger quotes—"'Tuvia's' story makes sense."

"Why you?" she whispered.

"Patriarchy," he said, apologetically. "If I get caught, it will cause fewer ripples."

"I'll cover for you," she said, rolling her eyes.

Rabbit spun on his heel and trailed the initiate and his charge, scanning the building for the best place to eavesdrop. The classroom gathering space had windows (without glass, of course) that opened onto the courtyard. Rabbit would be visible to the brotherhood if he walked by them. Feeling like an idiot, he crouched low and crab-walked under the open portals until he reached a spot close to where he and Helen had been addressed.

Isaac and Malachai were still arguing within.

"We are the Yahad. The brothers of light. This battle is coming to us. The last battle wherein we shall crush the darkness forever."

"So you say," Malachai responded.

"The scroll says—"

"I know the scroll as well as you, Isaac. We all do. It says nothing of *when* the great battle will come."

"Rome marches on Jerusalem while the Sadducees and Pharisees bicker over money and power. The Zealots and Sicarii rape the land for supplies and recruits. What more sign do you need?"

"And what do you think we can do about any of that?" Malachai spat.

"We can rally the people! Bring them together under the banner of light. Don't you see? This is the moment Teacher spoke of."

Rabbit cringed at that nickname. *Teacher*. That was one of the names Aaron had called himself during his rise to power. *Don't be paranoid. Aaron's stretch using that title wouldn't come for another 350 years.*

Isaac continued. "In the face of doom, the people will open their eyes to their own iniquity. They will turn their faces back to God and unite as one people."

Another voice rose among the brotherhood. "Ask the Sadducee."

There was a moment of silence. Rabbit imagined all eyes turning to Tuvia ben Antipas. When the visitor spoke, he sounded irritated.

"I'm not here to talk about fighting some lost cause."

Isaac growled his response. "No just cause is a lost cause."

"Can these Romans be beaten?" Malachai asked.

But Isaac was the one who answered. "We have already beaten legions on our own soil."

Tuvia audibly sighed. "Joseph ben Matityahu . . ."

"Who?" asked a voice from the crowd.

Another voice jeered, "Josephus the Roman."

Josephus wasn't really a Roman, but Rabbit understood the slur. The man who would become known as Titus Flavius Josephus was a Judean national, born to a priestly family. The Jewish government had appointed him to lead the resistance in Galilee. It was a controversial choice; Josephus was considered by many to be too pro-Roman even before the war. He would go on to become the only historian to write about this time-space from a firsthand perspective. Generations of Jews would question the motivations behind his descriptions of the war, especially since he would live out the rest of his life after the conflict ended as an expat in Rome.

"When Yodfat fell, Joseph was captured and brought to the general Vespasian. He said he'd had a vision in which Vespasian became emperor of Rome."

"Just trying to save his own skin, probably," said a voice from the group.

"If he didn't turn the city over, himself," muttered another.

"My point is," Tuvia said, "Vespasian is no Gessius Florus. He won't be so easy to defeat. He and his son lead veteran legions who have proven themselves against the Zealots and forces of the provisional government. Standing against these Romans is suicide."

You could have heard a pin drop.

Tuvia continued. "If you came to Jerusalem today, you would not recognize the city most of you came from. We are a splintered people. Zealots from the North and South, Sicarii, everyone vying with the army for control of the city and even the Temple. The city itself is carved into strongholds like a body divided from itself. Like you, I pray we will not fall. I pray the priests can talk sense into the rabble and we sue for peace before it is too late. But while we pray, we also plan. I am charged with keeping the treasury out of Roman hands. Should the city fall, we will need it to rebuild the Temple one day."

"You want to hide the treasury here?" Malachai asked.

"No. I want to hide a document here that will allow our people to find the treasury, should all who know its location perish. Secacah has always been known as a home of faithful preservation. I would ask that you steward the map and provide it to the priests when the time is right to rebuild."

Rabbit felt the hair standing up on his arms. He felt giddy that he was present for this significant conversation and had to remind himself that it might never have really happened this way. If Tuvia was Eshek, then all this was some performance of his devising.

"If this is the final battle, the Yahad will not be here to protect it." Isaac, of course.

"If this is the final battle, it won't matter." There was a little mirth in Tuvia's voice.

"Will it be safe enough here?" asked Malachai. "So much wealth all revealed by one scroll. You might be better hiding it—"

Tuvia interrupted. "The Copper Scroll is one of a pair. The locations listed in it are encoded, the translation is in a second scroll. Unless someone has asked you to house the key scroll . . ."

In the dramatic pause that followed, Rabbit could imagine the heads shaking no.

"Then it is perfectly safe here."

There was a little debate among the brothers, but not much. Despite their disdain for the priestly class in Jerusalem, they absolutely recognized the need to preserve the Temple. If hiding the document on their grounds would help in that aim, they were on board.

Rabbit was ready to return to Helen, but Tuvia had one more item.

"Before I go, I would like to speak to my brother, Tzephania."

Silence fell like a hammer.

"Tzephania?" Isaac asked weakly.

"He is an initiate here. He came a few months ago."

"Yes. Well . . ."

"Tzephania has been punished," Isaac said. "Expelled to the desert until the sun is high."

Rabbit thought it had been quiet before. *I wish I could see their faces.*

When Tuvia spoke again, his voice was simmering. "You sent my brother, the second son of a priest, into the desert?"

"The initiates . . ."

"Where . . . is . . . he?"

The mood in the room became suddenly animated. Rabbit stood up from his crouch and walked toward the dining hall, trying to appear nonchalant. As he heard the tramp of footsteps exiting the meeting room, Rabbit caught a flash of sunlight on bronze near the far corner of the building.

The brothers poured out of the room behind him. Tuvia stormed past Rabbit and into the dining hall ahead of the crowd, but Rabbit was still staring at the spot where he'd seen the glare of metal. Had he imagined it? Or had Leocharis been eavesdropping just like he was?

"Who among you thought it right to send my brother away?" Tuvia demanded. "Show me your hands." His voice shook with rage. "Who!"

Several of the initiates' hands rose.

Tuvia took two steps toward the nearest of them, knocked the covering off the young man's head, and seized a handful of his long hair. He jerked the initiate off his bench and dragged him to the door. "Find him." He released the young man's hair and kicked him in the backside. Then he turned on the rest of them. "Find him!"

They hesitated, caught between Tuvia's rage and their adherence to the word of the brothers. Malachai broke the deadlock. He stepped up beside the young Sadducee. "Organize a search. Two-man teams." At his word, the initiates rose as a unit and filed out past a fuming Tuvia.

Rabbit approached Malachai. "Can we help?"

The stocky brother nodded, rolling his eyes when he was sure Tuvia's back was turned. "Thank you."

The brothers and initiates poured through the main gate and fanned out across the plateau. Helen was following them, but Rabbit tapped her shoulder and indicated with his eyes that she should follow him back into the compound.

"What happened in there?" she asked.

Rabbit relayed the essentials in a whisper, concluding with, "The Copper Scroll is real, but it won't give you the locations without the corresponding key scroll to decode it."

"Is the key here?" she whispered.

"No. Tuvia implied it wasn't and let the brothers confirm that. It would be a smooth technique if he's one of us."

The compound was emptied out, so he led her into the classroom. On the table, forgotten, lay the scroll. When it was discovered in 1952, it was so badly oxidized that the only way to open it was to separate the semicircular pieces of green copper with a surgical saw. Here in

68 CE, the scroll was new, burnished, flexible enough to be unrolled and read in its totality.

He checked both doors, then unrolled it a few inches. Hebraic writing was stamped into the thin copper sheet. "Here. The last bit of the document says, 'In the subterranean shaft that is hidden on the north side of Kohlit, its northern entrance, there are buried at its mouth a copy of this writing and its interpretation and their measures, with a detailed description of each and every thing.' We need both scrolls to get the real map."

"You mean Eshek would," Helen said softly.

Rabbit paused. "Well, yes, obviously. The problem is, no one knows where Kohlit is located, at least not in modern day. If it's a city, we should be able to find out here, though. All we need to do is—"

"Rabbit."

He looked at her.

"That's all great but what I want to know is whether Tuvia is Einar Eshek."

He felt heat prickle up his cheeks. In all the revelations about the scroll, he had almost forgotten about the real quarry. He cleared his throat. "Right. I've certainly played some long games in my time to get what I was after. He could be doing the same."

Rabbit froze mid-stride, halfway through the garden gate.

"What is it?" she asked.

"Antipas. I just remembered why that name sounds familiar. The Temple treasurer is named Antipas. Tuvia and Tzephania must be his sons. If I was Eshek, I might assume they both know the location of the scrolls. So, the real question is—"

Helen finished for him. "Where the hell is Tzephania?"

That's when the screaming started.

QUMRAN

68 CE

Instinctively, Rabbit sprinted back into the courtyard, Helen right behind him. They skidded to a stop, ears cocked to the wind like a couple of hunting dogs.

A moment passed.

"That was nearby," she whispered.

She led the way through an opening in the low stone wall that shielded the mikvot from the courtyard.

Helen looked back at him from within and gestured with her head for him to follow. She had her knife out, held in stabbing position with the pommel facing forward. And she led with her other side, to ensure she kept control of the knife if she was jumped. *No time travel experience, but she's had combat training. What's your backstory, Helen?*

The first bath was big enough for a grown man to submerge himself. It was full to the top with what Rabbit knew to be rainwater, channeled in from a wadi nearby where the winter rains formed a seasonal stream. The water looked clean, but ominously dark under the shade of the thatch roof.

Its stone platform was empty.

Helen was already headed for the break in the wall into the next bath enclosure.

A few birds rose from the edge of the bath as they entered, circled under the thatch, and escaped through the space between the roof and stone wall.

Nothing here.

Helen sniffed the air. Rabbit smelled it, too. Metal and feces.

She ran headlong into the next room. "Helen!" he hissed, but it was too late.

When Rabbit cleared the door in the wall, he was assaulted by the view.

She was already squatting by the body, her knife discarded on the stones. Blood pooled on the floor, ran into the mikveh. The body was splayed out on the stone, belly slit open, organs arrayed around it. Once again, it reminded Rabbit of an orchid.

Just like the body in Rome.

Helen's bloody hands were fluttering, as though her brain was giving her conflicting messages about what to do with them.

Rabbit put his hand on her shoulder. She flinched but didn't draw away.

A wadded cloth was next to the dead man's face. It was wet, probably with saliva. The killer had muffled the man's screams until the last one.

Rabbit was awash with pity, revulsion, and fear. The sick bastard from Rome was here. The display of the body was too similar to be a coincidence. And after he had gotten what he wanted, he made sure Rabbit and Helen would hear Tzephania's scream.

He had lured them in to investigate.

"Helen, come on, this is a frame-up."

Footsteps. Running footsteps approaching.

Too late.

One of the Yahad skidded to a stop in the doorway, hand flying to his mouth in a universal gesture of shock. He was jostled out of the way by Isaac, the tall brother so hungry for blood. He blanched at the sight of the real thing.

Tuvia ben Antipas pushed in behind them.

"Brother . . ."

He shoved them all out of the way and fell on the corpse. Kissing the dead man's face, sobbing, trying vainly to reassemble the parts of a puzzle that had recently been a living man.

"Tzephania! Brother!"

Isaac turned to Rabbit and Helen, took in the blood on their clothes and hands. The knife lying amid the gore.

A host of brothers and initiates was gathering, filling both doors.

The horror in the Yahad brother's eyes hardened into fury. He pointed at Rabbit and Helen.

"Take them."

QUMRAN

68 CE

They spent the next few hours locked in a windowless stone room filled with piles of loose wool while the men of the Yahad presumably argued over what to do with them.

To her credit, Helen was far more concerned with the poor initiate's fate than her own. Rabbit wished he could say the same.

"Who would do that to another person?"

"Unfortunately, I have an idea."

He told her about the murder in Rome, the results of which looked so similar.

"Christ. A time traveler did this? One of your people?"

"Yes and no. Time traveler, yes. Professional, no. Some rich Russian brat bought himself a time machine and was selling trips to the past. My guess is the killer bought rides so he can commit his murders without fear of punishment."

"A serial killer?"

"I don't know what counts as serial, but it's as good a term as any." Rabbit shifted his feet. Helen was sitting on the floor of the little room, while he stood close to the door, listening at the pitted wood.

"I've never heard of this Russian."

That's because he's operating in your future.

Rabbit lied, "Law enforcement has kept it quiet."

She didn't say anything for a few moments. Finally, a little grunt escaped her. "Why here?"

"What do you mean?" he asked.

"Doesn't it bother you that this guy ended up in two places with you?"

"I don't love it."

"No, I mean, doesn't that seem like an awfully big coincidence?"

Rabbit pondered that. "Yeah, I guess so."

"Maybe it's not. Maybe this prick has it out for you specifically."

"Me? What for? I've ticked a few people off in my time, but not enough to make them want to frame me for murder . . . I think."

"Maybe he's pegged you as his nemesis. You got away from him once."

"That wasn't due to any skill on my part. He knocked me out and left me for the fire."

"But you saw him."

Rabbit shrugged, a pointless gesture in the dark closet. "Barely. It was dark and he was masked. It's not like I could pick him out of a lineup. Hell, I actually saw a lineup."

"You said he spoke to you in English."

"Right."

"Did you respond?"

Rabbit had to think about that. "No, I was too beat-up to talk at all."

"So, he might not know you're from the present. The future. Goddammit, you know what I mean."

"I suppose that could be true. Does it matter?"

"I don't know," she said. "There's something there, I just can't make it out yet."

"Better get about it. We don't have much time." *Or did they?* Rabbit met Helen when she was older than she was now. Didn't that imply she had to live through this ordeal? If she didn't, it would be a splinter, right? Of course, that didn't guarantee Rabbit must live. What if, when Helen encountered him in Alexandria, she had already seen him die? Jesus, that would be messed up. He still hadn't fully processed the notion that the Helen who started robbing him in 2017 had already had this experience with him. She had already sat in this cramped closet awaiting death. Already picked up the sound of . . .

"Do you hear that?" she asked.

Rabbit nodded ineffectually in the dark. "Horses."

Helen jostled him as she got up and they both pressed their ears to the door.

The wood was thin. Rabbit was sure he could kick it open if he braced against the back wall of the closet. It was the enraged cult outside that had kept him in. Now he could hear angry voices through that flimsy door but couldn't make out the words. "Can you hear what they're—"

"Shh!"

Apparently, she could.

He was bursting inside as she listened intently, occasionally whispering a summary.

"It's the Zealots."

He opened his mouth to ask a follow-up, but she put her hand on his chest and he stopped.

"They're recruiting. For Jerusalem."

"Are they—"

She slid her hand up to his mouth. How did her skin smell so good after days in the desert?

"The Sadducee kid—"

"Tuvia," he said around her hand.

"Tuvia is arguing with them."

Rabbit lifted her hand away. "What's he saying?"

"Oh shit."

"What?"

She grabbed Rabbit and pulled him back from the door just before it flew open. Tuvia stood there, flanked by Isaac and a couple dusty militiamen in draped tan and white robes. Unlike the cultists, the militia were armed. Gladii, the short swords emblematic of the Roman legions, hung from their belts. Looted from the slaughtered garrisons at Rome or Masada most likely.

"That's them," Tuvia spat, pointing at them. "They murdered my brother."

One of the militiamen pointed at the ground in front of him, staring Rabbit hard in the eyes. All the fear drained out of Rabbit like water, replaced by anger at the arrogant prick's expression. He came forward all right, faster and more assertively than the militiaman expected. The soldier took an inadvertent step backward at Rabbit's approach. The recruiter's face flushed red.

"This man says you and your wife murdered his brother. Is that true?"

"No," Rabbit replied simply.

"Liar!" Tuvia shouted. "You were found bathed in his blood!"

"Do you deny it?" said the militiaman.

"We heard his scream and went to his aid. My wife"—Rabbit turned to Helen, who had assumed an unyielding but not aggressive expression—"tried to help the man as anyone would. And yes, she was bloodied in the trying."

Tuvia wasn't about to let it go. "And what about her bloody dagger? Did she intend to use that to help him?"

"We both drew our blades when we heard the scream. She dropped hers in the blood."

"Why didn't you say any of this earlier?" The militiaman clearly thought this Perry Mason stumper was a master play, judging by the smug expression on his face.

"We were given no chance to. The brothers locked us up immediately."

The militiaman looked at Isaac, who shrugged his assent.

Tuvia picked up on the nonverbal exchange. "Don't listen to him," the Sadducee demanded, his voice growing shrill. "He's clearly a sorcerer."

"A . . . now he's a sorcerer, too?"

"I mean he is twisting your thoughts with his words," Tuvia explained condescendingly.

"So, you think this weak-minded soldier couldn't possibly withstand the verbal assault of this Galilean farmer," said the militiaman.

"I didn't mean—" Tuvia stammered. He was still furious, but the tides were turning against him, and he knew it.

The militiaman held up his hand to silence the Sadducee and returned his gaze to Rabbit.

"Trader," said Rabbit.

"What?"

"Not farmer. Trader." He suspected the militiaman was trying to figure out Rabbit's class alignment. This whole conflict had been predicated on the tensions between the wealthy elites of Judea and the poor working class. Rabbit couldn't pass as a farmer, his smooth hands would give him away, but a trader could work. To improve the impression he'd made, Rabbit added, "And sometime soldier."

The militiaman raised his eyebrows.

"Where did you soldier?"

Rabbit frantically searched his brain for something in the right time frame. "In the North, under Jacob and Simon." It was a gamble. The uprising had been twenty years ago. Would they believe he was old enough to be part of it?

The militiaman nodded. "A righteous cause born too early."

Rabbit was half-relieved, half-offended.

"Can you still hold a spear?"

"As well as most," Rabbit replied.

The soldier pondered for a moment, then concluded, "Pack up your things."

"What!?" Tuvia exploded. "This man should be put to death! At least six of us saw it all!"

"You saw what you feared to see. And no one seems to back you. I'm sorry for your loss, but you won't slake your bloodlust here. Jerusalem needs this man as much or more than it needs you."

Tuvia took a step toward him, puffing up like a rooster. It might have been aggressive; it might have just been posturing. Either way, the soldier had been primed by Rabbit's similar move. Instead of backing down, the recruiter shoved Tuvia, knocking him to the ground, and drew his sword.

"Step to me again and you will meet the point of this sword. Do you understand?"

Tuvia's face was clenched, barely holding back tears of frustrated rage. "You think you're threatening me? Do it. Find out what happens in Jerusalem if you kill me. My father is Antipas the Treasurer."

The soldier sheathed his short sword roughly, staring at Tuvia.

Tuvia stared back at him, cocky as only a rich man's kid can be.

The Zealot chewed his lip for a moment. "You said it was the woman who was nearest the body?" he asked Isaac.

The Yahad brother nodded.

The soldier looked from Tuvia to Rabbit to Helen. "And his arm was in that sling before the attack?"

Another confirmation.

He said to Isaac, "Pack up your food, gold, and arms. Everything that can be of use. We're going to Jerusalem."

Isaac looked shocked. The brother opened and shut his mouth, then he began to carry out the Zealot soldier's orders. Being commanded by a grunt clearly wasn't part of his lifelong fantasy of military grandeur.

Rabbit felt relief settle on him. Crisis averted. He took Helen's hand.

The militiaman shook his head.

"You fall in with the others, Tiberian. Our ranks are too thin to spare a veteran. But someone must answer for the Sadducee's brother." He offered his hand to Tuvia and hauled him to his feet. "I'll give you the woman. You can throw the first stone."

QUMRAN

68 CE

Helen stared at the militiaman and the Sadducee blankly. Her face was drained of color, but she made no sound. Rabbit's heart hammered against his ribs. What if Helen could die? Would that be some kind of splinter? Some new kind? He took a step forward, but she caught his sleeve.

"Don't," she said. "Thank you, husband, but don't. These men are wrong about us. Don't make them right." She straightened and looked directly at her accuser, radiant in her righteousness. Everyone felt it. The men led her away as though she were a queen, not a criminal. Tuvia followed, fire in his eyes.

"Get to work, Tiberian," the soldier said to Rabbit, more gently than the words would imply.

"Surely you won't make her go to her death alone?" Rabbit didn't know what he could do to help her, but he damn sure couldn't do anything if he was carting supplies while she was being stoned to death.

The Zealot sighed heavily. "You don't want to see this. Have you ever been to a stoning? It's not fast and it's not pretty."

The soldier could have guessed Rabbit had not. Capital punishment was extremely uncommon in first-century Judea. When it was done, it was usually carried out by Romans for offenses to Roman citizens in the method made famous by the most-read book in world history. Crucifixion wasn't a unique punishment for prophet carpenters.

"She's going to her death for us. For a crime she's innocent of. What kind of husband would I be if I let her die alone?"

The soldier sighed again. Nodded. "I'll do my best to make it swift."

He and Rabbit left the compound. On the plateau to the west of the building, Helen was standing with one of the guards while the others wandered around in circles, picking up rocks. A small cairn was already growing a literal stone's throw from Helen.

"Bind her hands and feet," the soldier ordered the guard supervising her. "Trust me," he told Rabbit. "Everyone runs. It doesn't matter how brave you are, everyone runs. It just drags it out. Quick and clean, that's what you want."

Something occurred to Rabbit in a flash.

"Stop!" Rabbit yelled. The guard complied, holding a bit of rope dumbly in both hands. Tuvia and the others also stopped and stared. "My wife is as fierce a woman as ever lived. She won't die trussed up like a sacrifice on the altar." He bared his teeth at the militia leader. "You say everyone runs? You watch. My wife has faced the slings and arrows of fortune unflinchingly and she will again today."

He made direct eye contact with Helen, trying to speak into her mind. Her brow knitted with confusion. *Come on, the answer couldn't be closer to you.*

The militia leader scrubbed a dirty palm over his face in frustration. "Fine, get on with it," he barked and waved the men away from her. "Be it on your head," he growled at Rabbit.

Tuvia lined up at the pile with the other men. He carefully picked through the rocks.

The line of Yahad brothers, initiates, and Zealot soldiers had all stopped to watch. Rabbit saw faces displaying horror, fascination, eagerness. The six carts brought from Jerusalem were filling up. One was mounded with weapons, another with food. A pyramid of green squash rose from the center of the food cart, and Rabbit absently noted that they would roll all over the place as soon as the cart started moving.

"It's not a feast day, Sadducee, pick one," the militia leader barked.

Tuvia selected a rock about the size of a racquetball. He squared his shoulders and arranged his feet like a big-league pitcher, glaring balefully at Helen.

Rabbit held his breath.

The Sadducee wound up and let the rock fly with all the power he could muster.

It missed by a mile. There were a few chuckles that the soldier in command stifled with a backward glance.

Cheeks red with embarrassment, Tuvia selected another rock.

Wound up and threw.

Another miss.

The soldier exhaled noisily. "Why don't I . . ."

"No!" Tuvia cried. Then, quieter, colder. "She's mine."

He selected another stone.

Tossed it back and forth between his hands.

He blew out air between his pursed lips.

Wound up.

Threw.

This one sailed straight at Helen's midsection. But instead of getting hit, she softened her knees, spread her hands in front of her, and received the stone with a smack against skin like a catcher at home plate.

In the surprised pause that followed, she whipped out her sling, dropped the stone into the pouch, and spun it—once, twice.

Men cried out warnings. The soldier near Rabbit dropped to a crouch.

She let the stone fly. It hissed through the air at head level, passed harmlessly between Tuvia and the closest soldier, and went straight to its target.

The top squash on the wagon pyramid exploded in a soggy splash of orange.

Helen let the sling complete its rotation and hang at her side.

Rabbit grinned like an idiot.

The Zealot recruiter slowly rose to his feet. He looked back and forth between Helen and the dripping remains of the squash.

Tuvia was the first to recover himself. He bent and grabbed another rock.

"Throw that and I'll kill you myself," growled the soldier.

He strode over to Tuvia and took the rock from him. "Can you do that again?" he asked Helen.

She nodded.

He threw her the stone underhand. It landed in the dirt in front of her and she scooped it up. Dropped it in her sling pouch.

The soldier looked around. "You." He pointed at an initiate carrying a bleating lamb. "Put that down."

Unsure of himself, the initiate did what he was told.

Already agitated from the commotion, the lamb broke into an unsteady run back toward the compound. The militiaman pointed at the animal.

"Romans don't stand still."

Rabbit looked at Helen. Her face was pinched with anguish. The sling was spinning over and over.

Come on. Come on.

The lamb was halfway back to the safety of the compound.

Three-quarters of the way.

Throw it!

Helen let the stone fly.

It sailed in a clean arc and hit the lamb with a sickening, heavy thud.

The animal slid face-first into the dirt. It tried to continue, but only its front legs worked. She had broken its back. It let out a terrible, whimpering cry like a human infant.

Everyone was still.

Finally, the lead soldier waved at one of his men, who strode over to the mewling animal. Rabbit looked at the ground and heard the agonized noises cut off.

Helen stared at the pitiful creature, face wet with tears.

The lead Zealot stared at her. He looked at Tuvia, who was already holding another stone.

"Put that down."

"You said—"

"An arm like that on top of the city walls is worth more than gold to me."

"She killed—"

"Maybe she did." The Zealot studied Helen, who was wiping tears from her eyes. "Maybe she didn't. What you saw isn't proof. I'm sorry for your brother, Sadducee, but I'm reversing my order. She'll come with us."

Tuvia choked with anger, but there was little he could do. He strode away.

"Let him go," the Zealot said. "Get those carts loaded. You, too," he said to Helen.

Rabbit crossed the space between them in a few steps and wrapped his good arm around her. Helen's heart was beating fast, but her hands on his back were steady.

He squeezed her tighter. "Well done."

"If that was Eshek," she said, "I'll fucking kill him."

JERUSALEM

68 CE

The caravan passed between the Mount of Olives and the Mount of Corruption at sunset, revealing a tableau straight out of a Maxfield Parrish painting. The sky above the walled city was splashed with orange and pink clouds floating across a fading azure sky. The tallest landmarks of the eastern side of the city, the Antonia Fortress and the Great Temple, rose above the walls, glowing amber in the fading sun.

True to the name, the low mountain ridge through which they passed was carpeted with olive trees in bloom. The air smelled fresh and sweet and green.

"Something just occurred to me," Rabbit said to her softly. "When you find Eshek, what are you supposed to do with him, exactly? I mean, okay, he goes back home and steals the Copper Scroll treasures. But what are you supposed to do about it? Capture him?"

She glanced behind them. "That's at my discretion. As long as I can stop the thieving asshole from getting the treasure back in the present, it's a win for me."

"Do you know what they'll do if they catch him?" Rabbit asked.

"I didn't ask. I suppose I didn't really want to know."

Rabbit nodded. There was no one in the present to do the dirty work for him. Rabbit would have to deal with Eshek himself.

"Well, situation unchanged," he said. "We still need to track him down."

"I mean, maybe," Helen said.

"Why maybe?"

She answered him with a question. "He's looking for the secret decoder ring for the Copper Scroll, right?"

"Yeah."

"So, who knows where it is?"

"Antipas, the Temple treasurer. I assume, anyway."

"Anyone else?"

Rabbit thought about that. "Maybe Tuvia—if that's the real Tuvia. But I'm not convinced of that either. We're talking about the future of Judea. If it was me, I would tell as few people as possible."

"Me too. So, let's assume for now it's just the treasurer who knows."

"Antipas," he added.

"Right. Wouldn't it be smarter to set up a stakeout on the one dude?"

"That's the one place we know Eshek is bound to go."

She nodded. "Am I missing something?"

Rabbit pondered that. "No. Well, maybe. Do you know when Eshek's trip decays?"

"When he has to go back, you mean?"

Rabbit nodded.

"Not precisely. I assumed they sent me back just before he came through, but I could be off. I never saw him in the valley after all."

"That's the wild card, then. If his trip decays after yours, we might have to abandon the stakeout before he strikes."

"Fuck. Yeah, okay, I hadn't thought of that. In that case . . ." She chewed her lip for a moment, wheels turning in her head. She stared at the olive grove. "You ever see chimps hunt a monkey?"

"Uh . . . no. No, I have not."

"There are a bunch of videos online. Hurl-worthy but addictive. Don't watch them." She made a disgusted face. "Point is, monkeys are faster than chimps—the predators don't have a prayer of catching one, especially in the trees. So, what they do is, they form a big V shape around the prey, far apart, you know, far enough apart that the monkey doesn't know they're there. And then one of the chimps starts to chase the monkey from the wide part of the V toward the narrow part. If the monkey tries to veer off course, the chimp bastards on the sides make a bunch of noise to direct the monkey back to the desired line."

Rabbit nodded, getting it. "Where it eventually runs into the point of the V. You're proposing one of us drive Eshek toward the other one, to make sure he acts before you have to go home."

"Right. Make him go for Antipas as quickly as we can, where I'll be waiting."

"Why you?"

She stared at him. "He's my monkey, Ward."

Rabbit put up his hands, acquiescing. "He's your monkey."

"Is there anything we can use to force him to make a move?"

"Depending on what's happened already, yes." Rabbit paused as a Zealot rambled past them toward the front of the wagon train. They were starting the climb from the bottom of a steep valley up toward the southeast side of the city walls. The pack animals were slowing with the strain.

Rabbit resumed once the soldier was out of earshot. "A few years ago, the local Roman procurator executed a bunch of citizens because he felt they had disrespected him. Stole a healthy sum of gold from the Temple, too. Like so many idiots before him, he thought what the people needed was a good show of force to bring them in line. It had the opposite effect. A former priest turned rebel leader named Eleazar ben Simon raised a Zealot army and slaughtered the Roman garrison in Jerusalem. And the procurator, too, of course."

"Obvi," she said.

"So, the governor of Syria, I can't remember his name, he sent in his garrison legion to put down the rebellion. It fared a little better, but owing to bad generalship, it got ambushed and slaughtered, too."

"Jeez."

"I know. So Eleazar's Zealots are now armed and armored like professional soldiers. But by this point, all this violence drew the attention of Emperor Nero, who sent General Vespasian and his son Titus with four legions to put down the Zealots. They landed in Galilee last year and started a city-by-city campaign, stomping out resistance as they went. The historian Flavius Josephus came over from Rome to take over as the titular Jewish general for the northern theater, but he got captured or surrendered—hard to tell the truth of it from his narrative. Meanwhile, a separate rebel force of Zealots, unconnected to the provisional government, was holed up in a walled city called Gischala where they held off Titus in a long siege. Their leader, who typically goes by John of Gischala, fled in the night with his forces when he was convinced the city was going to lose. So, they're in Jerusalem now, too."

Helen shook her head like she was trying to rearrange a bunch of marbles into some sensible position. "So now Jerusalem is jammed up with Eleazar's Zealots and John's Zealots?"

Rabbit nodded. "Right. But that's not all. There are also official soldiers who report to the provisional government, the priestly class, essentially. And there's another group that may be in the city called the Sicarii."

"Sicarii. Like Sicario? The Spanish assassins?"

"Same word. Spain adopts it from these guys. These 'dagger men' are another rebel force, but they specialize in guerrilla tactics, especially assassination. All those groups are milling around the city at this point, gathering up anyone who looks like they can hold a spear from the surrounding countryside." He indicated their caravan with a wave of his hand. "Like us."

She raised an eyebrow. "That's a lot of words," she said. "How does this get my damn monkey in motion?"

"Sorry. The point is, John of Gischala at some point arrests Antipas the Treasurer and, after an undisclosed period, kills him. We don't know right now where we are in that timeline. Antipas might have been arrested; he might not have. Hell, he might already be dead. I sure hope not because then Eshek has no reason to stay in town. If Antipas is still alive? Well, we could . . . nudge things along. Eshek must know the history, too, so if he thinks Antipas is in imminent danger of being assassinated, he'll be forced to move in. If he's not in custody yet, well . . ."

Helen looked at Rabbit as though seeing him for the first time.

"I know how that sounds," Rabbit said. "But the man's death is a foregone conclusion. Josephus said Antipas was killed by someone called John the son of Dorcas while being held by the northern Zealots. We can't change that."

"So, we might as well use it to our advantage," she finished for him.

He thought about trying to spin it somehow to sound less cold-blooded but couldn't come up with anything. "Right," he concluded.

"Okay," she said at last, nodding. "You'll do whatever you can to speed up the treasurer's death and I'll do my best to get in a position to catch Eshek when he comes to claim him."

"Right," Rabbit agreed.

"Before you put your foot on the accelerator, let me get into position."

"Of course. I'll need to find out the status with Antipas first anyway."

"I take it back," Helen said. "You're no Boy Scout."

"Sorry to disappoint."

"I didn't say I was disappointed."

They continued their climb up from the Valley of Kidron up to the city walls. As they walked, Helen studied the hills to their north, the imposing city walls. Her mouth tightened into a thin line.

Rabbit saw the worry settling in on her features and thought of his own first mission. He had prepared for six months, learned the first of the ancient languages he would eventually acquire. He had read everything he could find from the era, although little contemporary text had survived. It was 773 BCE, Olympia, Greece. The first of the Greek Olympics he would attend in his career. He was so nervous, he had almost left his decay point without marking its location. The first day, he didn't speak to a soul. Too nervous that his crash course in ancient Greek would fail him. The enormity of the task before him had been so overwhelming, he had been tempted to discard the whole career and just wait it out until the portal opened back up to rescue him.

Somehow, he had worked up the nerve to put one foot in front of the other and begin the task at hand. Twenty days later, he returned to the present and bragged to PJ through bloody, grinning lips, "Got it." That mission had officially launched chrono archaeology as a profession. Laws would be passed on time travel, intergovernmental structures established. Competition entered the field. But what Rabbit remembered was how much he transformed between day one and day twenty.

He had been afforded the privilege of solitude, like a goddamn butterfly. Helen, he supposed, had been afforded the privilege of company.

"You're gonna be fine, you know."

"Fuck you," she said, somehow imbuing those two words with simultaneous appreciation and dismissal. A moment later, however, she spoke quietly. "You really think so?"

"I know so," he replied. "I've seen people in this job come and go. Not everyone has what it takes. You do."

A grateful smile tugged at the corners of her mouth. Her shoulders released their tension.

"What's that?" she asked finally, looking north up the length of the valley to a geometric garden dotted with orange terra-cotta buildings.

"That?" he replied. "Oh, it's just the Garden of Gethsemane." Helen had been raised Catholic. Even though Rabbit suspected she was no longer observant, there was no way this sight wouldn't be impactful.

Helen stared at the garden. The warm light of sunset made her skin glow and her wide eyes glitter like drops of rain.

She rounded on him. Based on her body language, and the content of their previous conversation, Rabbit prepared for a slap. Instead, she darted forward and kissed him on the cheek. Her lips were warm and soft and left the tingling memory of the kiss cooling on his skin as she turned back toward the city with a sigh.

An initiate bumped into him, and Rabbit realized he had stopped in his tracks.

"Sorry," Rabbit said.

"Never been to the city?" the young man replied. It was Enoch, the blue-eyed initiate from the night before. He seemed to think Rabbit was starstruck by the towering walls of the capital.

Rabbit shook his head.

"Where are you and your wife going to stay?"

"An inn, I suppose."

"The way these soldiers have been talking, there are no spare beds anywhere. The whole city is filled with refugees from the countryside."

"Didn't you say you're from Jerusalem?" Rabbit asked. The young man seemed amiable enough. Maybe Rabbit could score a bed for himself and Helen like he had with Andor's family in Constantinople.

Enoch's lips pressed into a hard line. "I am, but I don't think I'll be welcome back home. I didn't part from my family on good terms."

Rabbit caught the tinge of worry in his voice. Right. The kid wasn't offering a bunk, he was asking for assistance from two adults who he supposed had it more together than he did.

"That's tough," Rabbit said sympathetically. "Maybe you could stay with one of your friends from the Yahad." He didn't particularly want to adopt a stray.

"Maybe." Enoch looked at the looming city walls, his worry growing more obvious. "If you find somewhere good, you'll let me know, right?"

"Of course," Rabbit assured him, and gently extricated himself to rejoin Helen.

A few moments later, the caravan passed through a towering gatehouse, its dark mouth wide enough to admit their wagons with ease.

As they passed through, Rabbit looked up and saw flickering light through the capped murder holes. Never storm a castle, Rabbit reminded himself.

Tonight, however, the iron-banded doors at both ends were open for the caravan. The wagons rumbled through the tunnel unmolested.

Inside the gatehouse was a spacious courtyard next to a huge black pool of water, the Siloam reservoir. Palm trees waved above the reservoir, illuminated by fires set in open braziers to chase away the cold of the desert night.

A soldier awaited the leader of the caravan.

"Is this all of them?" he said to the militiaman who had spared Helen, swiveling his head to take in the Yahad brotherhood.

"I'm afraid so. At least they come with their own supplies." To prove his point, the caravan leader walked the other man to the nearest wagon and pulled back the tarp covering the vegetables and bags of grain within.

Rabbit and Helen mimicked the uncertain restlessness of their fellow travelers while trying to remain close enough to the two soldiers to hear what they were saying.

"How many wagons?"

"Six."

The officer brushed his hands off on each other. "Won't go nearly far enough, but good." He glanced around at the milling crowd. "Any problems with this lot?"

The caravan leader shook his head. "They were eager to come. Well"—he looked around them—"except for one. Turns out both the sons of Antipas were there. One of them joined the cult."

"Antipas the Treasurer?" the militia leader asked. "Where are they?"

"Well, one's dead."

The soldier stared at him. *Seriously?*

"We didn't kill him! He was dead before we got there. The other one is here somewhere, a redheaded dandy with the temper of a wet cat."

"We'll send him home. If he wants to complain about it, he can complain to somebody else."

Rabbit leaned close to Helen and whispered, "Sounds like things are about to accelerate. Are you okay to follow the crowd wherever they are directed? I'll follow Tuvia."

She nodded and whispered back, "I'll keep an eye on Leocharis."

"Quiet down, everyone!" The soldier had mounted the tongue of one of the wagons so the throng could see him. "Every man hailing from Jerusalem should return to their homes for the night. I expect to see you at the Hippodrome tomorrow after morning prayers. The rest of you will go directly to the track with Tanchum here." Another soldier waved his hand in the air. "We'll try to find you a place to lay your head."

"What about the women and children?" someone from the crowd called.

The soldier scowled and searched over the heads as if demanding proof of their existence. "If you have relatives in the city, go to them. Otherwise report to the Hippodrome as well. There is plenty of honest work to be done."

As the crowd broke up, Rabbit nodded to Helen, his eyes already crawling through the crowd for Tuvia.

Helen caught him by the arm and leaned in close. For a moment, he thought she was going to kiss him again, but instead she whispered, "Remember. He's my monkey, Ward."

"Scout's honor," he said.

She rolled her eyes as they parted.

JERUSALEM

68 CE

Rabbit slipped away from the milling crowd and followed Tuvia into the Lower City.

Named for its position on the steep decline of a long hill, the neighborhood was a sprawling maze of mostly two-story apartments of tan limestone. The blocks crawled up and down the hill following the topography, creating a monochromatic hive navigable only by the locals. It smelled of rotting garbage. Small wonder. Since the war began, refugees had more than doubled the city's population. There was no way the infrastructure could support the overcrowding.

Full night had settled as Rabbit climbed another of the narrow stone staircases that connected the switchback streets. The moon was bright enough to keep Tuvia in sight a block or so ahead, but the twists and turns of the neighborhood were so tight Rabbit was concerned about losing him at every step. The only saving grace in his pursuit was how empty the streets were. This Jerusalem was no place to wander after dark.

Robbers and worse came out of the countryside and did not limit themselves to stealing, but proceeded as far as murder, Josephus had written.

Rabbit remembered the first English translation of Josephus he had ever read. It was a red, faux-leather hardback library edition he had found at Stanford. He couldn't recall the translator or much of the commentary. Still, out of nowhere the book's cover had appeared in his mind's eye. Strange thing to come up at a time like this.

He shook his head, emerged from the stairs, and picked up Tuvia turning left at the next intersection. Rabbit had to hand it to the guy, he walked with the confidence of a local. No hesitation, no "checking his six" as they said on the cop shows. Just a brisk pace, head held high, walking like he owned the city. *Cocky*, Rabbit thought. A safer but less direct path would have avoided the Lower City in favor of main arteries that led to the Upper City, where no doubt the Antipas family made its dwelling. So Tuvia was either in one hell of a hurry, or he simply felt confident enough to take the shortest path through the city.

Stepping around a corner, Rabbit realized how close he had gotten to his quarry as he studied him. Close enough to be recognized if Tuvia turned around.

He paused, and as he did so, the sibilant sound of leather on sand behind him lit up his senses. Rabbit reached for his dagger, spinning.

"Helen?"

Instead, it was the wide blue eyes of the Yahad initiate, Enoch, that stared back at him.

"Who's Helen?" he asked.

"Dammit, Enoch! What are you doing?"

The initiate cringed at his anger. "I'm sorry! I thought you were going to find somewhere to lodge."

"I told you—"

"I know. I will. Really. I'll go see my parents . . . tomorrow."

Rabbit looked over his shoulder at the junction down which Tuvia had disappeared. Gone.

Rabbit considered running after him, trying to pick up the trail again, but it was no good. Sound carried too well in the abandoned streets. The Sadducee had probably heard them and taken off.

"Are you looking for someone?" Enoch asked.

"Do you know this neighborhood?" Rabbit asked, ignoring his question.

The initiate shook his head, glancing around warily. *Of course he didn't. A kid like this. Child of privilege.*

"What are we going to do?" he asked Rabbit, looking jumpier by the second.

"It's a damn fine question," answered a new voice.

Both men turned to see an older woman striding toward them from the direction of Tuvia's escape.

"You're likely to get yourselves killed out here," she continued as she halted before them. Fists balled on her hips, the woman struck the perfect image of a fierce matriarch. She rose no higher than Rabbit's chin and was as thin and hard as a broomstick.

She glanced around at the neighbors who had begun opening doors and shutters at the sound of her voice.

"Go back inside," she said. "And bar your doors. I'm not scared of these two lost lambs." She looked at Rabbit. "Any particular reason you are troubling the peace tonight?"

"Me?" he asked, legitimately indignant.

"Lions only go where they can find a lamb. If people stayed behind closed doors after sundown, we might see the last of the Zealots prowling our streets."

"How do you know I'm not on the prowl myself?"

She snorted. "You may not be a lamb, but you're shepherding one."

Rabbit looked at Enoch, who was clenched up so hard he might implode.

"I'm Joseph. From Tiberias. My . . . acquaintance and I were conscripted by the militia."

She grunted. "Miriam bat Sarah. Tiberias, eh? And where do you belong tonight?"

"I don't. That's my problem."

She looked him up and down.

"Well, now, I suppose we can't leave you out in the cold with the . . . maybe not lions. Feral curs, anyway. For tonight, you'd better come inside."

JERUSALEM

68 CE

Light from the oil lamp cast an amber glow around the main room of the little apartment, which was decorated everywhere with textile art. Surprising for a humble apartment in the Lower City. Several layers of fabric covered the shuttered windows as well. All that fabric provided some decent heat insulation; Miriam's place was almost too warm.

Of course, it wasn't being warmed by the lamp. Besides Miriam there were two other women and six rambunctious children under the age of five bustling through the house.

"Joseph and . . ." She pierced the initiate with her stare.

"Enoch," he squeaked.

"These ladies are Judith and Leah. Their husbands are in much the same company as you. Drafted into the Zealot militia."

"If not for Miriam, we would have been beggared," said Judith.

"At least there is a proper fighting force in the city now," insisted Leah. "The Zealots defeated the Romans at Gischala before heading south to rally Jerusalem."

Rabbit snorted.

"What's funny?" Leah demanded.

"Well, it's not funny, exactly." Rabbit shrugged. "But I think the Zealots may have painted a sunnier picture of their successes in Gischala than is strictly truthful."

Leah, the Zealot supporter, sat up a little straighter, implicitly demanding more.

"The Zealots put up a good fight, but the city fell. The resistance fighters fled south in the night."

"They ran?" Leah asked, deflating.

"I'm afraid so."

"What became of the city?"

"Burned," Rabbit replied.

Leah was no longer looking at him. Her eyes had strayed to her children.

Miriam pointed at the bedroom. Leah shepherded the kids into it. Rabbit noticed that the old woman's fingers were a rainbow of dye stains. He glanced at the colorful hangings on the walls. Fabric dyer, he decided. Maybe she gets to keep the off pieces.

"I knew it," Miriam said. "Their story never made sense. Why abandon Gischala if they won?" She fixed Rabbit with her dark eyes. "This is how they have tried to win over the people of Judea. The great saviors of the North. If people knew what they really were . . ." Something occurred to her. Her attention went inward for a moment before she returned. "If you came in with the Zealots, what were you doing in the Lower City?"

"I foolishly chased after a young Sadducee hoping he might house us. Tuvia ben Antipas was his name. I don't suppose you know him?"

"I know him," Miriam said, simply. "You're not family of his, are you?"

Rabbit shook his head. "He seemed like a generous young man. Do you think you could direct me to his residence?"

"You might take some lumps from his house guards if they catch you harassing the family, but I'll set you on your way. Tomorrow, though. Too dangerous after dark. You and your friend are welcome to the roof, at least until you sort yourself out in the morning."

Rabbit nodded. "That's very hospitable. Thank you."

She went over to a tiny kitchen. "I don't have much in the way of board. A little bread?"

Rabbit shook his head, although his stomach was growling. "Save it for the little ones." Leah had returned to caretaking the children, who were contentedly playing now. "Is your husband in the militia as well?" he asked Miriam.

She raised her eyebrows. "My husband? He died seven winters ago."

"I'm sorry."

"I'm glad he didn't live to see this. He was as hard as eastern silk, that man." She looked at Rabbit intently. "Are you set on this plan to see Tuvia ben Antipas?"

"I don't know what other options I have."

"Of options you have plenty. You could go to the Council House and join the army. The real army, that is. You could go to the Hippodrome as planned and throw in your lot with the northern Zealots or to the Temple and join the southern Zealots."

"So many factions," Rabbit said, feigning surprise. "Who do you support?"

"I support Jerusalem." She looked fierce. "The Zealots rattle their spears and demand war. A war we'll surely lose. The Sadducees advocate for peace with Rome. Of course, they do. Who benefits from the system more than they?"

Rabbit sensed her anguish. "And you?"

"Me? I would have a different peace. A better peace. Rome will always be Rome." She studied Rabbit, and he could feel her trying to plumb his intelligence as though she had engaged in this debate many times and was striving to determine whether it was worth the breath. "I would have Judea be a friend and ally of the empire, not part of it. I would have lower taxes for all, and the heaviest burden carried by those with the most to give, not the least. I would have farmers and merchants and craftspeople sit on the court of elders along with the priests and landowners. I would allow any woman unburdened with children to hold office."

Half point. Still, any one of these ideas put her well ahead of the curve.

"I would have a world in which anyone of merit is able to rise above their birth."

Rabbit accepted that with a nod. "Well, Miriam, I think I would like to live in this world of yours."

"Would you? I wish more people agreed. Some days I think I would have been exiled to the desert if I weren't just a harmless old crackpot."

Given Enoch's expression, a mix of horror and sympathy usually reserved for the insane, the young man agreed with the harmless crackpot theory.

"That's the thing about the world," Rabbit said. "Most of the time, nothing much changes. And then every once in a while, everything does." He thought of Aaron.

"May it change for the better," Miriam said. Then shrugged. "Only God has all the answers. And some days I'm not even sure of that."

Later that night, Rabbit sat on the roof of Miriam's house, looking up at the stars. Rooftop bedrooms were a common feature of the architectural landscape in the Lower City. In the summer, they offered a respite from the baking interior of the stone homes. Tonight, it was cold enough for Rabbit to see his breath. Still, it could have been worse. Miriam had given him a couple of ragged sheepskin rugs and a dense mat that reminded him of a removable chair cushion.

Nearby, Enoch's breathing was steady and deep. He twitched in his sleep.

Gazing down over the city, Rabbit found himself wishing Helen were with him. He had spent so much of his life alone, or pretending to be someone else, which is the deepest kind of isolation. Rabbit had grown accustomed to it over the years. Now? The jobs he had done with Helen had changed his relationship with himself, which he found very curious. He missed her ribbing, her insight, the way she challenged his preconceptions.

As he began to doze, Rabbit found his thoughts drifting to the Temple treasures. What would it be like to go where he wanted in time and place? To set his own course, under his own sail, with Helen beside him. Not dependent on fickle sponsors to pay his way.

He drifted away dreaming of gold bars and Helen's voice.

"Billions, with a *B*."

JERUSALEM

68 CE

The next morning, Rabbit and Enoch trekked through the maze of the Lower City, mentally noting the path back to Miriam's as they made their way through the crowd to the chariot racing track. Jerusalem had seemed abandoned in the night, but daylight had revealed the city's overcrowding and the tensions it caused. The two men were cursed and shoved more than once for no greater crime than shouldering their way through the masses just like everyone else.

"Where are we going?" Enoch whined, dusting off his clothes after an encounter with a filthy beggar.

"*I'm* going to the Hippodrome. You should go home."

"I told you, my parents—"

"The whole country is under siege," Rabbit snapped over the din. "Do you really think they're going to hold it against you under these conditions that you joined the Yahad?"

"You don't know them," the young man insisted.

"They're going to impress you into the militia if you go with me," Rabbit said.

"Then what are you doing?"

"Meeting my wife."

Rabbit had directions to the Antipas family home from Miriam, but that would come later. First, he wanted to check in with Helen and see what she'd learned.

The Hippodrome stood at the north end of the Lower City at

the feet of the Temple. Rabbit looked up at its walls and wondered if Herod the Great had a sense of humor.

Racetracks were common in Roman cities and were often a dominant feature of the urban landscape due to their sheer size. Not in Jerusalem. The Hippodrome of Jerusalem looked like a child's toy left at the mighty feet of the Great Temple. It didn't even reach the height of the platform that led to the Temple's lowest entrances. Was the juxtaposition intentional? It was hard to believe otherwise.

Oh, Herod. You should be glad you didn't live to see what became of your greatest building achievement.

Rabbit preceded Enoch into the racetrack through a tunnel at midfield where his senses were assaulted.

The steep bowl of stadium seating captured and amplified the smell like an olfactory soup tureen of sweat and smoke and shit and infected flesh. A tent city sprawled over half the track and up the sides of the bowl while the open area of the other side was reserved for drilling the militia. The clatter and shouts of the active Zealots melded with the moans of the injured and dying. Fighting the urge to escape, Rabbit steadied himself by searching for the women of the Zealot camp.

At the first turn of the track, a stream of Zealots was flowing into one end of the stables. At the other end, the stream was exiting clutching food in their hands.

Bingo.

Enoch trailed Rabbit to the back of the line that snaked into the shade of the building, where the stench of the track was replaced by the comparatively wholesome smell of hay and manure.

At a row of tables, each man was given a small loaf of bread and a swallow of water from a slimy barrel with the same ladle. Ian would lose his germaphobe mind at the very idea.

"I beg your pardon," Rabbit said to the back of a tall woman unloading bread from a basket. "I'm looking for my wife."

The woman flinched at the sound of his voice and flashed a fleeting glance over her shoulder at him. She was veiled. Only her eyes were visible. Without a word, the woman looked down at the ground and pointed at the far exit of the stables.

"Don't mind her. She doesn't speak, poor thing," said another woman, wiping her floury hands on her apron. "We think she was at Ein Gedi. Hasn't spoken a word since she got here."

"Oh," he replied lamely. He felt a little guilty. The woman must have been one of the refugees at Secacah. He'd never spoken to them.

"Who are you looking for?"

"Rachel."

"You'll have to be a little more specific, man."

Dammit. When they had picked their alter egos, they hadn't chosen parental surnames, and Rachel was a very popular moniker of the time—hardly a distinguishing feature.

"I'm her husband, Joseph," he ventured.

She brightened. "Oh, came in last night? The mad slinger?"

"That's her," he said, relieved.

"She's out by the ovens in the courtyard. Come on, I'll take you." The woman headed for the stable door. "That's a good woman you've got there, Joseph. She was like a breath of spring air around here and no mistake. You be good to her."

Rabbit smiled. "I'll do my best."

"I don't know how a body can stay so witty and bright amid all this."

"It's a special talent of hers."

They passed through a walkway that separated the stables from the stands. Fresh air was passing through the breezeway from the outside, carrying with it the toasty smell of baking.

"She had us all up late last night telling our stories of the war and before. I'm as slack as an empty grain sack this morning, but it was worth it."

Rabbit felt a flash of pride. He'd have bet his life Helen had extracted more information than she'd given. She was a natural at this work. Proud though he may have been, Rabbit couldn't forget that she was his primary competition here, too. *Don't underestimate her.*

They passed into the sunny courtyard outside the stables where several brick ovens had been constructed. They were firing and smoking now, attended by several women cranking out the thin loaves of bread as efficiently as any factory.

The women were chatting as they worked and seemed perfectly coordinated and at ease.

Amid the conversation, he picked up Helen's distinctive snorting laugh.

"Here she is. Look who turned up, Rachel."

Helen beamed at him. The scarf covering her hair was floury and smudged with soot. Still holding a handful of dough, she strode over and hugged him tightly around the middle, pinning his arms to his sides. She held him longer than she strictly needed to for appearances, then stepped back, appraising him.

"How are you?" she asked.

"Oh, don't tell me you were worried," Rabbit's guide said. "All last night, it was, 'there's no one more canny and hard than my man,' and 'pity the thief that finds Joseph in the dark.'"

Pink crept up to the tops of Helen's cheeks. "I don't recall saying that last part."

"You never heard such bragging. If you're everything she says you are, woe be to the Romans." The woman laughed.

"She esteems me higher than I deserve," Rabbit said. He hadn't taken his eyes off Helen's. "Ma'am, could I borrow my bride for a few minutes?"

"We've nowhere private, lovebirds," she teased.

"I won't keep her long," Rabbit assured her. With the woman's assent, Rabbit and Helen walked to the edge of the courtyard.

Enoch began to trail them, but the woman caught him. "How about some bread, my young man?" She led him a few paces away, but the initiate refused to be led out of sight of Rabbit.

Rabbit and Helen tucked into a corner of the stables. "Are you okay?" they said in unison. And laughed.

"The women had a lot to say last night."

"I heard."

"You were right," she said, rushing in her excitement. "Antipas, the Temple treasurer, was 'arrested' yesterday evening. More like kidnapped. The pricks are holding him and a couple other city officials in a house next to where John of Gischala set up his headquarters."

"Where's that?"

She pointed. "Just up the hill from here. That terraced area overlooking the track. The same two women deliver food to them every day. I think one of them might be getting frisky with Gischala. She looks suspiciously cleaner and better fed than everyone else. Oh, and Dinah, that woman who brought you over? She kind of looks down her nose at her. I'm going to try to get assigned to that job myself. Then I can keep an eye on the place."

"Quick work."

She grinned. "What about you? Did you track down Tuvia?"

He shook his head. "I got waylaid."

"Muggers?"

Rabbit jerked a thumb at the initiate, who stood chewing his bread and staring at them from a distance. "The Yahad kid, Enoch. He's like a lamprey. I got us housing with a widow in the Lower City. You'd like her. Badass broad in her sixties or seventies. Seems to be some kind of local revolutionary. I have to admit, I may have encouraged her."

Her eyes narrowed. "Aren't you afraid of changing history? Causing a splinter?"

"Doesn't really matter. Eshek isn't part of this history."

"Well, thanks, but what about the Book of Esther? You might lose it."

He shook his head. "I got it while everyone was packing up the wagons. Tucked it away in a little crevice a dozen yards from the mouth of cave five." It would really be the icing on the cake if his hiding spot was effective. It might even help him patch things up with PJ.

Helen sighed. "Well, at least one of us got what we came for."

"You'll get your guy. You're doing great so far. Anyway, Miriam invited us both to her place tonight. It's not fancy but it probably beats group quarters.

"As soon as I shake my shadow, I'm going to see whether the militia bagged Tuvia. I'm still more than half-convinced he's our guy."

"What about Leocharis?" she asked.

"I've got an idea about that. Do you want me to hold off on driving your monkey?"

"Fuck it. Pull the trigger. I'll get that job. Don't worry about me."

"I'm not."

"Meet me back here for the evening meal?"

"If not before," he said.

She hugged him, hard. "For appearances," she whispered in his ear.

Rabbit returned to Enoch with a thin loaf of bread in his hand and a warm buzz everywhere else.

"Come on," Rabbit said, leading Enoch back through the stables.

"Where are we going? Are we volunteering? Do you think I should find the brothers?"

Rabbit scanned the crowds until his eyes caught what he was looking for. A flash of bronze plate mail.

"Leocharis!" Rabbit said, approaching the dashing Macedonian, who had apparently made quite an impression on the locals; a unit was focused on him as he drilled them in the proper way to form a phalanx using the eighteen-foot-long sarissa spears someone had dredged up from the storerooms of old weapons.

The mercenary pushed sweaty blond curls from his forehead and beamed. "What have we here? My fellow vagabond!"

"This one is eager to join the ranks," Rabbit said, thrusting Enoch between them.

"What?" the initiate sputtered.

"More grist for the mill. Delightful! Grab a spear, lad."

"But I . . ." Enoch looked at Rabbit like an orphaned puppy. As Leocharis strode into the line to grab arms for the new recruit, Rabbit leaned close to the dismayed initiate.

"Do me a favor. Keep an eye on him." Rabbit tilted his forehead toward the Macedonian. "Don't ask why. I just need to know what he gets up to during the day. Can you do that for me?"

Enoch started to protest, but Rabbit cut him off. "Help me out with this, and I'll help you with your parents. Deal?"

The initiate turned his big blue eyes on the phalanx with trepidation.

"Deal?" Rabbit repeated.

"Deal," Enoch choked out.

"Good man." Rabbit clapped him on the shoulder.

Leocharis returned cradling two of the massive spears in his hands.

"Not for me, thanks," Rabbit said. "I have business up the hill. Good luck!"

Before either man could answer, Rabbit slipped away into the crowd.

All right, Tuvia. Where did you land last night?

JERUSALEM

68 CE

Rabbit made his way through the throngs of people clogging the streets of the Lower City up to John of Gischala's headquarters. Nestled into an outcropping in front of an impassably steep section of the hill, it reminded Rabbit, just a little, of the Kahan mansion in Malibu. Only instead of the Pacific, it overlooked the Hippodrome. Compared to the Lego pile of nondescript apartments that carpeted most of the hillside, John's home base was fairly grand. Two stories, a little peristyle garden, and a great view. It shared the outcropping with a companion home of the same size and design.

The dead-end outgrowth of a plateau afforded the two homes a uniquely private space. It was kept private by a gang of Zealot muscle loafing around the hill as a visual deterrent to trespassers. Sure beat running a sarissa up and down the stinking bowl of the Hippodrome. Rabbit would have bet his life these guys were all relatives of the northern Zealot leader to have gotten this cushy assignment.

He smiled inside as the next part of his plan came into focus.

He followed the switchback roads to a higher point on the hill. From that perch, he watched the milling Zealot guards for a while. Long enough to observe their patterns—or lack thereof. Their full attention, when they paid any attention at all, was on the road approaching the twin homes. No one paid any heed to the scrubby cliff at the back of the plateau. It was too steep for a group approach, and a group approach was all they were thinking about.

Rabbit quietly slipped down the face of the hill, clinging to the stunted trees that protruded from the rock face, until he vanished behind the back wall of the second home's peristyle garden.

He listened for voices or footsteps that might indicate he'd been spotted. But the interior of the garden was so quiet he clearly heard a rat before it poked its nose up through the nettles near his feet. Rabbit slipped his right arm free of its sling and hauled himself over the wall.

In contrast to the clearing outside the houses, the home's courtyard had fared well enough. Flowers and shrubs dotted the garden. A gnarled little olive tree bent its limbs over a gnarled little man sitting on a wooden bench cradling a cup in his hands.

"Good morning," Rabbit said, walking up to him.

"Is it?" The man's long face was seamed by time and sun and care. He didn't seem at all surprised by the unannounced appearance of a stranger in his midst.

Rabbit glanced at the door to the garden. "I'm still alive."

The seated man slowly nodded. "I'm glad that's a comfort to you."

Rabbit introduced himself. "Joseph ben Joseph."

"Antipas ben Moishe," the man replied.

"Antipas, the treasurer of the Temple?"

He nodded. "I was."

"I think I met your son."

That got his attention. Antipas leaned forward, eyes widening. "You saw my Tzephania? Where? Is he back in the city?"

Rabbit's stomach dropped. He had been so focused on Tuvia-maybe-Eshek he had forgotten all about Tzephania, dead in the Yahad stronghold. Shame prickled the skin of his neck and face like raw wool.

Rabbit always tried to keep it in his mind that the people he met on his missions were shadows of the past. He couldn't alter their fate. But had his job really numbed him to the point he could forget a young man's murder so easily? Meanwhile, another, far colder part of his brain concluded that if Antipas didn't know that Tzephania was dead, that also meant Tuvia hadn't been here since returning from Jerusalem. So, the answer was a resounding maybe.

Antipas stared up at him, his eyes alight.

This man would be dead soon himself, unceremoniously murdered for political convenience. Was there any point in making his last days more miserable than they already were? Rabbit remembered being told, just before leaving for a vacation with his grandparents to the Appalachian Mountains, that his beloved dog had died. He had never understood why his parents couldn't have delayed that news until after he returned. He would have preferred a gentle lie than that cold truth. He'd been mopey and short-tempered the entire vacation. His grandparents would also die, not long after that and in quick succession.

Antipas the Treasurer had enough worry and pain right now. Rabbit would spare him this.

He shook his head. "I saw him in Secacah days ago. He was fine."

The treasurer heaved a sigh. The weary, calm demeanor he displayed when Rabbit entered the courtyard was replaced by sick relief. Antipas closed his eyes and whispered a grateful prayer. When he opened them, his face returned to the expression of resignation.

Rabbit knew a little of what Antipas was feeling. Twenty years ago, when Rabbit had lost Aaron in ancient Rome, he had lost all hope with him. It was done, and no act of Rabbit's could undo it. People could hate him all they wanted, and some of them did.

When he had returned to Constantinople through Helen's decay point rather than his own, it had kindled hope in him and thereby reminded him of hope's natural companion—fear. Hope and fear were twin sides of a coin that could never be separated. The idea of Tzephania being back in Jerusalem had sent those twin feelings thundering through the treasurer.

Antipas cleared his throat. "Why are you here?" he asked. "Please make it entertaining, at least."

Rabbit knitted his brow in confusion.

Antipas continued. "You're not the first spy John has sent to earn my trust. It's all right, we can play the game. I prefer it to the intervals of threat and pain in between." He gestured to a second bench. "Sit, tell me how you, too, are captive. Or whatever tale you prefer."

Rabbit sat, the corners of his mouth turning up in a little grin. He had to admit, he liked Antipas the Treasurer. "I am not a captive. I left Galilee a week ago and have information that is helpful to the Zealot leaders but not the Zealot cause."

"I see."

"It's no mystery why you're here. They want you to turn over the hidden location of the Temple treasury."

"No, no, not like that," the man chided. "You can't give away the game all at once. This is where you ask me unrelated questions to put me at ease, pretend ignorance, convince me that I have nothing to fear from a simple, purehearted rustic like yourself."

Rabbit laughed. He couldn't help it. "Sorry, I don't care where it is."

"That's better. Feign disinterest. Just the thing."

"And I'm neither purehearted nor rustic." Rabbit glanced up at the house. "There is something else I wanted to ask you, though. You mentioned Tzephania. What about your other son?"

"Ah, so that's to be the angle of the blade. Fair enough. My son Tuvia is safe. Far away from here as it turns out."

Rabbit shook his head. "He's back in Jerusalem."

"You lie. He had instructions and was committed to them."

"The Zealots had other plans. That is," Rabbit said, as something occurred to him, "if the man I met was your son. What does he look like?"

Antipas just studied Rabbit, as though trying to peel information off his face, so Rabbit volunteered. "Red hair and beard. This tall. A little . . . sure of himself?"

The lines of the old man's face settled more deeply, telling Rabbit everything he needed to know before the man's nod confirmed it. So, the person they met as Tuvia matched the description of Antipas junior. Of course, Eshek *might* have imitated Tuvia's look and manner if he had been able to study him, but this was one more strike against Tuvia being the suspect.

"I imagine you will threaten my son unless I tell you about the Temple treasures." The seamed face had settled again into that Zen-like resignation it had worn when Rabbit first arrived.

"Not at all. You don't need to tell me anything. I was just curious if you had seen your son. I mean, I already know you inscribed the locations on a copper scroll and entrusted its keeping to the Yahad brotherhood. What else is there to know?"

A flicker passed over the treasurer's face, implying that he considered even this part of the plan secure until now.

"Don't worry, I won't tell anyone about that. Let alone the companion scroll."

The flicker turned into a twitch.

"I did want to warn you about something, though," Rabbit continued. "At some point soon, a man is going to find you who is very interested in your secret. If you have any way of moving the second scroll through an intermediary, you should. Preferably an intermediary who can keep the secret of its location from you."

"And you would volunteer for the job, I suppose?"

The treasurer had resumed his knowing look, seeing through Rabbit's clumsy ploy. Rabbit shrugged, smiled.

"I don't think so," the gnarled treasurer concluded.

Subconsciously, Rabbit had been fantasizing about where he might go if he could fund his own missions from just a taste of the Copper Scroll treasure. The siege of Troy? Caesar's Gallic campaigns? Or maybe somewhere peaceful. Spend a little time with the Mycenaean Greeks.

Rabbit sighed. There it was again. Hope and fear.

He rose to his feet as the door to the garden swung open on pleasantly squeaky hinges.

A guard stood in the door staring at Rabbit for a frozen moment, the gears of his brain ticking over. Click, click, click. Nope, they concluded, that guy should not be here.

"Hey!" the guard shouted, fumbling for a spear he had deposited to open the gate.

Rabbit smiled at Antipas. "Nice chatting with you. But I must be getting on with my day."

He calmly walked toward the point of the young man's spear, leaving the bemused treasurer to his own conclusions.

"How did you get in here?" the guard demanded. He was just a kid with a whisper of a beard and a gawky height he hadn't yet grown into.

Rabbit slowly deflected the point of the spear away from his midsection with one index finger and offered the guard the most beatific smile he could muster.

"One doesn't get to say this every day, so . . . Take me to your leader."

JERUSALEM

68 CE

The teenaged sentry enlisted a few cousins in the trampled yard outside the garden. Rabbit had factored their youth, inexperience, and relation to John of Gischala into his plan. In his many travels, Rabbit had encountered plenty of guards who would have stabbed first and asked questions later. These kids were molded different. Eager to please in a world of unclear expectations, they deferred all important judgment calls to their commander in chief. The decision to murder Rabbit was above their pay grade, a fact he was happy to have calculated correctly.

Rabbit expected to be frog-marched through the dusty prison yard between the two houses. Instead, his captor, whom Rabbit mentally nicknamed Champ for his eager uncertainty, collected his bros and led the way back down the dead-end lane whose terminus housed John's headquarters.

Before they reentered the busy streets of the Lower City, they passed two figures trudging up the lane toward the houses carrying weighty baskets draped in cloth. One was veiled, the tall silent woman from Ein Gedi Rabbit had run into by the Hippodrome. The other was Helen. Both women nodded at the teen guards as they passed but avoided eye contact.

Nice job, partner, he thought.

As if on cue, Champ's stomach growled. He gazed wistfully over his shoulder at the retreating food bearers and tightened his grip on his captive's right arm. Rabbit winced.

It turned out they were in for quite a walk. The boys entered the bustle of the neighborhood, shoving anyone who got out of their way too slowly, brandishing their weapons at anyone who looked at them too long, and generally acting like the pack of curs Miriam had named them.

When they turned north at the foot of the Lower City valley, Rabbit assumed they were headed back to the Hippodrome. But the guards marched him past that, too, then past the public gathering space called the Xystus and straight to the stairs of the Great Temple.

For all the trouble this job had cost him, Rabbit felt like he was finally getting a reward. He hadn't been able to justify a trip to Herod's greatest achievement, but now the job was taking him there. Oh, he might die there, sure, but at least he'd die with a good view.

With much the same sense of awe as he had felt when he first saw the Pyramids of Giza, Rabbit stared up at the magnificent structure that dwarfed everything else in sight. *How the hell had this never been classified as a world wonder?*

Limestone steps as wide as a modern city street ascended halfway up the towering façade to "the porch," a balcony that served as an open market where hundreds of vendors hawked their wares to Temple visitors.

Rabbit and his dishonor guard ignored the merchants and money changers, stepping through a vast door into the interior of the Temple Mount. The Mount wasn't merely a hill clad in stone, it was a complex of underground chambers and passages Rabbit was dying to explore. Just inside the mouth of the porch were hallways penetrating deeper into the building.

Champ yanked his arm.

"Hey," Rabbit snapped inadvertently. "Take it easy."

The kid's mouth fell open at Rabbit's temerity. When he caught his cousins' looks, however, he yanked even harder. Rabbit felt like he had jammed his finger in an electrical socket.

After another long climb up the steep interior stairs, they stepped out into the sunlight and Rabbit forgot about his pain.

The scale alone was shocking. A perfectly flat floor that could house twelve football fields with room to spare. He turned his head to take in the Royal Stoa, a three-tiered colonnade, each tier supported by columns the size of oak trees.

Despite his research to the contrary, Rabbit had always envisioned the Temple as expressing the classical Greek aesthetic with its white and buff stone austerity. Instead, the Temple was an eruption of color. The vast floor was tiled with polished stone in more hues than language could name, like Joseph's fabled coat, like a field of flowers. And much like those flowers, every Roman foot of the Temple Mount contained a mathematically constructed geometrical design. Starbursts, concentric squares, and the frequent motif of Herod's triangle.

Rabbit stared at the stone pattern at his feet. A square enclosed by the iconic triangles, enclosed by more triangles, finally making a square again.

Three points of a triangle. Me, Helen, and Einar Eshek. Trapped together in the past. Triangles and triangles making a square. It's so subtle you might miss the fourth point, but there it is. And who is our fourth point? Who makes us square? Helen in the future, competing with Helen in the past? The murderer, with his bloody body count? What am I missing? It feels like it's right there staring me in the face if only I can look at it the right way . . .

They were in motion again, crossing the Court of the Gentiles for the stoa on the other side of the Mount.

Levite musicians were playing in the shade, a light, peaceful tune that seemed to permeate the air, despite the crowd. The trilling of the strings sounded traditionally Greek, the drums had the roll of northeast Africa, while the pipes spoke of something else, perhaps a Babylonian influence. In that music, Rabbit heard the various cultures that had impacted the Jewish people over the centuries.

Sweet, spicy incense smoke drifted through the air, complementing the rich smell of roasting meat, evidence of the sacrifice being performed in the Temple even now. Rabbit turned toward the scent and was almost blinded by what he saw.

The Mount and its surrounding stoa were a grand framing device for the Temple itself, which shone from the center of the colorful tile flower patch, all white marble and gold plate reflecting the sun in Rabbit's eyes so brightly they watered.

He was gazing through the yawning main entrance, its solid bronze doors hammered into a relief of a castle. Through those open doors, Rabbit could see through the Women's Court to the Court of Priests, the high sacrificial altar within, the gleaming gold face of the Holy Place, a collection of frames within frames laid out with mathematical precision. The whole structure had been designed for this breathtaking view.

Could the Temple treasury really be as vast as the Copper Scroll implied? One look at this majestic building wiped all doubt from Rabbit's mind. Hell yes, it could.

As they turned and started up the stairs into the Temple proper, Rabbit took in everything to which the splendor of Herod's architectural masterpiece had blinded him.

The Mount was crowded, but not with religious visitation. From the balcony overlooking the Kidron Valley on one side to the gate leading to a raised walkway to Herod's Palace on the other, the complex was crowded with soldiers. They were camped out under the roofs of the colonnades, drilling in the Court of the Gentiles. Thousands of them. Unlike the Zealots in the Hippodrome, these men were clad in Roman armor, wielding Roman weapons. They could have been legionaries, if not for their full beards.

These must be the southern Zealots led by Eleazar ben Simon, who turned the Temple into his barracks against the protests of the priests and the provincial government.

Rabbit tripped up the stairs into the Women's Court, passed the great gold donative vessels, their insatiable mouths hungry for coin.

Bantering soldiers crowded the Court, likely the lieutenants of the Zealot force. They paid him little mind as Champ ushered Rabbit into the cool, dim enclosure of one of the square, two-storied chambers that formed the corners of the walled Women's Court.

It took a moment for his eyes to adjust but, on the way, his nose told him where he was. The chamber of incense was heavy with fragrances he associated with his few trips to church. Frankincense? Myrrh? He had no idea what composed that odor, only that he was now experiencing it in a way he never had before, so strong it was like a miasma in the air stirred by his passage.

"What now?" rumbled a voice so low it vibrated Rabbit's sternum.

Its owner was a bear of a man dressed in simple wool clothing similar to Rabbit's own. The bear's companion, standing across a table covered by a crude map, was comparatively splendid in his brightly colored clothes and neatly groomed appearance.

"Sir, I caught—" Champ mumbled, voice pinched and high with tension.

"Speak up!" the man boomed in that same bass voice. Impressive asset for a general, that. The man was big and square all over. Big square head, big square torso, like someone had hewn his body out of stone blocks, then carpeted it with hair.

If the bear had intended to stiffen poor Champ's spine, he'd be disappointed. The barked command had the opposite effect. The nervous teen tightened up so hard, Rabbit swore he heard a sphincter squeak. His answer was inaudible.

"I was caught talking with your prisoner, Antipas," Rabbit said with casual factuality. "Well, to be accurate, I waited for someone to find me talking to your prisoner. It took longer than I was satisfied with."

The blocky general gaped at Rabbit but the well-dressed man across the table was fixing the bear with his steady gaze. "John?" the man asked in polished tones, but Rabbit didn't give the general time to reply.

"I'm sorry for the intrusion." Rabbit gave a short bow of the head and touched his chest. "Joseph ben Joseph. From Tiberias."

"Well met, Joseph ben Joseph," replied the bear in his tectonic rumble. Then, to the young guard: "Leave his body in the desert for the crows."

Champ, eager to get the hell out of there, grabbed Rabbit's right elbow, which sang with pain. Rabbit winced but held it together.

"Wait," said Rabbit. Not a plea, an instruction.

The big shaggy eyebrows of his sentencer rose.

"John," the smooth companion pressed again.

"John of Gischala," said Rabbit, taking a leap. "You hired my brethren to bring you something. Someone actually."

"Sicarii," John whispered.

"John!" his companion insisted. "Tell me what this is all about. You arrested the Temple treasurer? On what grounds?"

"On the grounds," growled John, glaring at Rabbit before shifting his headlights over to the dandy, "that he has hidden the Temple treasury."

The man's full lips turned down in disappointment. "Oh, John, no."

John smacked his big fist down on the table. "Don't get sanctimonious with me, Eleazar, as you sit here with your army huddling in the Holiest of Holies."

Eleazar sniffed. "No one is encamped beyond the Men's Court. The priests are still admitted to perform the rites."

Rabbit slid a few more puzzle pieces into place. Eleazar ben Simon, conqueror of two Roman legions, had taken over the Temple Mount with his Roman-equipped forces. But he and John hadn't enacted their takeover of the priesthood yet.

Rabbit hadn't intended to reveal John's secrets to his partner in crime. The two of them were colluding, Rabbit knew, while John played double agent with the provincial government. Only John had kept his abduction of Antipas secret, and Eleazar was only now finding out about it.

John continued. "You sit up here catching the breezes on the Mount while my men sit in squalor down there. Ill-armed. Ill-equipped. You keep telling me you will supply my troops, but have I seen a shekel? No. So I took matters into my own hands."

"But the Temple treasury?" Eleazar chided. "How will we hope to rebuild after the siege?"

"There won't be anyone left to rebuild if Vespasian breaks our walls!"

Rabbit thought the bass rumblings, amplified to eleven, might shake the cakes of incense off their racks.

The two militia leaders glared daggers at each other over the table. Eleazar broke first, sighing and looking down.

"How did you know the treasury contents were missing?"

"An informant sold me the information a week ago. He knew about the plan but not the location. How did you know?"

Eleazar paused, appeared ready to refute the implication, then changed his mind. He sighed and smiled. "I searched the building, of course."

"You should have told me," John growled.

"As should you." He blew out a long breath. Threw up his hands. "Neither of us did and here we are."

As if on cue, both men turned to Rabbit.

He inclined his head politely.

"My understanding," Rabbit said, picking up on their unspoken question, "is that the treasurer is disinclined to share the details of his plan. Which is why you contacted my brothers." He glanced pointedly at the guards. "Might we dispense with the peripheral ears in the room?"

John signaled for them to exit.

"But sir!" protested Champ. "He could be an assassin!"

John rolled his eyes. "He slipped past the lot of you unnoticed. If he was after murder, he wouldn't have allowed himself to be captured." He shooed them out again, and they complied.

"Good boys," John muttered.

"Bad guards," Rabbit replied.

"All right, dagger man. What do you want?"

"You have hired a very valuable asset of mine," Rabbit said. "Also a John, sometimes called the son of Dorcas." At Eleazar's blank look,

Rabbit explained. "A cunning man at extracting pearls from tight oysters."

"A torturer," John said, simply. "They say he learned his trade in the courts of the Parthian kings. You know how those eastern potentates love to hear people scream."

The smooth militia leader stared at his shaggy peer in horror, but John would have none of it. "If you'd been at Gischala, Eleazar, you might have a different view of what is necessary."

"I am not here to debate wartime ethics," Rabbit interrupted. "I am here to ensure that my asset, who again is worth quite a lot in trade, is adequately protected while he does his work."

John bristled. "My compound is guarded by two score loyal men."

"Loyal, maybe, but not very good at their jobs. They seemed to be more focused on keeping your captive contained than in keeping undesirables out."

"Why do you care so much about my captive?" John argued.

"I couldn't give a week-old fish for your captive. I want to make sure you keep my asset safe. He's valuable to me."

"Him safe?" The general laughed. "From whom?"

"First, from you. Once his work is done, you might be tempted to close his lips to ensure your secret doesn't spread."

John started to protest, but Rabbit held up a hand.

"Second, from the Antipas family. They know their patriarch has been abducted, and they know where he is being held."

The wild beard dropped along with the jaw. John looked at Eleazar.

"Don't look at me. Until a moment ago, I didn't know you'd taken him myself," said the rival Zealot leader.

Rabbit continued. "They have appealed to the provincial government for military support. They will be on your doorstep soon."

John looked panicked for the first time. "How soon?"

"Soon."

The general began to pace the room, his mountainous shoulders hunched.

Rabbit caught a hint of a smile tugging at Eleazar's lips as he observed his peer's dismay. They may have been co-conspirators, but there was no love lost there.

Finally, the bear turned to Eleazar and barked a command. "We accelerate the appointment."

"What? When?"

"Tomorrow."

"To . . . No. Absolutely not."

John swelled to his full height and puffed out his chest. He was clearly used to intimidating other men with his size. But despite his urbane appearance, Eleazar was a veteran of several successful battles and wasn't one to be cowed. Nor did he flex back, he just cocked an eyebrow that deflated the northern Zealot. John continued in a more respectful tone.

"It will throw the city into chaos. The army will be too busy trying to keep the peace to lean on my operation."

"Whose operation?" Eleazar said sweetly.

John was about to answer, when he interpreted his rival's question. "You don't need more funding."

"How did Cicero put it? 'The sinews of war are infinite money.' Of course, you're welcome to try out our little scheme without me from the Hippodrome but I don't think many people go there to pray."

"How much do you want?"

"There are two of us. Some quick arithmetic tells me . . ." He glanced up left in a dumb show of thought. "Oh yes, half."

"What are you going to do with it?"

"Not truly your concern."

The two men locked eyes in a silent battle of wills.

Well, Helen, this is certainly going to speed things up.

"Half," John agreed.

Eleazar's smile widened as he extended a hand to shake on it.

Job done. Now Rabbit was ready to get out of here. "I don't know what any of that is about, but can I take it you will be able to ensure the safety of John bar Dorcas?"

"Rest your mind, Sicarius."

A knock at the door.

"Come!" said Eleazar.

A soldier in full Roman gear entered, leading a man in humble workman's clothing.

"Simeon ben Ephraim," the newcomer said with a little bow of his head. "Of the Sicarii."

The rival generals looked from their visitor to Rabbit and back again.

Oh, hell.

Rabbit ran.

JERUSALEM

68 CE

Rabbit shoved past the Sicarius, sending the man crashing into the doorframe, thinking to himself unhelpfully, *Well, apparently the torturer really has arrived in town.*

He burst into the Women's Court, riding the wave of the generals' protests.

How the hell am I going to get out of here? Rabbit was smack-dab in the middle of a thirty-six-acre complex, surrounded by thousands of Zealot loyalists armed to the teeth.

He dodged right then left around soldiers whose brains hadn't converted what they were seeing into action.

The Temple Mount wasn't an option. Too much ground to cover. They'd cut him down before he got to the Court of the Gentiles.

A Zealot warrior lunged at him. Rabbit hit him with a stiff-arm as he passed, feeling like a football player if the defense were armed with swords and the price for not making first down was beheading.

A clear booming voice filled the court. "Stop that man!" John shouted.

Rabbit ducked another Zealot. This one had his gladius half out of its sheath.

A mirror building to the one he had just exited stood, door open, in his path—a two-story square of stone built into the walls surrounding the Women's Court, black inside.

Get to the door, his brain screamed. The door was goal, home base, safe. Just reach the door.

A man stepped between him and his target.

Rabbit lunged low, sliding across tile floor. *Thank you for sparing no expense, Herod.* The tiles were fitted so well they created a surface as smooth as glass. Rabbit took out the soldier at the knees, saw him flash overhead, heard the grunt as he landed hard.

Blackness.

He was inside.

Problem was, this wasn't home base and this wasn't an evening game of tag.

Scrambling to his feet, Rabbit kicked shut the bronze door with a clang, then slammed his shoulder against it. Something hit it outside, driving Rabbit back a violent few inches before clanging back to the frame.

Wood. There was wood everywhere. Stacks and stacks of wood, racked on wooden shelving to cure. Wood for the sacrificial pyre. Appropriate.

The door had no locking mechanism, not even arms for barring it shut.

He snatched a sliver of olive wood that looked like a shim and rammed it into the narrow gap where the door met the floor. Kicked it home as another soldier crashed into the bronze. It held, but barely.

The shouting was quieter in here. He could think.

Think.

Another clang. A crack of light appeared around the door.

Rabbit backed away, scanning the room. Bumped into a shelving case taller than he was.

Felt it move.

Not much. It wasn't unstable, per se. But it had moved. That meant it wasn't fixed to the floor.

Clang. The light got brighter.

Rabbit darted around the shelving rack and threw his shoulder against it. The rack moved, fractionally.

He leaned on it, hard, planted his feet against the base of the adjacent rack and pushed. The shelving tipped toward the door slightly.

Clang went the bronze door.

Just like getting a car out of the snow, Rabbit thought. Just like a car.

The rack fell back toward him, tipped toward him a fraction of an inch, then Rabbit threw himself at it again, his legs shaking with the strain. It rocked toward the door, but didn't fall.

Clang. An arm came through the door, groping for whatever held it in place.

Rabbit let the rack fall back toward him again. This time, it hovered on its edge, a few pieces of wood toppled to the floor around him, and for a split second, Rabbit thought it was going to fall on him, crushing him under its weight.

Rabbit threw his weight into it one more time. This time the rack tipped on its far edge faster than before, hovered, then finally toppled over. "Clear!" he shouted stupidly, desperately hoping it would prompt the groping soldier to remove his arm from the gap.

Rabbit fell, riding the rack as it tipped into the door, slamming and sealing it shut with the sound of an explosion.

Rabbit heard muffled screaming through the bronze. He didn't look down, afraid of what he might see.

He'd bought himself a moment, no more. *Use it.*

The room was filled with closely spaced wooden shelving like the stacks of a library. There were windows cut into the stone for airing the timber, but they were blocked with heavy bronze shutters. No entry points there.

He quickly stepped through the racks. Wood, wood, more wood.

Then a sight that almost brought tears to his eyes.

A stairway descended into the Mount, which spelled escape.

And a second flight descended from the room above, which spelled pursuit.

On cue, he heard footsteps. Running, sandaled feet appeared above eye level on the stairs in that familiar, controlled fall Rabbit had executed a million times on staircases just like this one.

He reached out instinctively, grabbed the ankle, and turned it into an uncontrolled fall.

The soldier tumbled ass over elbows down the steps and crashed into the opposite wall.

Rabbit tried to do it again with the man's companion, but the second Zealot leaped over his grasp and landed clumsily on the tile floor, drawing his sword as he got his footing.

Rabbit snatched a log from one of the drying racks and parried the gladius. The steel bit deeply into the wood and Rabbit twisted it, trying to wrench the blade from the soldier's grasp. No good, the sword slid free and the man wound up for another overhand slash.

Rabbit backed out of the path of the steel's arc and whipped the piece of wood at the man. It went end over end like an ax and smashed into the man's helmeted head, knocking him off-center with a pained grunt.

Grabbing another log from the rack, Rabbit launched himself down the stairs two at a time.

At the bottom of the stairs, a stone passage split in three directions. Feeble flames from wall sconces suggested long hallways, but didn't reveal much beyond his immediate reach.

Wood-soled sandals clattered on the stairs behind him, and Rabbit reflexively took off down the left passage, trying to keep his footfalls soft and silent, sure he was doing a bad job of it.

He glanced over his shoulder when the sound of the Zealot's labored breath changed pitch. The man had cleared the stairs and was peering down the passages.

Rabbit slowed to a backward creep, eyes intent on his pursuer.

The soldier was lit by a square of weak sunlight penetrating the stairwell. When Rabbit had hit that spot, he couldn't see more than a few meters into the darkness. He was hoping the militiaman's eyes were no better than his own and, by the looks the man was shooting up all three halls, Rabbit was pretty sure they weren't.

The Zealot's partner, whom Rabbit had tripped down the stairs in the Chamber of Wood, joined his hesitant companion, and the two of them conferred in murmurs. Rabbit slid his hand along the clammy stone wall as he continued his stealthy retreat.

The newcomer pointed down an adjacent hallway, and the first soldier started in that direction. Before he'd taken two steps, however, the newcomer swung something hard at the back of the man's head. The thud of wood against skull was followed by the clangor of armor on stone as the soldier collapsed in a heap.

The newcomer then peered down all three passages as keenly as his hapless companion had done before, calling in a stage whisper:

"Ward! Rabbit Ward, is that you?"

JERUSALEM

68 CE

Rabbit stared down the hallway, mouth agape, struggling to process what he was seeing. A Zealot soldier who knew his real name and addressed him in modern English.

The soldier was squinting down the hallways.

True, the newcomer had just saved Rabbit's bacon, but the enemy of your enemy isn't always your friend. Rabbit wasn't sure whether to slip into the darkness or take a gamble on the newcomer.

He might have debated that all day when the Zealot announced himself. "It's Nazarian!" he whispered.

If Rabbit's jaw was slack before, it fell all the way open now. Yeshua Nazarian, Israel's lead chrono-archaeologist, was dead. Killed by Aaron a year ago on a mission to sixth-century Constantinople. The figure haplessly trying to see Rabbit down these dark tunnels was a ghost. If Rabbit hadn't been interacting with a past version of Helen for days, he might have assumed he was being played, but the voice did sound like Nazarian's—sharp as a knife blade on flint.

I can't believe I'm doing this. Rabbit whistled softly through his teeth.

Nazarian followed the sound toward Rabbit.

"That's close enough," Rabbit said, stopping the man a few body lengths away.

"What are you doing here, Ward?" he demanded. Silhouetted by the dancing flames from the sconce, the Israeli glared up at him.

Nazarian was half a head shorter than Rabbit but wore his size with the aggression of a pit bull.

"I could ask you the same thing. I don't recall seeing your trip on any registry."

The international registry of time travel was meant to prevent collisions like this one. Rabbit studied it before every trip and, for some reason, the names, times, and places always stuck with him. For example, he remembered clearly that Nazarian visited the Roman siege of Jerusalem two years from now in 70 CE. He was confident the man had never taken an official trip to the civil war that preceded the Roman incursion.

Nazarian's jaw muscles bunched as he clenched his teeth silently, confirming Rabbit's suspicions. The flex went all the way up the sides of Nazarian's bald head. Direct hit.

The Israeli turned and spat. Something Rabbit thought only happened in the movies.

"You're welcome," he said, wiping his mouth on the back of his hand.

"For that?" Rabbit pointed at the fallen Zealot. "I was already gone."

"As soon as those dopes get through the door I jammed back there, this place will be swarming with soldiers after your hide. And I'm not going to blow my cover to protect you."

"I didn't ask you to."

Nazarian shifted his feet and his tone, softening. "Listen, Ward, I don't know how you found out about the cave, but you've got to give it up."

Rabbit stared, uncertain as to how to reply.

"Come on! It was emptied out. We found the tunnel. Are you telling me you didn't arrange that?"

"I have no idea—"

Nazarian stepped forward with alarming speed and jabbed a blunt finger at Rabbit's chest.

"That gold belongs to the people of Israel."

Rabbit put both hands in the air. "Hey, man, I agree with you."

"Don't insult my intelligence. You lost your innocent card the moment you showed up here. Tell me you're not looking for the key to the scroll."

"Okay, I'm not looking for the key to the scroll."

The flickering corona of torchlight around the Israeli's head displayed a pulsing vein and a bead of sweat that followed its path. "Prove it," he growled through clenched teeth.

"I don't have to prove anything to you, asshole. You're here on an unsanctioned treasure hunt. There's nothing of historical relevance in the scroll treasures. You want to know why I'm here, look it up when you get home. My trip is on the registry just like yours should be."

The clatter of distant feet descending the steps rang through the hall, increasing in volume with every moment.

"Have it your own way, Ward. But like I said, I'm not blowing my cover for you." As the first soldiers appeared in the subterranean hallway, Nazarian's voice cut through the darkness. "This way! Over here!"

As Rabbit turned on his heel, he heard the sharp whisper chase him into the darkness. "Time to run, Rabbit."

Bastard.

Rabbit ran.

His eyes were better adjusted to the dark than the Zealots pursuing him, which should give him an edge. He hoped.

Down the passage he sprinted, skidding at a T junction that seemed to come out of nowhere. Cut right. Another flickering wall sconce appeared down the hallway.

There were doors all along this hall, but Rabbit didn't dare try one. The Zealots might run past, sure, but they might not. Rabbit couldn't risk getting trapped in a dead-end room. A glance back revealed no pursuit until he reached the next junction in the hall. They were chasing him methodically, which was almost worse. It meant they had probably split up in an attempt to cut him off. They certainly knew this warren of underground chambers better than he did.

He had to beat them to an exit, or they'd tighten the noose until they had him.

Rabbit slowed, crept down the passageways as quietly as he could until he spied the cool glow of sunlight ahead.

He resisted the urge to run for it, instead slowing down even more as he approached the corner around which the light was glowing.

A quick glance revealed an open door to a small platform with descending stairs outside. Had to be the north side of the Mount, near the fort.

He held his second glance longer. No one on the platform. No one in the hall to it.

Go.

He ran for it, sandals hissing on loose sand that dusted the stone floor.

He was halfway to the exit when it suddenly filled with bodies, pouring in from both sides of the open door.

Trap.

Rabbit skidded, tried to get purchase on the stone, his hard-soled shoes pinwheeling.

There were more closing in behind him in the hallway. Two, no, three. Swords bare.

Can't give in.

Give in and you die.

Fewer opponents inside than out. That decided it. Rabbit ran back up the passage, watched the men set their feet to receive his rush.

He veered right, watched them shift their weight, then at the wall, he pushed off and spun left, ducked and darted low around the trio. A blade whistled over his head as he passed.

Back into the darkness.

This time they had his scent and gave up on caution. The clatter of their armor followed him, close behind.

Happily, all that armor slowed them down.

At the end of the passage, Rabbit had opened the gap. Twenty paces behind, at least.

He cut right, ran.

His lungs were starting to strain. Couldn't keep this pace much longer.

He saw more light ahead. Was it his imagination, or was it pink?

Lungs heaving, he ran into a wide, open chamber, its high ceiling a stark contrast to the rest of the cramped underground.

From the opposite entry to the chamber, he could hear running footsteps.

Trapped.

He stopped.

A steady stream of red fell into an open pool lit by the sunlight entering around the liquid. And the smell hit him. Blood. He must have been directly below the slaughter tables in the Inner Court. The blood from the sacrifices was falling as though from a faucet into a pool. Light penetrated around the stream, bathing the room in that curiously rosy glow.

The footsteps grew closer.

No way out.

Wait. The blood had to get out, didn't it?

His eyes tracked a stone trough that crossed the room and disappeared into a round-bottomed tunnel in the stone wall.

Without another thought, Rabbit darted for it.

It was barely wide enough for his shoulders, and nowhere near tall enough for him to crawl. But what other option did he have?

Rabbit dove into the dark orifice and its river of blood.

Commando-crawling with his forearms, he shimmied as quickly as he could, aided by the surface made slimy from the endless gore that had passed down its gullet in the decades since its design. The stench was unbelievable. He fought to hold down his gorge, even as his face dipped into the spongy muck.

He paused to see if anyone was following him, stupidly turning his head, but the passage was utterly without light. Not to mention the tunnel was too small to allow him to look over his own shoulder.

Now I know what toothpaste feels like, he thought, and held back a frantic laugh.

A new fear struck him as he wormed his way forward. What if the tunnel turned? He'd never be able to navigate a sharp bend in this tiny space.

Don't think about how small this tunnel is.

Rabbit thought about it.

What had he done? He'd selected the most horrific way to die he could think of, jammed into this narrow tube under tons of stone.

Just keep going.

The only way out is through.

He squirmed and shimmied for what seemed like hours until, suddenly, he was stuck.

It had happened so gradually, Rabbit hadn't felt the tunnel narrowing. Only now it was too small for his shoulders. He tried to back up, but he couldn't get traction on the slick surface. And the pressure in his head told him he was facing downhill. Of course he was, how else would the blood exit the tube?

He started to hyperventilate.

He dug his fingers into the slime but they wouldn't catch. Tried to get his arms ahead of him to narrow his profile, maybe slide through, but there was no room to work them free.

How long would it take to die like this?

There was air, so he wouldn't asphyxiate. Dehydration then. Three days. Three days trapped like this? And how long before the thirst got the better of him, before that trickle of blood started to seem appealing?

No. No, he refused to die this way. He could beat his head against the roof of the tunnel, kill himself that way. Now he did laugh, a sick, bubbling sound.

Bubbling.

Why was there bubbling?

The blood level behind him was rising. Rabbit was jammed into the tube so tight he was blocking the flow. It had been building up behind him and he hadn't even realized it. The blood crept up his back, slithered in tendrils down both sides of his neck, racking him with a disgusted shiver the space was too small to allow.

The pressure behind the tendrils built up to a font, and then the font began to spray. He could feel the droplets splash his cheeks as the pressure of all that blood splashed it over his ears, into his eyes.

That was too much. Rabbit lost the war with his reflexes and convulsed, the vomit spraying out of him to join the blood fountain.

At the apex of the convulsions, something about the involuntary pulsations of his torso and the mass of liquid pressing down on him suddenly and violently freed him from the narrow point of the tunnel. Like a cork from a champagne bottle, he shot down the slick stone tube on a frothing column of gore.

JERUSALEM

68 CE

And then he was free. Flying, tumbling through the air. Splashing into a pool, colliding with the edge of that pool with enough force to drive the air from his lungs and replace it with metallic brine he spat out in retching revulsion.

He had landed in an oversized wooden vat at the center of a little compound of shacks and tents at the base of the Temple Mount. The four towers of the Antonia Fortress cozied up to the corner of the Temple to Rabbit's left, which put his location on the north side of the Temple, the Lower Bezetha section of the city.

Rabbit rose shakily to his feet in the slippery confines of the vat, gripped the rim for support, and looked down over its edge.

Two men were filling a barrel from a spigot at the bottom of the vat. Matching barrels crammed one of the tents. A handful of men were arguing near the barrels.

"Last week you charged me half that for twice as much!" one man was insisting, gesticulating wildly. "I can't make a profit fertilizing my crops like this!"

"You exaggerate," his adversary replied in a weary voice. "Yes, the prices have risen some. Eleazar ben Simon takes a larger cut than the priests."

"The high priest should . . ."

The man had stopped mid-sentence, staring at Rabbit, his mouth hanging open, frozen around a word he would never utter.

The blood salesman followed his gaze. Gasped.

In a chain reaction, the two barrel-fillers looked up. One of them screamed, then they both ran. Their panic was infectious. In moments, all the men from the compound were running, falling over each other as they stumbled away from what must have appeared to be a terrible apparition.

Rabbit climbed out of the vat, aching in every joint, wrung out from retching.

Looking down at himself, he could understand their fear. A slimy red coat covered him like a second skin. Or like he'd misplaced the first one.

"How did you get clean?" Helen asked, when he rejoined her near the Hippodrome bread ovens, the sun low in the sky.

"That's your first question? Not, 'did they pick up pursuit at the fertilizer camp' or 'are they going to jump us any minute?'"

She shrugged. "We all have our priorities."

"Turns out, they water down the blood before they sell it to the local farmers, so they had some at the camp."

"Did they pick up pursuit at the fertilizer camp?" she said, echoing his intonation perfectly.

"Funny."

"Were you hurt?" she asked, this time with genuine concern.

"No broken bones or holes that shouldn't be there," he said, thumping himself on the chest. That hurt. "I want to check back in with Enoch—"

"You need to sleep, dumbass. Where does this hostess of yours live?"

"Lower City. Ten blocks or so. But first—"

"No 'but first.' Come on." She led him around the periphery of the women who were breaking down the breadmaking operation for the night. "Dinah," she called to their leader.

"What?" The woman looked harried.

"I'm taking my husband back to our lodgings for the night. If that's all right."

The woman nodded, distracted, and shooed them away.

"What's wrong?" Helen asked.

Dinah shook her head. "That silly girl, Deetza. No one's seen her since this morning. She's such a hopeless flirt, I thought she might have made a fool of herself over some soldier. But I was sure she would have shown up by now."

Helen explained to Rabbit, "I filled in for Deetza today, taking food to the prisoners and guards up on the hill. Do you want help looking?" she asked the leader of the ovens.

"No. It's near dark. Wherever you're going, you should get inside. We'll find her soon enough." The lines of her face disagreed with the words.

"If you're sure," Helen tried again.

"Go on," Dinah insisted. "Be safe."

Reluctantly, Helen and Rabbit left the bread ovens and merged with the crowd heading home for the night. But they had barely exited the shadow of the Hippodrome when a hand tugged at Rabbit's right sleeve. If he hadn't thought about his aching right arm before, that reminded him. Rabbit turned. "Enoch."

"Why are you wet?" He shook his hand, looking mildly disgusted.

He should talk. The initiate looked filthy and smelled worse.

"Do you need something, Enoch?"

"Well, I thought, if you're going back to Miriam's . . ."

"Go. Home," Rabbit intoned clearly.

"I will, I will. But I can't tonight, it's too late."

Rabbit was about to tell him off, but Helen placed a hand on his arm. "It's all right. You said there was plenty of room on the roof, right?"

Begrudgingly, Rabbit agreed, and the three of them set off. "Did you keep an eye on Leocharis today?"

"I tried to. Honestly! But he disappeared before midday, and I never saw him again."

Rabbit and Helen exchanged a furtive glance.

"Well," said Rabbit through tight teeth, "thanks for trying."

Enoch beamed.

The crowds thinned as the sun dipped below the horizon, but not everyone was at home tonight. The trio made out voices drifting down from Miriam's windows as they climbed an impossibly narrow staircase between the apartment blocks to her street.

". . . you have the ear of the Lower City and of Bezetha. They will listen to you."

"I am an old woman with new ideas. Since when have either of those things been popular?" Miriam. For sure.

"It is because you don't cling to the old ways that they listen. The common youth think the only route to change is with the sword."

She laughed. "Most common people would back a goat if he promised lower taxes. The Zealots preach revenge, which is tempting meat to young men raised on plates of humility. And the message of peace is owned by the Sadducees, who those young men hate almost as much as the Romans."

"But you're not aligned with the Sadducees—"

"What is this?" Miriam interrupted. In the moment of silence that followed, Rabbit and Helen looked at each other curiously. Pressed together under the window, ears cocked toward the voices, like intimates brought together by a shared voyeurism. Enoch stared at them, clueless. "It's not a trick," Miriam pressed. "What is it?"

"A . . . a coin?" her companion said.

"And how many sides does the coin have?"

"Two," the other voice answered hesitantly, knowing he was playing into her rhetoric and not wanting to go.

"What is on this side?"

"Miriam—"

"What is on this side?" she demanded.

"A palm tree."

"What is on this side?"

"The fruit."

"Here, now I'll flip it. What will I get?"

"The fruit or the tree."

"What if I flip it again?"

"The fruit or the tree."

"And—"

"It will always be the fruit or the tree."

"Keep it. Now you understand power."

"But I—"

The old woman continued patiently. "Power is a coin. A trick invented to convince you that there are only two sides to an argument. You align with one or the other. The fruit or the tree. Now the voice of power only needs to combat one thing, not the bounty of true possibilities. I am neither fruit nor tree, but the vying powers would paint me as one or the other and my voice would end there."

"Will you think about it, at least? I must get home." A hand slapped a table. "Use it at the Temple at tomorrow's Sabbath."

The door opened and shut loudly.

Rabbit, Helen, and Enoch continued up the steps to Miriam's and knocked.

"I told you, I . . ." Miriam barked as she opened the door. "Oh, it's you. Well, come in." She pursed her lips. "You appear to have multiplied during the day."

"My wife, Rachel," Rabbit said, gesturing to Helen.

The old woman huffed. "There's room on the roof for you, too. But everyone's bellies will be a little lighter."

"I don't need food," Helen said. "In fact"—like a magician, she pulled out a small bundle wrapped in cloth—"I brought some for your house. Just a little bread, but I hope it will help."

Miriam softened a little. "Well, it certainly won't hurt."

Judith, Leah, and the children appeared to have been hiding from Miriam's debate with the political rabble-rouser. The two women glanced warily at Rabbit, Helen, and Enoch as they entered the common room.

Miriam went back to her kitchen without another word. She violently stoked the fire in the floor hearth.

The coin sat on the table. A well-worn shekel. Rabbit picked it up.

Don't get involved. These people are all dead and their stories are over. Don't get involved.

"Miriam," he said.

"Hnh?"

Rabbit stood in the doorway to the kitchen, rolling the shekel over in his fingers.

"Well? What is it, man? I haven't started the evening meal."

He waited until she turned and looked at him.

When she did, Rabbit flipped the coin with a flick of his thumb. It spun in the air until he snatched it. Then, gently, he stood the coin up on its side on the table. It stood there, threatening to roll away as Miriam looked quizzically at Rabbit.

"Even a coin has three sides."

She looked between the coin and him.

"A change is coming," Rabbit said. "Something big. Who knows, maybe it's the opportunity you've been waiting for."

"Who says I'm waiting for anything?"

"Maybe it's the opportunity others hope you'll take." Rabbit flicked the coin, knocking it over on its side again. "Or not. Your choice."

Rabbit, Helen, and Enoch climbed up to the roof under a starry sky.

Rabbit and Helen lay side by side on thin mattresses, shoulders barely touching, while the initiate occupied the corner furthest from them.

"I'm not tired," Helen said.

"Me neither," Rabbit replied.

"I am," Enoch said in a bleary voice.

They lay in silence in the chilly night air, listening as the young man's breathing slowed and deepened. Occasionally his breath would catch in gasping hiccups.

Quietly, and in English, Rabbit updated Helen on what he'd learned. The Sicarii torturer had almost certainly arrived in the city, given the embassage that had revealed Rabbit to be a fraud. The Israeli Authority was hunting down the Copper Scroll key, too, and without official sanction.

"It's getting pretty fucking crowded around here," she said.

Rabbit agreed. "Eshek will make a move soon. He'll have to. That Antipas is a cool customer, though. It'll be hard to get anything out of him."

"I like him," Helen said.

"Me too."

"Do you think . . . Maybe we could save him," she suggested.

Rabbit shook his head no. "That's the hardest part of the job. Good people die. Monsters get rewarded. There's nothing you can do about any of it."

"That's a grim outlook."

He shrugged, and the simple gesture felt like it wrenched a thousand piano wires in his body. "It's the truth."

"It's *a* truth."

"What do you mean?"

She was silent for a few moments, then pointed at the sky. "The light from most of those stars. Not the light we see now, but the light leaving them now, it still won't have reached Earth by the time we go home."

"Sure," he agreed. "They're millions of light-years away."

"But will it ever? I mean those exact stars. You might have inspired a whole progressive movement tonight almost two thousand years too early. We must have splintered this timeline by now, right, which would mean those aren't the same stars we see in our sky. They're . . . copies, in an alternate timeline. An alternate universe."

"Maybe I did. And maybe I didn't. I didn't invent Miriam. She was already here, dreaming up a radical change to her society. Who knows, history might be littered with these little candles of ideas that just don't manage to catch fire. What made the ideas of Jesus of Nazareth take hold now, persist and grow? How many other world-shaping radical flames just"—he puffed air like a kid at his birthday—"blew out in the wind?"

"Then again, maybe she changes the whole goddamn world in this timeline. Wouldn't that be kind of amazing?"

Rabbit thought about Andor, his friend from Constantinople, who might have steered the course of his history for the better. "This may sound selfish, but I'll never see that world. No matter what I do, I always go back to my own timeline. It has a certain inevitability that's . . . oh, hell, I don't know. It makes me sad sometimes."

Another long pause, as the stars wheeled overhead.

"Why are you still here, Rabbit?" she asked finally, her voice small. "Why are you really here? You already got what you came for."

Rabbit sighed. The lie that came next wasn't a lie at all. Oh sure, it wasn't the whole truth, but it wasn't complete fabrication either. That realization worried him enough that he would have stayed silent about it to anyone else but her.

"Billions with a *B*," he said.

He felt her head turn toward him.

He continued. "You don't know me that well but . . . I'm not always this easy to get along with."

She didn't laugh at his joke. Neither did he. Somewhere, a cricket filled in for them.

"I'm a proud man, Helen. 'Arrogant,' maybe, is a better word. What I do for a living, very few people can. But back in our world, that doesn't matter. I'm still beholden to people with money. Captains of industry. Trust fund recipients. Lucky investors. It doesn't even matter if they earned it, people with money view themselves as a superior species, and people without it agree with them."

"You want to be rich?" she asked.

He sighed. "No. Not really. I mean, I don't want money for money's sake. I don't want yachts or country clubs or whatever rich people indulge themselves with. I just want . . . I want . . ."

"Freedom," she concluded for him.

"Freedom," he agreed.

"What would you do if you got it?"

At first, he thought she was being provocative, but the quizzical look on her face told him the question was sincere. "This," he said, waving his hands at the city. "Time travel. Why would anyone want to do anything else? I'd set my own mission objectives, just to learn about the past, not to always be trying to bring back some trophy to justify the expense."

Helen made a little grunt of acknowledgment, then fell silent again.

A shiver went through her and she shifted her body, pressing against his for warmth.

It felt good.

Rabbit couldn't get involved with her. It was unethical, using secret knowledge about someone to, was there any better way of saying it, seduce them?

Then again, what did Rabbit really know about Helen? He had never so much as laid eyes on her in present day. He knew very little about the organization for which she worked. Even less about the life she lived when she wasn't on a mission. For all Rabbit knew, she could be married with three kids. He cringed a little, picturing her kissing some handsome man goodbye, suitcase in hand. *See you when I get back!*

He and Helen were work friends. Nothing more.

When he and Ian were just work friends, he knew Ian was snarky and smart, cautious and integrous. A germaphobe. But he hadn't known Ian was a rabid movie buff who had once considered becoming a film editor. He didn't know about Ian's tragically romantic sensibility or how truly afraid he had been for his own safety throughout his youth. How he had developed his sense of humor as a kind of armor to convince the world he didn't care what anyone thought of him.

Rabbit could fill a book with unanswered questions about Helen.

Sure, he knew a lot about how her agile mind worked. She was quick to draw conclusions, quick to act on them, quick to recover if she was wrong. He knew she valued right above rules. That she was light of spirit, quick to joke. She didn't take life too seriously even, or especially, when the stakes were high.

He also knew Helen was *always* on her game. Rabbit thought of himself as an open book outside of missions. Helen, by contrast, appeared to be in deep cover all the time. Rabbit could make inferences about her life from context clues, the way you could sometimes tell where a rock was in a river by the way the water eddied around it. And that part of him said there was no husband or kids waiting for her at the end of missions.

Or was that just hope and fear again? Yeah, he didn't believe she was coupled up, but he feared it. Which told him plenty about what he hoped.

He kicked sand out of his shoe and shook his head.

Why did it have to be Helen? Was there anyone less practical to want? She pissed him off frequently. She had robbed him blind, almost ruined his career. She wasn't even his type. Rabbit had always been attracted to emotionally distant intellectuals.

"Funny bitches," Ian had once told him.

"What?" Rabbit had been surprised.

"Come on, it's just the truth. You like 'em smart, witty, and mean." As Rabbit began to protest, Ian counted off evidence on his fingers. One, "Jennifer."

"Yeah, she was funny but—"

Two, "Christine."

"She wasn't funny, she was just mean—"

Three, "Bianca."

"I wasn't into Bianca."

"I tricked you! Bianca was a sweetie." Four, "Jennifer two."

"Jesus . . ." Rabbit said, seeing the pattern.

"So just give it a try with Karyn. She's a hundred thousand percent your type."

Karyn. Three dates and one athletic but transactional roll in the sheets. Most notable for being the boss of the snitch who almost landed Ian in jail.

It hadn't worked out, but Ian hadn't been wrong either. She was funny. And mean.

Helen was different. Just as smart as anyone he'd been with, just as funny, but with a sincerity and earnest heart that . . . well, what? That he didn't trust, he supposed.

That was it. Maybe he didn't trust kindness in women. Some part of him was always sure he was being played. When a mean woman wanted to bed you, you knew there was no ulterior motive. Everybody knew what they were getting into. Right?

Maybe . . . maybe he didn't think he deserved anyone being kind to him.

Rabbit sighed. *What the fuck is wrong with me?*

His eyes were beginning to get heavy when a shooting star cut a path across the constellations.

"Make a wish," he said softly.

But Helen was asleep.

JERUSALEM

68 CE

Rabbit and Helen were up at dawn. There wasn't much choice, when the rising sun shone directly in your eyes.

Enoch whined about the accommodations, accepted too much of Miriam's scant food, and generally acted like the spoiled kid he was from the moment he rose until Rabbit introduced a detour into their path to the Hippodrome.

"It's twice as far that way," Enoch complained.

"That's an exaggeration," Rabbit said. "I want to swing by the market and get something to eat that doesn't rob those kids of food."

"She offered," Enoch protested. If anything, a good night's sleep had made him more entitled.

"Of course she offered, she's a normal person. That doesn't mean you have—"

Helen interrupted. "Enoch. Why don't you go that way? You're right, it's faster and we don't want to make you late for muster."

"Fine," he snapped, and walked away into the crowd.

"That kid's really getting under my skin," Rabbit said.

"You have a thing for lost souls, don't you?"

"Me?" He laughed. "I don't think so."

"I do. You could have cut him loose, but you keep letting him tag along. Only you're irritated he doesn't see the world the way you do."

"He's an entitled brat."

She smiled.

"What's so funny?"

"For someone who says you can't change anything, you sure do try."

He changed the topic. "I'm going to check on Tuvia this morning. See if he came back to his house overnight," Rabbit said, navigating them down the tiers of streets to the market lane. They had plenty of company. Farmers headed for the olive and fig groves outside the city walls, tradespeople, craftsmen, shop owners, and domestic servants making their way to the Upper City, the Mishneh, or Bezetha. "It sure would have been helpful if your people had shown you a picture of Eshek."

Helen nodded. "The crowd she runs with seems to be big on anonymity."

"She?" he asked. "Come on, this way."

He took her through a narrow alley, scaring off a couple of skinny cats from a pile of offal in the process.

"Where are we going?" she asked.

"Getting breakfast. You said 'she.'"

"There's bread at the Hippodrome."

"Man does not live on bread alone," he intoned.

"Shall not," she corrected.

"Are you sure?"

"Eight years of Catholic school. I'm pretty fucking sure." But she didn't resist as he led the way to the little food stall from which the thickest plume of smoke rose.

"What do you have this morning?" Rabbit asked the vendor, a stooped man with a leathery face etched with sleepy smile lines.

The man's little stove was semipermanent, with a brick base for the fire. A copper pot on top was already emitting a cloud of spices that smelled something like harissa.

"Two?" the old cook asked, raising his fingers, one of which ended at the second knuckle.

At Rabbit's confirmation, the man pulled out a flat loaf from the lower tier of the chimney. As it steamed, he deftly sliced it in half on a board, slathered the insides with a scoop from the pot, and finished it with a swipe of deep red pulp from a jar.

Rabbit paid the man his inflated price and took a bite. The hot bread crackled between his teeth and flavor exploded in his mouth. Sweet tart pomegranate honey. Rich, spicy vegetable paste from the pot. It was the best thing he had eaten in a long time.

"Worth it," Rabbit declared, chewing.

The food demanded they walk a little slower, as did the thickening crowd. As the sun broke over the mountains, the Temple came into view, sparkling gold against a backdrop of shaded olive groves on the mountain slopes.

He glanced at Helen. Fine lines crinkled the skin around her eyes. She nodded in acquiescence. "Worth it."

They were walking alongside other militiamen now. Rabbit recognized a few of them from the Hippodrome.

"Is she why you're doing this?" he asked.

Helen chewed a bite of her bread far longer than it required. Swallowed. "Yeah."

"Friend?" he asked.

"Sister."

Rabbit waited. It seemed interminable.

"Olympia," she said, finally. "My older sister. Idiot got mixed up with a bunch of"—she side-eyed Rabbit—"questionable individuals."

"Questionable?"

"Criminals, Ward."

"Is she a . . ." Rabbit didn't know how to say *hostage* delicately. "Are they holding her against her will?"

Helen shook her head with a look on her face like she just drank spoiled milk. "She works for them. Kind of a big shot, it seemed like when I saw her last. Everybody deferred to her, and she was rolling in money. Picked me up in this tricked-out sports car. I think she was trying to impress me."

Something clicked in Rabbit's head. The woman with the glasses who was running the show at Helen's organization. She had the same laugh as Helen, that little snort she did when something funny caught her off guard. He couldn't believe it hadn't occurred to him.

Sister, eh? Well, that put a new spin on things.

"How did she get involved with them?" he prompted.

Helen finished her bite. She seemed to be at an inflection point. Would she tell the story or not? With a little sigh, she decided. "She wanted to do what you do. She was in grad school for history when she heard about an opening"—she pursed her lips—"at the Smithsonian."

Helen's disdain for the Institution suddenly made sense. "Of course. And she asked you to apply with her."

"Right. I didn't even want to. I already had a job in Europe at that point. But she wanted it so badly. She thought maybe they'd hire us as a team. Olympia was studying classical history and archaeology and thought my, uh, my more practical skills might balance her out. I resisted for a month, but she wore me down."

"Let me guess. They offered you the job but not her," Rabbit concluded.

Helen nodded. "She was so fucking mad at me."

"At you? Why?"

"Jealous, I guess. Anyway, she blamed me for showing her up. Like I meant to do that. I didn't even want the damn job!" she protested.

"Did she get over it?"

"We barely spoke for a while. My Christmas card got returned. She'd moved and left no forwarding address. She would answer texts now and then, so I knew she wasn't dead or anything, just pouting. Then about six months later she popped up again. Called me out of the blue sounding almost manic she was so excited. She had met this guy—"

"A boyfriend?" Rabbit asked.

"More like a mentor. But the way she talked about him gave me the creeps. She was obsessed with him. Quoted him all the time. He was a godlike father figure slash guru slash lover."

"So, they were lovers?"

"Mmm. No, I don't think so. Not physically, anyway. I got the impression he kind of kept her at arm's length. Anyway, she told me he had recruited her to run his time travel operation and wanted me to be their . . . well, their you."

"Why wasn't she doing it herself?"

"Seems like she decided she was better at management. She pitched it like we could finally be the team we'd always said we'd be."

"Did you? Always say that?"

"No. It was icky the way she put it. Like she was offering me a chance to make it up to her about the Smithsonian? I don't know. I sure as hell didn't like it. And when I asked about the legality of the operation, she dodged that hard. Said it was a 'privately operated concern.'"

"That's not a thing. All licenses go through government channels," Rabbit said. The Hippodrome came into sight over the rooftops of the market stalls, and he intentionally slowed his steps a little. He didn't want the destination to end the conversation prematurely.

"I know," she said.

"So, you rejected the offer."

"Not right away. I wanted to see if I could talk her out of it. I met up with her, just once, in a hotel in Switzerland."

"Neutral territory."

Helen smiled. "Ha. Right. I tried to find out more about this guy she was so obsessed with."

"How'd that go?"

"World War Three would about describe it. She accused me of trying to steal yet another thing from her, said I was weak-minded, manipulative."

"This guy really got his hooks in her."

"Yeah. Although this all kind of lined up with her modus operandi anyway. In the end she kicked me out of the hotel room and went silent again."

"For how long?"

"Two years."

"No shit?"

She nodded. Licked drips of honey from her fingers. "Last month, I was working in Ankara. I came home and found her in my apartment. Trust me when I say it's no fucking joke, getting into my apartment unnoticed. She'd changed so much. She was wearing this outfit that cost more than my car, but it wasn't just that. There was this . . . coldness in her I hadn't seen before. Maybe it was always there, maybe I just never noticed it before. She explained that their jumper, that's what she called Eshek, had stolen a lot of money from the organization and could I help her find him."

"And you said yes?"

"I said I had to speak to her boss first."

"Damn. No, I mean I'm impressed," he said in response to her suspicious look. "Did he agree to it?"

"He wouldn't meet me in person, but he did agree to a phone call. I told him I would get his runaway thief in exchange for my sister's release. And not just 'you're free to go.' He had to pay her off and send her on her way, *Shane*-style. Buh-bye, bitch."

"I guess I haven't watched *Shane* in a while."

"What was I supposed to do? Eventually, she was going to get hurt, one way or another."

"You're right." Rabbit thought of Olympia and Helen, the speed of their organization, the mercs armed with submachine guns. Like she said, it was bound to catch up to them badly at some point. "And he agreed?"

"He agreed." There was hesitance in her voice.

"What's the catch?"

"That if I don't find Eshek, then I work for him, too."

"We won't let that happen," he said even as he realized that's exactly what would happen.

She looked up at him, eyes full of vulnerability and gratitude. "Thank you."

So, there it was. This was how Helen ended up with the company. This same organization would order her to steal his takes out from under him a few years later. He imagined her face when he first met her in Alexandria. The fire raging around them as she held hostage the scrolls he'd been sent to rescue from the conflagration. She had been smiling, had teased him. But there was no joy in that smile. She was enjoying her revenge, enjoying ruining his career one theft at a time.

Since then, they had become friends. Not intimates, Rabbit wasn't sure she trusted anyone enough for that. But friends. He had hoped that by coming back here to help her, he might take their friendship to the next level.

Unfortunately, between now and then, she would learn to hate him.

Rabbit cleared his throat. "Don't thank me yet."

Rabbit and Helen arrived at the bread ovens to find them abandoned.

The fires were still hot. Smoke rose in clouds from the chimneys. Dough lay abandoned like limbless babies in the bowls, but no bakers tended the hearths.

Rabbit poked his head into the shade of the racetrack stables, but they were empty, too. He could see the usual crowds of men in the Hippodrome beyond the stables; only the women were gone.

Anxiety prickled over Rabbit's skin. He and Helen trotted the length of the stables, poking in and out of the doors, looking for some sign of the missing bakers. It wasn't until he got to the other side of the courtyard that he spied the first of them. A lone woman—he didn't know her—stumbling in the direction of the ovens, her eyes wide and wet, mouth open in a silent O.

When Rabbit approached the woman, she flinched away from him.

"Where is everyone?" he demanded.

Helen spoke more softly. "Sarah." The baker's eyes focused on Helen. "Where are the others?"

Sarah glanced over her shoulder toward the end of the stables.

They went in the direction she had indicated, around the corner of the building. Across an open clearing, at a row of low stone buildings, the women were gathered.

They rocked, clung to each other in a ghastly imitation of prayer.

Rabbit and Helen pushed through as carefully as they could to the nucleus of the group, gathered around the mouth of a three-sided midden, piled high with manure.

Nestled in that bed of filth, he saw exactly what he feared he would.

JERUSALEM

68 CE

The body had been vivisected, just like the others. The victim was a woman, although that was barely discernible in her condition. Rabbit knew at a glance she hadn't been killed here; the organs had been roughly jammed back inside the open torso, not arranged in their usual petallike configuration. Her legs were still buried in manure where the killer had hidden her. A gash had peeled away her cheek, but that wound was bloodless, almost certainly delivered long after death. A shovel lay on the ground nearby. Someone must have been emptying the midden when they hit something that shouldn't be there.

"Who is she?" Rabbit asked softly.

"Deetza," Helen replied. "She disappeared yesterday. I got her job." She was squeezing his hand in a punishing grip. It felt welcome.

Two women were gently unearthing the corpse from the midden heap. The rest were sighing, rocking, holding themselves or each other.

"An animal attack," someone whispered behind him, desperate to make the atrocity slot into something that belonged in the natural world.

Rabbit understood the sentiment. Why would someone resort to such . . . creativity? Of all the creatures on Earth, humans were the most adept at murder for no natural reason. Packs of young male orcas were known to kill baby whales for sport, taking a bite or two and letting the rest sink to the ocean floor. But as with speech, humans had applied their remarkable intellects to the act of killing in a way that was totally exceptional. Humans made an art form of death.

The woman who invented that rationalization was doing her best to put her world order back together into something recognizable through the force of her imagination.

Rabbit admired it, but he lacked the capacity himself.

He just wanted to erase the source.

Head buzzing, hands tingling, Rabbit wove through the crowd. Then he was in the stables and now the racetrack floor, walking through crowds he was hardly aware of.

Someone was shouting. Maybe at him, he wasn't sure. He didn't care. He had caught the glint of burnished bronze across the track, and everything else was mist.

He burst into a circle of fools ringing Leocharis, who looked like a Greek god in his shining armor, his stupid, handsome face bright with mirth. Rabbit wanted to grind that godlike face into the dust of the track.

Somehow, he managed to speak in Greek and not revert to English when he growled, "Did you kill her?" He closed the gap quickly, coming for the Macedonian without weapons or shield, whereas Leocharis had both.

The mercenary pivoted gracefully out of the attack path and lightly shoved Rabbit with his round shield. It was effortless but sent Rabbit stumbling a few steps before he righted himself.

"Did you kill her?!" Rabbit shouted, spittle flying from his lips.

The amused smirk never left the Macedonian's face. "Kill who, old man?"

Rabbit stepped forward again but pulled up short to stop from impaling himself on the merc's weapon.

"Yes or no? Did you kill her?" Rabbit shouted.

"Specifics!" Leocharis said brightly. "I've killed a lot of people."

"Deetza," Rabbit said, the point of the lance touching his sternum. "John's serving girl."

"In that case, no. I haven't killed any serving girls. In fact, I haven't killed anyone in Jerusalem yet. Does that satisfy you?"

Rabbit didn't answer. He was coming off the rage adrenaline, thinking more clearly. This wasn't going to get him anywhere. If he'd been able to calm down he would have realized that, but the animal had taken hold of him.

Helen was beside him, holding his arm. When had she appeared?

Before Rabbit hit his high school growth spurt, he'd been the target for every bully in school. It was then he learned that predators aren't fierce. The very act of predation is cold. Meditated. It's their prey who are fierce, tapping into a kind of wild, unpredictable energy needed to survive overpowering odds. In Rabbit's line of work, he was usually the predator, methodically knocking down the obstacles between him and his quarry. This mission was different. He felt the presence of that graceful, masked killer hovering at the edge of his perception all the time. This time he felt very much like the prey. Jumpy, hypervigilant, twitching with rage. It didn't take much under those circumstances for that wild, hunted beast to take over the better angels of his nature.

Leocharis coolly waited for an answer. Now there was a predator. He was Eshek. Rabbit was almost sure of it. But how the hell to unmask him?

"I'm satisfied," Rabbit grumbled.

"Good!" The merc turned back to his trainees like Rabbit was no threat at all.

Rabbit was inclined to agree with his assessment.

"Come on," Helen said. She tugged his arm. "Joseph."

He allowed himself to be led away.

In the lee of the Hippodrome, near a blind alley, Helen finally stopped.

"Better?" she asked.

He nodded. His heart was still pounding against his ribs, and he didn't trust his voice not to croak.

Helen squeezed the bridge of her nose with both index fingers, took a deep breath.

"I want to kill him," Rabbit said.

"No, you don't," she said. "Not really. You just want him to stop."

Rabbit scrubbed a hand over his head. "Yeah," he admitted. "You're right. Why kill an innocent girl like that? What's the point?"

"I don't know. Yesterday I was glad she was gone. It got me the job I needed. I hate myself for that."

"Not your fault."

She began to pace. "Are you sure the murder in Rome was the same man?"

"Positive. The method is too distinctive to be more than one."

"So, what now?"

Rabbit steeled himself. "The murder's a distraction. We follow the plan. I'll go to the Antipas household and sic them on John's headquarters like I planned to do yesterday. If Eshek is paying as much attention as I think he is, he'll know his time is almost up. He'll move."

She nodded. "I'll be waiting."

Rabbit knocked on the front gate of a beautiful domus after a walk that bordered on a run. Antipas the Treasurer made his home in the Upper City, the wealthiest neighborhood in Jerusalem. It was a stark contrast to the monochromatic warren of Miriam's neighborhood. Orderly, right-angled streets connected blocks of gleaming walled gardens and Greco-Roman homes that wouldn't have looked out of place on the Palatine Hill in Rome. Owing to its position on the high side of the mountain city, it even smelled better.

A peephole the size of a mail slot opened in the stout door to the Antipas garden revealing the upper half of a face pinched with suspicion.

"Yes?"

"I have a message for the family of Antipas."

A hand spread near the peephole, inviting Rabbit to push it through.

"A verbal message. My apologies. I would give you the message, but my master was quite explicit," Rabbit said. "Only to the head of the household."

"Master Antipas' brother is here. Will that suffice?" the man on the other side of the door said. Rabbit had expected imperious annoyance, but the servant seemed too rattled to flex his position. His voice shook slightly as he spoke.

"Thank you, yes," Rabbit said.

"Wait here."

A few moments later, Rabbit was admitted to the home and escorted to the study.

The brother of the treasurer stood to greet Rabbit. He was younger than Antipas, his face less seamed with time and cares, but he shared the same angles to his bones. "You have a message? Is it about my brother?"

Rabbit nodded.

"Two nights back, he went to the Temple and never returned. We feared the worst. The boys are gone. Tuvia and Tzephania both."

Rabbit knew the man was rambling only to delay the news he feared to receive, but he didn't stop him. So, Tuvia had not come home after all. Where the hell was he?

"The elder went to fetch home the younger from that cult he'd taken up with. There was no one but me to look after things. I'm doing my best. I kept hoping he would walk through the door."

"I have bad news for you, but it's not the worst. Your brother is alive."

Antipas' brother sagged in his chair with relief.

"But he has been arrested, imprisoned by John of Gischala."

"Arrested? On what grounds?"

"None that have been stated. I know he's being held against his will, that's all."

The man rose to his feet. "Do the priests know?"

Rabbit shook his head. "Only John's intimates are aware of his fate."

The worry on the man's face was slowly being replaced by anger. "He's gone too far. The provincial government has given a long leash to his Zealots. No one wants the city to turn on itself, especially not now with the Romans in the North. But this!"

"What will you do?" Rabbit asked.

"Tell them. Immediately. My brother has many friends. John won't get away with this. The army will come to our aid."

Rabbit nodded, satisfied. "I'll show myself out."

"No, wait!" he said. "I'll call the family together. It won't take long. I want them to hear this from you."

They assembled quickly, dozens of relatives from the Antipas clan who made the spacious courtyard feel cramped. Cousins, in-laws, even a few highly placed servants heard Rabbit's information, including the location of the makeshift prison and its protections.

He was almost done answering their questions when he saw something that stopped his tongue. At the edges of the family crowd stood a black-bearded man wringing his hands.

Hands stained a multitude of colors. Dyer's hands.

Miriam.

Gears turned over in his head.

What had Miriam been doing out after dark the night he arrived? He hadn't thought much of it at the time. But she had been coming from the direction Tuvia had disappeared. Rabbit imagined her intercepting the young man on his way home, directing him to hide. She knew about Antipas' disappearance by then.

"Does the family own a textile mill?" Rabbit asked, injecting the question into the middle of his own sentence.

Antipas' brother looked perplexed by the question, but answered, nonetheless. "Of course. Our family is the oldest importer of Tyrian—"

Rabbit didn't hear the rest. He made his excuses and slipped away from the crowd, confident that his work was done. The family would march on John's prison, forcing Eshek to make his move.

But it wasn't Eshek he was worried about right now.

Rabbit sprinted to the gate in the wall dividing the Upper and Lower City neighborhoods, skidded down narrow alleys, and burst through the door to Miriam's home, panting like a dog.

The old woman came out of the kitchen with fire in her eyes, a cooking knife in her hand. She stopped short when she saw Rabbit.

"Young man, you have some explaining to do!" Her glare moved between him and the leather strap she used to lock her door that now hung broken and useless.

Rabbit deftly dodged Miriam's kitchen knife and hugged her.

"I'm so glad you're . . . here," he said, biting back the word *alive*.

"It's the Sabbath, of course I'm here," she said. "Now about that door."

"Do you work at the Antipas fabric manufactory?"

"Yes, what of it?"

"We can talk on the way."

"My husband worked as a dyer for years. He was a mixer, one of the most respected men in the business."

They were walking as fast as her legs could carry her through the crowded streets, Rabbit chafing at the constraints of her speed like a whippet on a leash.

"I was nursemaid to the boys, Tuvia and Tzephania, until they were too old to need my care. Antipas let me work at the mill after my man died. He wouldn't have let me go hungry in any case, but I needed occupation."

"So, you knew when Antipas didn't come home the other night," Rabbit said. They passed through the archway in the first wall, the one Herod had used as his personal raised sidewalk between his palace and the Temple.

On the far side of the wall was the Mishneh neighborhood, which housed much of the city's industrial complex.

"I knew," she admitted. "And I was worried for the boys. I caught Tuvia before he went home and hid him in the storerooms of the factory."

"Which is why you were coming home so late," he finished for her.

She stopped in her tracks.

"Joseph, what do you want with that young man?"

"There's no way for me to explain this to you, but I know he's at risk. Tuvia and his father are both aware of . . . certain pieces of information that make them very valuable to the Zealots. Please." He gestured her to move again.

She didn't. "You're a smooth talker. Got me walking this way before I even knew where my feet were taking me. How do I know you're not the real risk to that boy?"

Rabbit sighed. "You don't. You don't know and nothing I can say will give you the certainty you want. So, you're going to have to trust your instincts."

She glared at him, fists balled on her hips.

"Time is a factor," Rabbit said.

She huffed. "Come on."

The dye works was empty on the Sabbath. The sprawling, two-story building was festooned with long strips of brightly colored cloth hanging from lines around brick dye baths. It was beautiful but smelled atrocious.

She guided him up a ladder to the second floor. The shorter-ceilinged second floor was filled to overflowing with bales of cloth and amphorae of all sizes, arrayed in neat rows as far as the eye could see.

Miriam led Rabbit through the rows to the farthest point in the attic. A sort of pillow fort had been built into the corner, stacks of fabric assembled to enclose a small square of floor.

What wasn't there was Tuvia.

The air drained out of Miriam.

At one end of the enclosure, the bales had been tossed aside to open the space. The sleeping mat was crumpled in a corner and littered with remnants of food, evidence of a struggle.

"Where is he?" she asked, the strain evident in her usually sharp voice.

"I'm sorry," Rabbit said. "I think I know."

JERUSALEM

68 CE

Rabbit left Miriam with the instructions to join the Antipas clan. He would do his best to intervene on Tuvia's behalf. If he was lucky, he might free him before he ended up in the same prison cell as his father.

Rabbit didn't feel lucky.

The crowded streets slowed the closer he got to the first wall and stopped completely before he reached the gate. Despite the antipathy rampant in the city, the bloated populace was descending on the Temple for the Sabbath. Nothing could get in the way of that.

But somewhere on the other side of this crowd, a man was about to be tortured to death. Before that happened, Einar Eshek would get information from him that would send Helen to a prison cell if Rabbit couldn't get there first.

He scanned the wall that bisected the city from the priest's gate of the Temple all the way to Herod's Palace on the west side. It had once been the northernmost defensive barrier of Jerusalem. Since the building of a second wall far to the north, the protective integrity of this one had been somewhat neglected. A hive of hovels had been erected along its northern face made of scrap wood, cloth, anything that could provide shelter for refugees. Rabbit turned away from the gate and pushed upstream, shoving and being shoved by the hordes of men and women trying to reach their holy sanctum.

At the corner of a square tower that provided sufficient structural support for taller hovels, Rabbit scrambled up the rickety wooden frame of the makeshift building and onto its roof. It swayed under his weight.

A horn blew in the distance, low and resonant, followed by more distant instruments at the corners of the Temple. Tens of thousands crowding the Mount fell silent.

Rabbit strained for the lip of the parapet wall, but it was just out of reach.

A voice pealed over the crowd. It couldn't be the original speaker. No, this would be a crier, one of many repeating the message for all to hear. "For generations too many to remember," the speaker began, slowly and clearly so that his words wouldn't get muddied by their own echo, "the Temple has been under the control of the priestly families. I am from such a family, as you all know. But was it always the way? The priests would have you believe so, benefit as they do from this arrangement."

Eleazar ben Simon.

Rabbit softened his legs and jumped for the top of the wall. As he did, the roof of the shack splintered under his feet with a sound like bones breaking. His fingers caught the sharp edge of stone as the hovel crumpled beneath him.

"But it is not so!" Eleazar continued through his crier. "We have found evidence of an older way. Long before the priests convinced us that only they had the divine right to perform the sacrifices, the offices of the priests were held by a drawing of lots."

Rabbit pulled himself up on the lip of stone that bit his fingers.

All around him, the vast crowd erupted in a cacophony of disbelief and dismay at what they had just heard.

Rabbit managed to get his left elbow on top of the parapet and lever himself up, trying not to look down at the twenty-foot drop or the splintered wood that awaited him at the bottom should he fall.

The horns blasted again, silencing the crowd. Eleazar spoke again.

"To some of you, this will sound like blasphemy. It would have to me before I read the truth as well. I defy you, Kohanim of Jerusalem, to show me scriptural evidence that only members of the old family may serve. Where does it say only they may be priests? Nowhere. It is tradition, but it is a new tradition."

Rabbit reached with his right hand, got a secure hold on the inside of the parapet stones, and pulled himself up and over the lip of the wall. It hurt like hell, but that drop was one hell of a motivation.

Eleazar let the echo of his words fall completely silent before he resumed.

"Do we need a high priest in the Holiest of Holies? Yes! Of course! Does it need to be Ananus ben Ananus? That, it does not."

The tower to Rabbit's right was empty. To his left, soldiers and priests crowded the raised walk all the way to the beautifully arched entrance through the west colonnade. At the arch were massed armed Zealots, holding the priests and their bodyguard at bay.

"I have here the names of all the men of eligible age in the land taken from the last census. This is how our forefathers intended us to govern our religious lives. I will draw the lot, but it is a more powerful hand than mine that guides the selection, I assure you."

While the crowd was no longer shouting, it was far from silent. The disbelieving murmurs of tens of thousands takes on its own character, not deafening, but pervasive.

A long silence followed. Rabbit could fill in the visual. Eleazar ceremoniously reaching into some vessel to withdraw a token. "Mattityahu ben Shemai of Artas!"

Word spread through the crowd like a wave on the water. Artas was a backwater. A rural nowhere with more goats than residents.

If the idea of selecting a high priest by lottery inspired outrage, the selection of a country rustic as that priest inspired something worse. The howl from the men on the skybridge and the crowds in the streets crashed over the walls of the Temple.

At the arched entry from the walkway, the first club was swung.

The Zealots and soldiers clashed at the gate. It didn't look like swords were being drawn, but the violence was still deadly. Rabbit watched as a man went over the edge of the wall into the crowd below.

Down in the Xystus at the foot of the Temple, another skirmish broke out. Rabbit couldn't tell who was fighting whom, only that the tensions that had been building in the city for months had reached their boiling point.

From his position on the wall, Rabbit could see John's headquarters perched on the rocky precipice across the Tyropoeon Valley. But between him and his destination lay thousands of rioting citizens. By the stables of the Hippodrome, John's northern Zealots were pressing out into the crowd like the pseudopod of some immense sea creature of myth.

Impassable.

Rabbit had no choice but to go around. In the distance, the tidy streets of the Upper City were empty. That was his route.

He ran west along the wall, away from the worst of the violence. The din chased him mercilessly, shouts of anger, screams of pain, the ringing percussion of arms against armor. He thought of Miriam getting caught in the middle of it all. Of her neighbors. Of the Yahad brothers, so eager for the end of the world. He fought the urge to help, to try to soothe tempers or defend those less able to defend themselves.

Not my war, thought Rabbit. He hated himself for it, but it was true. He kept running.

A tower high on the Upper City hill promised an easy descent to the street level in the deserted part of town.

Or, almost deserted.

Movement caught his attention as he ran. He doubled back a few paces to confirm he hadn't been imagining things. Hadn't seen that telltale glint of sunlight on polished bronze.

Only he hadn't imagined it. Leocharis, unmistakable in his stupid antique armor, was bobbing away from Rabbit on one of the wide brick streets with a companion.

It had to be him. Had to be. Miriam had led Tuvia to shelter the night he arrived. She had known him since he was a kid, which ruled him out as a suspect. That left the would-be Macedonian, with his terrible cover story and his movie-star good looks.

Rabbit sprinted for the tower and erupted into the street a moment later, backtracking a few intersections just in time to see the duo round a corner. He caught up with them as they opened a garden gate at one of the Upper City mansions.

"Wait!" Rabbit called out.

They turned at the sound of his voice. As soon as Rabbit identified the merc's companion, he shuddered. Enoch. Of course.

Just like Deetza, the killer would go after anyone who had gotten close to Rabbit. Enoch had been stuck to Rabbit like gum to a shoe for two days. Rabbit jogged toward them as both men smiled in greeting.

"Leocharis said he would help me talk to my parents." Enoch's tone carried a touch of recrimination for Rabbit.

"Nice of him," said Rabbit to the handsome face. Furious as Rabbit was, some fraction of that anger he reserved for himself. If he'd helped Enoch earlier, the kid wouldn't have made such an appealing target.

"Nothing makes me happier than helping those in need," Leocharis said, smiling.

"I bet."

Rabbit gestured the mercenary toward the open garden gate. "After you."

JERUSALEM

68 CE

Whatever convinced you to join the Yahad?" Leocharis asked Enoch as they walked through the garden toward the house, glancing over the kid's shoulder at Rabbit.

Rabbit snorted softly. Enoch was such an instinctive follower, he was a shoo-in for cult manipulation.

"I did it to impress my friends," the youth admitted. He had the good taste to look embarrassed at least.

"Go on," Leocharis prodded. He looked like an illustration from a kid's mythology book. Apollo in the sun chariot. Enoch was certainly entranced.

"We all talked about how our parents were out of touch with the problems of the real world, living in their mansions with all their servants and slaves. They barely ever said prayers unless they were in public. I probably shouldn't tell you that. Please don't repeat it to them."

Rabbit almost said, *Scout's honor*. Instead, he just shook his head. "So, you hung out with a bunch of radicals, huh?"

"It's not even radical. Our parents are leaving us such a screwed-up world. The olive yields are lower than ever due to over-farming. Most of the people I grew up with didn't make their wealth, they inherited it and just used it to make more. Of all of us, you know I'm the only one who actually had the guts to go to the Yahad? The rest of them talked big, but when they became men, they all followed in their parents' footsteps."

"But you decided to take a real stand, eh?" Leocharis asked. He kept smirking at Rabbit behind the cult initiate's back.

They were following a winding cobblestone path. Cyprus and fig and palm trees swayed in the breeze over the walled garden ten times the size of John's run-down little yard.

Enoch seemed to be slowing down with every step in his anxiety. "I met one of the Yahad when he visited my brother in Jerusalem. He's a Joseph, too, my brother. After they concluded their business, I spoke with him about life in Secacah, how differently they lived. A clean, simple, good life. After he left, I tried to convince my friends to join with me, but they all had excuses. I thought I'd lead the way and they'd follow."

"It doesn't always work out," Rabbit said.

Enoch blew air through his lips as he paused on the threshold. Preparing himself.

The walls of Enoch's family mansion were tall, white plastered stone with blue and gold painted tiles inset in a pleasing pattern across its surface. The porch offered no strategic choke points, unfortunately. *Wait for it.*

Leocharis' smile didn't mask his own searching, assessing eyes, either.

Clueless, Enoch unlocked the front door with a heavy bronze key.

"Hello?" he called. "Ima? Tata?" The place was silent. "Well, we might as well go."

Rabbit gave him a gentle shove. "Go look for your parents."

The young man took a deep breath and nodded, wandering off into the house, leaving Rabbit and Leocharis in the atrium. It was a spacious rectangle with an open skylight in the center that admitted midday sun and reflected it off the tiled rain pool in the center of the floor, dry now. Windows with painted wood shutters, now standing open, offered a view of the garden.

Finally alone, Rabbit and Leocharis slowly circled one another in the shadowy perimeter of the room.

"I've come to take you back," Rabbit said.

"Back where exactly?" the Macedonian replied. Rabbit cursed himself for having confronted Leocharis after Deetza's death. This would be a lot easier if the Macedonian didn't know Rabbit was after him.

"To 2019. Whatever connection you have to Misherenko, you're going to have to come clean. Personally, I don't care what you're up to with the scroll treasures, but a friend of mine is in trouble, and you're going to help."

"You say the strangest things, Jew." He leaned his face into the light well. "I don't know you. I don't know your friend. But you're obviously crazy, and I appreciate crazy. As a matter of fact, it's what I'm known for."

Jewel-toned couches were arranged in two squares around low, figured wood tables to the left and right of the reflecting pool. The walls boasted complex mosaics and tapestries, and on the far wall, clamshell insets in the plaster framed lifelike, Greek-style busts of family members on plinths. Rabbit went closer to examine Enoch's clan, one eye firmly fixed on his adversary.

The first two busts were of middle-aged men, with a strong family resemblance to one another and none to poor Enoch, the youngest son of the family. At the third bust he stopped. And stared.

A young man sporting Roman-style short curls. Arched bridge to the nose. Sharp jaw angle from chin to ear. A neutral expression he had seen before.

Rabbit could have slapped himself.

He had been thinking of his first translation of Josephus all week and couldn't figure out why. But it wasn't the red leather cover that had been trying to break through to his consciousness. It was the inside liner page with its print reproduction of a Greek-style bust.

This Greek-style bust.

This Greek-style bust of Flavius Josephus.

Rabbit had also seen that face in person although he didn't

recognize it at the time. In Rome, 64 CE, Rabbit had seen it begging for death at the conclusion of unimaginable torture.

Help me, Josephus had pleaded.

This was his home. But in this timeline, Flavius Josephus had not been tortured to death. People had spoken of him in the North. Rabbit had seen him die in a splinter.

And just like that, the incongruity of the murder in Rome fit into the puzzle with a click. There was no serial killer. These murders weren't done for their own satisfaction, at least not solely for that. Nor did the killer have an ax to grind with Rabbit. He was merely an inconvenient bystander.

Josephus had been tortured for information.

Just like Tzephania.

Just like Deetza.

All the blood. All the pain. It all came down to the Copper Scroll.

"You tortured them," Rabbit said.

Leocharis shrugged. "That's the other thing I'm known for."

Rabbit stared at Leocharis and this time he spoke in English. "All those murders, they all knew something about the treasure, didn't they? Josephus told you about the plan he'd cooked up with Antipas. The others you thought might know the key to the scroll."

Rabbit realized his knife was in his hand. The mercenary's sword slid from its sheath with a quiet scrape.

"What are you babbling about?" Leocharis said in Greek.

"You know exactly what I mean," Rabbit continued in English. "You figured if one Antipas brother had the scroll, the other must have the key. But Tzephania was clueless. You thought Deetza might have learned something from all that time in the presence of the treasurer, but she didn't have any idea what you were talking about."

"Stop talking nonsense!" the mercenary barked in Greek and took a step forward, his sword catching the sunlight.

The Macedonian's last word was cut short by a thud like a rock dropped on concrete. Leocharis pitched forward and collapsed into the empty reflecting pool.

Enoch stood behind him, holding a wooden bat about the length of his forearm. He grinned, those wide blue eyes looking proud.

Relief washed through Rabbit.

But as he watched, the silly Judean youth appeared to transform.

The cramped anxiety, the weight of fatigue and fear that Enoch wore like a suit of clothes dropped away before Rabbit's eyes. His posture straightened and relaxed into graceful liquidity. Even his face, so pinched and pained, settled into the confident, unworried lines of a predator.

"He doesn't speak the language, you know," Enoch said in English barely tinged with vowels from the American South.

Rabbit wanted to beat his head against the wall.

"You're Einar Eshek."

The young man smiled.

JERUSALEM

68 CE

Thank you for distracting him," Enoch, no, Eshek said. "He's a lot more dangerous than you."

"You?" Rabbit said. He couldn't help it.

"Me," he replied.

"But he knew about the treasure."

"Mm-hmm." He shrugged. "He doesn't look like a John, does he?" Enoch tipped his head to one side, studying the fallen Macedonian. "Maybe Mother Dorcas just liked the name." He pierced Rabbit with those pretty blue eyes that suddenly looked like ice chips. "He's a smart fellow. Figured out he was likely to be executed the moment he finished the job with Antipas, so he did his best to find out what the treasurer was hiding without engaging."

"Did you swap notes?" Rabbit growled.

Eshek smiled, shook his head. "He's an opportunist, probably a psychopath. You might say he lacks the depth I seek in my compatriots."

Leocharis began to stir. Eshek pushed off the wall and delivered a sharp kick between the fallen soldier's legs. Even unconscious, Leocharis groaned.

Eshek flicked his eyes back toward Rabbit. "When I met you in Rome, I had no idea you were a time traveler. Imagine my surprise when you walked up to me in Qumran talking to the treasurer's boy."

Now that Eshek had dropped the Enoch routine, he looked ten years older. Rabbit placed him in his early- to mid-thirties.

Using only his peripheral vision, Rabbit began to scan the room for weapons that would allow him more reach than his dagger, choke points that would limit Eshek's movements.

"Who are you with?" Eshek asked. "Israeli Authority?"

"Smithsonian."

He grunted. "I thought Americans were just in it for the"—he raised his nose in the air and spoke in a nasal 1950s newscaster voice—"historical preservation! But then, nothing erodes high-minded ideals as quickly as a costly consequence or a great reward."

So, Eshek thought they were competing for the Temple treasures. No point in disabusing him of that notion.

"This whole time, I wasn't sure how close you were. Half the time it looked like you were right on my heels and the other half you'd stumble around like a blind man. You know about the second scroll though."

"Sure," Rabbit vamped, testing out his theory while playing along. "You tortured the plan out of Josephus four years ago. You splintered that timeline, but you didn't care. All you needed was the information. He's here, of course, alive if not quite well in Roman possession."

Eshek studied him for a moment, then abruptly shifted his posture and began to walk around the room, studying the mosaics. "He and the treasurer cooked up the plan even before Gessius Florus stole those talents of gold. Hid the treasury and created a two-part map to find it. They left enough in the Temple specifically so that the Romans wouldn't get suspicious if they came to loot the place. They really thought of everything."

"Sure."

"Well, not a couple time travelers coming to slice the gold out of their little Hebrew fingers, but they can hardly be blamed for that."

Rabbit nodded.

"So, where's the second scroll?" Eshek asked.

"I don't know." Rabbit felt a shift in the young man.

Eshek shook his head and came circuitously closer, all the while seemingly inspecting the rich furnishings of the room. "You and your pretty partner have managed to get in deep with John and his captives. It's the only reason you're still alive, you know. Lord knows I had enough to do on my own. Are you sure they didn't give something up?"

"Pretty sure." Rabbit felt the noose tightening. He adjusted his right arm, ready to free it from the sling. He kept his feet planted, however. Let Eshek waste his energy circling his kill, Rabbit would wait for the lunge.

"You could just tell me, you know. I could even cut you in on the profits at the other end. Even a fraction of the haul would buy you a healthy dose of . . . freedom." He smiled.

Rabbit cringed inwardly at Eshek's intimacy. It felt like bloody fingers groping his naked skin. "That's a good deal, but I don't have anything to give you." At his right side was a light end table he was ready to snatch up as a shield or a bludgeon.

"I guess we'll find out. You've seen my work, so you know we'll have plenty of time to get acquainted with the truth."

Rabbit tensed his legs, ready to spring, when suddenly there was a clatter at the door.

A small crowd was entering the house mid-conversation.

"They will have sorted everything out before evening . . ."

The man at the front of the pack blinked at Rabbit and Eshek, both poised with their weapons in hand. Leocharis on the floor. A clipped shout escaped the owner of the home, bringing the rest of the crowd pouring into the room. Two burly-looking men pushed past the family members. Bodyguards.

"Lucky again," Eshek said to Rabbit. Before the men could advance, he sprang out the open window into the garden.

Rabbit was grateful for the rescue, but his position didn't look any better than Eshek's.

"Sorry, folks," he mumbled as he followed the killer.

There was shouting behind him as he sprinted through the trees. To his left, he saw movement between him and the safe exit of the gate. He cut right, making for the wall. The damn landscape designer had done such a good job he couldn't see the white barrier until he almost ran into it.

Too high to jump. Had to be ten feet to the top.

Without thinking, he jumped onto the horizontal branch of a thick fig tree, took a few steps up the branch, and launched himself at the wall.

Both hands latched onto the stone, miraculously landing between jagged ceramic shards protruding from the top. He pinwheeled his feet, got one up on the lip, and threw himself over.

The impact with the street jarred his knees and hips, but he managed to keep his balance and break into a wobbly run that he maintained until he was convinced no one had followed him.

His route to John's headquarters was diverted several times as he skirted mobs of one faction or another. The violence hadn't dissipated, it had just dispersed into the streets. Rabbit's dread built with every step as the sun passed behind Herod's Palace and out of sight. All the while, Rabbit kept hearing one phrase run through his mind. *You and your pretty partner*. Eshek had spent the previous night not twenty feet away from them while they slept. He'd listened to their conversation, faking being asleep himself. Future and present, Einar Eshek knew far too much about Helen for Rabbit's taste.

But Eshek hadn't gotten what he came for. Not yet. He didn't have the Copper Scroll key. Rabbit was convinced the man wouldn't be willing to leave without it, which meant Eshek would finally take a stab at the one target he had yet to interrogate. Antipas the Treasurer.

Cutting him off at John's headquarters was Rabbit's last shot at Eshek, and he'd be damned if he was going to risk missing him.

He peered over the cliff's edge down to the plateau where the twin houses overlooked the valley. The same cadre of youthful guards patrolled the grounds between the buildings, only their numbers had been doubled since last time he'd paid a visit to Antipas. Damn if John hadn't listened to him.

He was regretting giving that advice when a spearpoint touched his neck.

Rabbit raised his hands and turned his head.

Champ stared down the shaft of the weapon with vengeful glee.

"There you are!" boomed John like a drum as Champ and his fellow guard marched Rabbit into the garden of the headquarters. Like the yard outside, its foliage had been trampled into the dust by all the militia foot traffic. It reminded Rabbit of a prison. "I told Eleazar you'd show up again. He owes me ten shekels."

"How about I pay you the same and we call it even," Rabbit offered.

John boomed laughter and punched Rabbit playfully in the stomach so hard his dental fillings almost popped out. The general threw an arm like a bundle of hams across Rabbit's shoulders and led him through the dusty peristyle into the public room of the house.

The room was crowded. Eleazar; a handful of senior Zealots; the Sicarii emissary; Dinah, the head of the breadmaking operation.

And Helen.

Rabbit didn't know whether to be relieved that Eshek hadn't gotten to her or afraid that John had. Her tense expression told him everything he needed to know. Helen wasn't there to deliver bread. John had made a connection between them.

"You made quite a mess of things, stranger," Eleazar said. "Interfering with well-laid plans, pretending to be someone you're not."

"I want to know why," John said.

"If I tell you, will you let me go?" Rabbit asked.

John snorted like a bull. "No, but I'll promise you a quick, clean death."

Rabbit pretended to consider the offer. He knew he shouldn't be glib, but he needed the next steps to go his way. "What's my other option?"

"Don't waste your time with him, John. He'll talk once he spends some time with the son of Dorcas." Eleazar smiled cheerily at Rabbit. "He'll be here any minute."

Rabbit ground down a mirthless laugh. He couldn't help it.

"Mad," muttered John.

"Enjoy your joke. It will be your last," Eleazar said.

That broke Rabbit. The blatant mustache twirling might have been original in the first century, but it sounded ridiculous to someone raised on movies and television. He laughed uproariously as the guards marched him to his death.

His laughter died when Rabbit heard them coming.

Bobbing torches were coming up the road, heralding the approach of a large group of people. Rabbit and his guards were crossing the space between the houses, Rabbit at the point of a spear.

"You might want to tell the general that the Antipas clan is coming."

"Keep your mouth shut," growled Champ. The other one scurried back to the headquarters.

The loafing gang of family members John had surrounded himself with were stirring into action in the space between the two homes. Leaderless and disorganized, they were generating a lot of motion with little result, like an agitated hive of bees.

Rabbit was led through them toward the makeshift jail as they quickly donned bits of armor and took up their arms.

At the head of the Antipas family parade was the brother Rabbit had met. Beside him, and close to the front, Rabbit spied Miriam.

John rallied his troops, using that impressive vocal instrument, while Rabbit passed into the makeshift prison. Time was going to be very tight for John of Gischala. Tighter still for Rabbit Ward.

Champ and a cousin led him into the house and slammed the door behind them, muffling the sounds of the Antipas family clashing, verbally for now, with John's soldiers.

Lamps gave the interior of the house an amber glow that failed to warm the icy chill of the people in it. Antipas, his son Tuvia, and two other men sat dismally on Roman couches arranged in a square around a table. Cups stood on the table, but only one of the men appeared to be drinking anything.

"You're back," said Antipas the Treasurer.

"So, it would seem," Rabbit replied. Since the guards didn't seem to care, Rabbit began searching the house. On the main floor were the common room, a small study, servants' quarters, and the kitchen. The windows in every room were shuttered securely and nailed in place, save the servants' quarters that had no windows at all. It wasn't an impenetrable enclosure, but an escape route this way would be noisy and sure to raise alarm.

"What are you doing?" Tuvia asked sharply. "Won't you sit down?"

"No, sorry, I'm not staying," Rabbit replied, going upstairs.

The second floor was dominated by bedrooms and contained a stairwell to the roof with a hatch that had been nailed shut as well.

He searched upstairs for weapons, but the best he came up with was a water ewer that had some heft to it and a big bronze decorative plate hung on the wall. He took the latter. Its leather hanging strap made it a decent little shield.

"Robbing the place? What a surprise," droned Tuvia.

"Decided you're going to kill me with sarcasm, have you?" said Rabbit as he checked the nearest shutter nails to see how tight they were. Answer? Pretty tight.

"I don't need to kill you. Or haven't you heard?" Tuvia said, sounding churlish.

"Is this how you want to spend your last hours on Earth, my son?" asked his father.

Tuvia ignored his father and continued. "We're all to be questioned like common criminals and then murdered."

"Apparently he does," Rabbit said to Antipas, who scowled as Rabbit sat down on an unoccupied horsehair stool. A stray mane hair, sharp as a needle, poked him in the ass.

"Like you murdered my brother," Tuvia went on.

Rabbit leaned back against the wall. "Let it go! I did not kill your brother."

"You're a liar," said the young man and closed his eyes as he reclined on the couch.

"He's telling the truth, you know," said a new voice.

All eyes turned toward the garden door where a lean silhouette stood, backlit by torchbearers at his rear.

"I know this because I did. Your brother didn't have the information I have been asked to obtain. I'm hoping you do."

He stepped into the room and the door closed behind him. "My name is John bar Dorcas. We're going to get to know each other better tonight."

Rabbit slumped on his stool.

"Hello, Eshek."

JERUSALEM

68 CE

You come last," Eshek told Rabbit. "There are some things I want to ask you, too. But first things first. Treasurer Antipas. You and Joseph ben Matthias, sometimes called Flavius Josephus, hatched a plan together to hide the Temple treasury. Don't deny it, I've already had the truth out of your conspirator."

The two prisoners unrelated to the treasurer looked at him with unveiled shock.

Eshek went on. "You sent your firstborn son east to hide the first part of the map with the Yahad brotherhood. But the locations on that map are encoded. I want the other half of that code."

Antipas sighed with his typical resignation. He had one foot in the grave and thought he was beyond fear. "There's no point to this. The treasury must remain hidden. Rome will destroy the Temple as surely as the winter brings rain. Without the treasury, how will it be rebuilt? You ask me to betray myself as a Jew, which I will not do no matter what skills you possess."

"Let's test that theory." Eshek looked around the room, sizing up the people and the space as though he was a real estate shopper at an open house. "The traditional tactic in this case would be to work with your son first. Let you hear his agony, knowing that you can end it. But I'm short on time, and I sense you to be a man of great resolve. So, I'm not going to do that. Instead, I will question you both simultaneously. That way, you can know firsthand what I am about to do to your flesh and blood, because I have just done it to your flesh. And blood."

He turned to the other two men. "I noticed from your reactions that your colleague's plans were unknown to you. That's exceptionally fortunate for you . . ."

Both men visibly relaxed.

"Because you have no value," he concluded. And with a smooth motion, he drew a long dagger and slashed the throat of the man seated nearest him. The official flopped over the back of his couch, clutching his spurting throat, choking on his own blood as he hit the floor.

The other man shot to his feet and tried to run, got tangled in his own garments, and tripped over them, falling heavily to the floor, too. As he scrambled to get up, Eshek sprang over the couch and planted a foot on his back, pinning him to the floor. Two quick jabs of his dagger and he was up again, leaving the man bubbling on his punctured lungs.

Everyone in the room was white with shock, including Champ and his cousin who still stood by the door. Eshek wiped spatters of blood from his brow, smearing red across his skin. He inhaled the deep stuttering breath of postorgasmic surrender.

"Please don't read into my efficiency that I am feeling rushed. The Zealots are more than capable of holding your family at bay outside, leaving us to do our work undisturbed." He turned his attention to the two white-faced guards. "There are two cots in the servants' quarters, just back there. Tie these two down, arms and legs spread. Here's rope." He tossed them a length of marine line. "They will fight you. Do not under any circumstances render them senseless, do you understand? If it takes both of you to do the job, then take care of the son first, then the father."

Antipas shook his head. "I will not fight."

Eshek grinned hungrily. "Everybody fights."

The two guards looked nearly as shaken as their captives. They had seen killing before, but this was likely their first experience of pure, cold sadism. Still, they did as they were told.

At the last moment, Tuvia did, indeed, try to run. They wrestled him to the ground, pinioned his arms, and practically carried him, kicking and biting, into the back room.

"I hope they don't bruise him too badly. It numbs sensation," said Eshek to Antipas. The treasurer didn't reply, he just breathed deeply. "Nothing to say?"

"I do not waste my breath speaking to wild dogs."

Eshek twitched. It was just there for a moment, but Rabbit caught it. A spasm of the muscles in his left cheek.

The killer turned away from the older man to face Rabbit.

"You could tell me now and spare yourself listening to this. Who sent you here, really?"

"I told you."

"You lied. I had some time to think about it. The Smithsonian wouldn't be able to keep the treasury if they found it. So why waste the money sending you? No, you were sent here by someone else. Who?" Rabbit might have imagined it, but he could swear Eshek looked worried.

"I've got a better question for you," said Rabbit. "What makes you think you're walking out of here once you're done? The Zealots hired John bar Dorcas to do their dirty work, not to benefit from it. The moment you pass along the information, they'll kill you."

Eshek smiled. "They can try."

His confidence sent a chill down Rabbit's spine.

The guards returned, sweating and winded. One of them was shaking his hand, imprinted with a red semicircle of teeth marks.

Antipas waved them aside when they reached for him, rose to his feet imperiously, and walked between them to the back of the house. He ignored Eshek as though he were an insect unworthy of contemplation. Rabbit would carry that image of self-control to the grave.

"I don't think you made much of an impression on him," Rabbit said, baiting.

Eshek glared at Rabbit, confirming his thoughts. "I don't need him to be afraid, I just need him to fucking talk." He had slipped into

English. Rabbit wondered if he was even aware of it. More importantly, he had lost his cool. Antipas' disdain had really shaken him. So, the fear was an important part of it. Noted.

"Since we have a minute, who do *you* work for?" asked Rabbit.

"I don't work *for* anybody."

Rabbit shrugged. "Okay, who do you work adjacent to?"

The guards came back. "Done," Champ said.

"Hold this man here. Don't hurt him. If we have time, that pleasure will be mine."

They nodded and Eshek went to the back of the house.

The guards stood rooted to the spot, unsure of how to carry out their orders. A cry pealed out of the back room. They blanched and looked at the floor, at the ceiling, anywhere but at each other.

"There is nowhere for me to go," said Rabbit. "You'll be no less men if you choose to watch the doors from the garden side."

They glanced at each other, but Champ shook his head.

"As you wish," Rabbit said.

Then the screaming began in earnest.

Rabbit had seen the results of Eshek's torture and had an inkling of how it worked. It wasn't just pain he inflicted. He teased his victims along a razor's edge of mortality. Exposing people to their own viscera meticulously, keeping them alive for as long as possible. The victim must think at every step, *I'm dying now but I might make it. If only I give him what he wants, I might live.* The closer you got to the precipice, the more precious life became.

Hope and fear.

Rabbit knew he was trying to think his way out of hearing what was happening in the other room. He knew it wasn't quite working. He tried harder.

Eshek had skills. Psychological and even medical, of a sort.

Where did he acquire the skills? Was he a doctor?

Maybe a veterinarian. He'd had plenty of practice on living bodies.

Rabbit clung to his intellectual analysis, trying to shut out the sounds of agony.

If not, where would he get medical training? How would he learn . . .

Why did the jibe about wild dogs . . .

Whimpering. Almost worse than the screaming.

Okay, being mocked doesn't shake him, but being despised does. Maybe dates back to a formative time of derision, debasement. He thrives on being feared. What formatively scared him?

Mumbled, wet words tumbled over each other from the back. Pleas. No. Not pleas. An offering.

Champ and his companion were gone. Rabbit hadn't noticed them leave. Hadn't heard it over the awful sounds from that back room.

Rabbit could stop this.

Eshek's voice, gentle, soothing, offering relief.

Rabbit stood on shaky legs. Picked up the bronze pseudo shield. *Don't kill him. You can't kill him. Eshek's no good to Helen dead.*

He deliberately tried to slow his breathing. He checked the front door, but no guards were in sight. He took the first steps toward the gurgling sounds in the back room. Strapped the shield to his arm with its little leather thong. *At the very least, you can end their suffering.*

He crept back toward the room, into the awful, humid cloud that smelled like a cross between a slaughterhouse and a sewer.

As he got closer, Rabbit started to make out words spoken in a ragged, gasping breath.

"Not Achor . . ." A groan. "Antonia."

"Antonia Fortress?" Eshek. "And the key?"

"I don't know . . ." The words were almost a whisper.

A long, high-pitched moan escaped the door, more terrible than any scream.

"Please."

The sound just kept coming.

"The key!"

"Five one. Five one."

A peal of laughter stopped Rabbit dead in his tracks.

"Thank you, Antipas." Eshek's voice was rapturous. "I'll make sure your treasure goes to a good cause."

Just as Rabbit reached for the door, it swung open.

The grin slid from Eshek's face as he registered Rabbit. Rabbit smashed it with the shield.

The killer stumbled back into the servants' quarters and fell onto the spatchcocked body of his victim. Rabbit pressed the advantage, stepped forward, and brought the shield over his head but, before he could bring it down, Eshek kicked him in the stomach just above the groin. He felt like his bladder exploded as he fell against the door. He managed to bring the shield back down in time to parry Eshek's dagger with a clang of bronze, then a slap caught him across the ear, setting his head ringing, and Eshek pushed past him into the hall at a sprint.

Rabbit shook his head, trying to clear the ringing, and ran after him.

In the garden, he pulled up short next to Eshek. Side by side, they faced a hedgerow of spearpoints.

"Well?" asked John calmly from behind the guards. "Did you get it?"

"I extracted what you asked me for." Eshek answered with the calm tones of an academic. The effect was slightly marred by the overly nasal overtone. Rabbit had broken his nose. *Good.*

"Where is it? Where is the map?"

"Could we sit? My work is very fatiguing." Eshek gestured to a ring of benches set awkwardly close together in a circle a few paces away.

John approached. The guards formed a ring around the men, one of them holding a torch aloft to light the space.

"Sit, and be quick about it," rumbled John. He and Eshek selected seats. Rabbit remained standing. He knew Eshek must have a plan to make a break for it, or he wouldn't be so calm. He wanted to be ready to follow him. In preparation, he squinted his eyes almost shut to prepare them for the darkness outside the glow of the torches. He softened his legs to sprint. What the hell did Eshek have up his sleeve? He didn't know, but there was no way that psychopath was getting away from him again.

From outside, voices of the Antipas family and the Zealots poured over the wall into the garden. It was low, indistinct, punctuated by the occasional shout. No Eleazar, Rabbit noted. He must have been deputed as negotiator with the family, allowing John to focus on the gold.

Eshek proceeded slowly, not seeming to feel the time pressure at all. "You know that Antipas secreted away the bulk of the Temple treasury based on a plan devised between himself and Joseph. The locations of the treasures are detailed on a weighty scroll stamped in copper, designed to last the ages should those who know about it be lost in the coming war."

"Where is it?" John asked, trying to hold on to his patience.

"Here in Jerusalem," answered Eshek, lying as smoothly as anyone Rabbit had ever heard. "In Herod Agrippa's Palace."

John began to rise.

Eshek raised a finger, halting him. "That's not all. The Copper Scroll is encoded. Without the accompanying key, its locations are meaningless."

"Where is this key?" demanded the Zealot general.

"Well, that was the piece of information that Antipas and his son deemed most precious. It took all my considerable skill to extract it."

John was losing his patience. "Spit it out!"

"Are you sure you want"—Eshek glanced around at the ring of guards—"everyone to hear this?"

This was it. Rabbit poised himself.

John looked up at his men. "Back off ten paces. But keep an eye on these two!"

The guards did as they were instructed. Rabbit noted that the torchbearer backed off toward the house, not the garden gate.

The Zealot general leaned in close. "Well?" John asked quietly.

Eshek didn't respond to his captor. Instead, he swiveled his face toward Rabbit and smiled the widest, most content smile Rabbit had ever seen.

Then he disappeared.

JERUSALEM

68 CE

John stared into the space vacated by his pet torturer, jaw hanging open. One moment his captive was there, the next he was gone.

Sonofabitch. His decay point was right there all the time. No wonder he was so confident.

Rabbit took off.

His eyes were pretty good, having prepped them, and now he was running as fast as he could down the winding lane of the garden to the gate, weaving between the stunned guards and bursting out onto the street at top speed.

The shouts and commotion in the garden only trailed him by a few seconds.

The clearing between the houses churned with people. Conspicuously, there were no governmental soldiers; the Antipas family leaders must have failed to sway the provisional governor. But the clan outnumbered John's Zealots two-to-one and provided Rabbit with good cover.

Rabbit sprinted through the crowd, cutting right and left to avoid the pushing, shouting knots of people. At the center, Eleazar was debating several older men in clangorous tones, declaring that the treasurer was a traitor to the cause, yada yada. Killing time for a man already dead.

As the wall of John's HQ garden came in sight, Rabbit almost collided with a petite figure. He grabbed her shoulders to avoid knocking her over and found himself looking into the grim face of Miriam.

"Come on."

He dragged her bodily through the last of the crowd.

The sole guard left to watch over John's garden barely registered Rabbit before he dropped his shoulder and hockey-checked the poor guy into the wall. The breath went out of the guard like a popped balloon.

Across the beaten-down garden, Rabbit kicked in the door to the house, which flew open and banged against the wall.

Miriam was excoriating him as he dragged her by the upper arm along in his wake.

"Hush," he said. "That's going to be a bloodbath in a few minutes. You're too important to be part of it. Helen!" he hissed in a stage whisper that carried. The front room was empty; so was the kitchen. But as he turned for the stairs to the second story, she was coming down them.

"Come on," they said in unison. Rabbit caught her arm as she ran for the garden and spun her around to face the opposite wall of the triclinium, where together they threw open the heavy shutters and jumped out the window practically carrying Miriam with them. John's guards were clattering into the garden behind them as Rabbit and Helen slipped and slid down the steep decline to the street below the plateau.

"The Essene Gate," whispered Rabbit to Helen, and they ran quietly through the maze of the Lower City.

Blocks away from John's HQ, Rabbit finally released the resistance leader.

"Go home," he demanded, interrupting her protests. "Fight another day."

"The fight is now!" Miriam said, looking over her shoulder up the hill they had just escaped. The sounds of violence were drifting down from the promontory.

He shook his head. "It's already lost. Antipas and his son are dead. I'm sorry."

She froze in shock.

"Why did you pull me away?" she said.

"You're one of a kind, Miriam. Who knows, maybe you'll see your new world after all. I hope so."

"Unfortunately," said Helen, "we won't be here to find out." She nudged Rabbit. He'd heard it, too. Some of the Zealots had broken away from the melee and were in pursuit.

"Goodbye," Rabbit said to Miriam and ran with Helen for the Essene Gate.

"How much time until your decay point opens?" Rabbit finally asked her a few hours later. The only thing keeping their pace lively was the chill desert night. They had outrun their pursuers, and the rest of Rabbit's coin had persuaded the gate guards to let them pass without molestation.

"A few weeks," Helen said.

"Qumran, then. We should be able to get there by dawn. We can wait out the time there."

She broke the next silence with a hesitant question, her eyes straight ahead. "Do you want to tell me what happened?"

He wasn't sure he did. The cool night air, the desert, and the woman walking beside him were all he wanted to pay attention to. Rabbit had never had a companion on the road. When he left the past, he left his horrible experiences there, taking only the good ones. Or so he told himself.

Still, he retold her what happened in the prison, leaving out only the fine details of the torture.

"You heard . . . everything?"

"Yeah."

She waited for him to say more but didn't push, for which he was grateful. Rabbit put a grim smile on his face, his best and most practiced response. "Anyway . . ." He told her about the conclusion in the garden.

"His decay point was right there the whole time?"

Rabbit nodded. "Which meant he arrived right in the middle of the damn garden. How's that for cocky?"

"Well, that's it, then. We lost him." Her words were hollow.

Rabbit had never seen her like this before. She sounded broken. Hopeless. He wanted to offer her words of support, but couldn't quite bring himself to do it, knowing that he fully intended to ensure the very eventuality that she was so dreading right now.

They walked in silence toward the Yahad compound, the moonlight guiding their path along the dirt road, stopping only for water at the mountain spring they had discovered earlier in their journey.

Rabbit had lost his waterskin along the way somewhere. He bent down and dipped his face in the stream, drinking long and deep once he was sure his skin was washed clean.

When he surfaced, Helen was staring into the night, immobile as a statue.

"You all right?" he asked.

The voice that answered wasn't Helen's.

"So, now that you have escaped the belly of the beast, I hope you came away with something useful." The smooth Greek of Leocharis.

The mercenary was standing amid the boulders leading up the slope, his javelin resting on his shoulder. Relaxed as he looked, Rabbit didn't doubt for a moment he could launch the weapon accurately before either of them could arm themselves.

Rabbit struggled to fire up his nervous system with one last jolt of adrenaline. He was so tired his heart rate barely ticked up. This seemed more like an inevitable nuisance than a threat.

"I didn't find the key," Rabbit replied. "You're wasting your time."

The Macedonian shrugged. "Is there such a thing as a waste of time? I figure you tell me what you learned, or I eliminate you as competition. Either way it's a win for me."

Helen chimed in. "Secret for a secret." Her voice made Rabbit flinch. Why was she talking so loudly?

The Macedonian merc stared at her, too.

She continued, again in that overly loud voice. "Secret for a secret. How did you learn about the treasure? And don't tell me you just happened to read the Copper Scroll at Secacah. You knew before that."

"I told you I worked for the legions."

"Yes . . ." Rabbit prodded.

"We captured their general. Up in Yodfat. Joseph was his name."

"We're familiar," said Helen.

"Real opportunist, he was. Is, I suppose, if he hasn't overplayed his hand. He offered to tell me where to find an enormous treasure if I helped him escape Roman captivity."

"Did you keep your side of the bargain?" Rabbit asked.

"And get crucified? I think not. But then, it turns out the information he gave me wasn't all that helpful, either. Just enough to persuade me to make a lifelong enemy of the Roman army with nothing to show for it. So, I suppose we're even." He adjusted his grip on the javelin. "I had done some work for the Sicarii a few years back. It was easy to renew that relationship and make my services available, but I didn't trust the Zealots to let me walk out with the information. I thought I'd played that little shit Enoch for a fool." He rubbed the back of his head. "Ah, well. That's all past now. Tell you what. You tell me what you know, and I'll cut you in on the deal. Three can dig faster than one, after all."

"You haven't exactly made a case for your trustworthiness," Helen boomed up the canyon.

Rabbit turned to look at her and almost missed the motion among the boulders. But Leocharis' yelp of surprise dragged Rabbit's attention back up the hill where the mercenary appeared to have doubled in size. He stumbled forward, batting at the huge shaggy head that had appeared over his shoulder and was sinking its teeth into the side of his neck. The merc fell to his hands and knees, his plea for help cut short as the battered old lion drove him down to the sandy ground and shifted its teeth from his trapezius to his throat. Its black eyes fixed on Rabbit and Helen, as if it dared them to interfere.

They ran. They kept running until they were well clear of the hidden valley.

The sky was pink when they caught sight of the building complex perched on the Dead Sea.

"Thank god," Helen said. "I feel like I could sleep for a week."

He agreed, but in fact Rabbit wasn't sure if he would ever sleep again. Their walk may have been silent, but his brain was an electrical storm. Replaying fragments of what he had witnessed. What he could have done differently.

"We should stay up," he said, barely recognizing it as his own voice over the roaring in his ears.

She groaned. "You're one of those people."

"If we go to sleep now, it'll totally screw up our sleep schedule."

"I don't care."

"You don't care now, but the sleep hangover from time travel is bad enough, you don't want to compound it by sleeping all day. Before you go, I'll teach you my method for getting good sleep after you get home."

He expected a snarky response, but, instead, she was silent. Her eyes were unfocused and far away. He watched her and waited. After a while she seemed to snap out of it and focused on him, which was worse.

"Come on," she said.

"Where are we going?"

By way of answer, she held out her hand and led him toward the water.

They walked along the Dead Sea beach under a dark sky beginning to warm, neither saying a word. The stretch of sand was thinner than in Rabbit's era, and they had to scramble along some tumbled rocks occasionally where the cliffs pushed into the water.

He wasn't sure what she was up to, and eventually he stopped trying to figure it out. He just rolled with it, picking his way along the water's edge with her until she abruptly stopped and looked out at the water.

Its surface was invitingly smooth and glossy, the moon doubled on its black surface.

"Are you ready?" she asked.

"For what?"

"Turn around."

He did as she asked, studied the southern coastline. They could have been the last people on the planet. The state of his fatigue was such that he didn't even consider what she was doing until he heard gentle splashing sounds behind him that made him turn.

She was wading out into the water naked, her clothes folded and stacked on a rock.

Rabbit was no blushing kid, but neither his age nor experience had prepared him for his own feelings at seeing Helen unclothed. Like the moon, her shape was doubled, real and reflection. Once in his eyes, once somewhere deeper within him. His eyes saw her compact musculature, her smooth skin, her long dark hair flowing down her back, hiding and revealing in turns like a magician's cape. But like the sea, that was only the surface. What the rest of him saw was a fathomless, unexplored world stirring in him for the first time. The sweet, precarious tipping into something new, something he had wanted and denied himself now being presented in the shape of a woman slowly merging with her own double as she descended into the water step-by-step until there was only one.

Goddammit, Ian. You win.

Swallowing hard, he pulled his robes clumsily over his head, mounded them on top of hers, and lumbered into the water after her, feeling as graceless as a beached sea cow. Not caring much.

She watched him unabashedly sink deeper into the brine until they were just two faces bobbing in the buoyant black. They gazed into each other's eyes, trying to find answers there to questions they were too afraid to ask. Then she grinned, and the spell was broken, leaving something more real in its place, like the sculptor's transference of a figure from clay to marble. From this point forward, whatever was between them would be real. It might be broken, but Rabbit couldn't deny it as he had been trying so hard to do.

"Roll over," she said softly.

He did, and the front of his body floated to the surface. He had never been particularly buoyant. In a pool he would simply sink until only his crown was above the waterline. But here in the Dead Sea he bobbed like a cork.

He heard water run off her as she followed him to the surface.

Her hand sought his, felt its way down his wrist and closed around his palm.

"If we fall asleep here—"

"Shh."

He shushed.

"Breathe."

"I am."

"No," she said. "Breathe."

He tried to take a deep breath and felt it stick in his upper chest. His abdomen was clenched tight, as though he was expecting a blow. His shoulders were high and bunched like a boxer wading into the ring against a superior opponent. He tried to relax them, tried to breathe, realizing suddenly this wasn't new. He had felt this way for years.

Screaming in his ears.

He started to rise. "I'm serious. If we—"

"Shh," she demanded. "Let go."

He tried again. Just breathe.

Wailing, screaming, mewling for death. The sight of them split open and emptied, blood everywhere. The smell . . .

He realized he was squeezing her hand too hard. He released his grip, but she held on.

"It's okay," she said and squeezed him back.

This time he started with the shoulders. Tried to force them to let go and hiccupped a breath. Ashamed of it, he clenched back up.

"I'm falling asleep," he said. "Let's—"

"No, you're not. You're scared. But you can't leave him inside you."

Rabbit tried to put his feet down. "He's not."

"Yes, he is."

Yes, he is. She was right. Eshek was inside him. And not just Eshek. They were all in there. Eshek's sadism, Aaron's fanaticism, Domitian's depravity. He had been tensing for years, hardening his mind and body for the inevitable blow that would finish him. But all he had done was lock them inside, holding those memories close, nurturing them the way a child picks at a scab.

Screaming. Aaron's guns tearing people apart in the box of the Hippodrome.

Antipas begging for release. For his beloved son's release.

Rabbit let his shoulders go. At first, they fought him. Hitched up over and over as his breath caught in his lungs. And then he truly did sob. Tearless, shuddering sobs shook his body from end to end. She might think less of him. Might think he was weak. For the first time in his life, he didn't care. He couldn't hold them in any longer. The battlefields strewn with corpses. The massacres of innocent people. The writhing bodies engulfed in flame. This was the price his job exacted from him. He never told anyone what it was like to be surrounded by so much brutality. Just made himself harder so it would never take him. Today, Einar Eshek had finally overwhelmed his tank. Overbore his ability to quietly hold the memories.

They billowed out in shuddering convulsive sobs like poison clouds. What he found underneath was worse still.

You didn't stop them. You let them all down. You let them all die. You let them all suffer.

But that wasn't the end. Guilt, too, was a shield against something he had spent his life too afraid to face. But it came up now, bubbling to the surface on his shuddering breath.

No. You tried. And you were powerless to stop them.

You failed. You lost.

As though she were reading his thoughts, Helen spoke. "You're not responsible for what he did. It's okay to be horrified. It's normal. He beat us this round." Her matter-of-fact tone held not a trace of pity or even sympathy, which Rabbit found infinitely more comforting than consolation. "Now we get to decide what we want to do about it."

Rabbit had never cried in front of anyone that he remembered. As he lay there, floating in the Dead Sea, he realized what an insult that was. He had been a shoulder to cry on for PJ and Ian many times. But he held those doors closed against his own intimates. Afraid of looking weak or incompetent, of being despised. Now, as he lay here, holding Helen's hand, he realized how ridiculous that was. Pretending to be made of iron was a profound act of cowardice and selfishness.

His body, fatigued as it was, felt liquid and powerful after being drained of all that acid. He wished he could face Eshek now. The killer wouldn't stand a chance.

He laughed, which dissolved into a cough.

"Share the joke?"

"Just feeling good."

Something suddenly came back to Rabbit so clearly he shot straight up in the water, floundered, and ended up spitting and coughing brine.

"Lost points on the dismount," she said, laughing.

"I heard them!"

"Who?"

"Antipas," he said. "His last few words. I heard them when I was walking toward the door."

"You didn't tell me you went back there."

"Yeah, I didn't really want to think about it. Sorry."

"No, no, I get it. What did you hear?" She managed to right herself and plant her feet on the bottom. Her hair was slicked back, and droplets of water stood out on her cheeks. He couldn't take his eyes off her. She raised her eyebrows, encouraging him to continue.

He shook the cobwebs from his brain. "Let's see. Antipas said, 'Not Achor. Antonia.'"

"The Vale of Achor? It's mentioned in the scroll."

"I assume so. Antonia must be the Antonia Fortress. And then he said, 'Five, one.'"

"Fifty-one?"

"Maybe, but I think it was five, comma, one."

"How did Eshek react to that?"

"It clearly made sense to him. He was fucking delighted."

"So, you do swear."

"What?"

"I've never heard you drop an f-bomb. I thought maybe you were too pure."

She reached out and brushed a little water from his brow before it dripped into his eyes. Her naked body this close to him, he didn't feel too pure at all. But for the dark water, she'd know it, too.

"The situation merits it," he said.

"That it does. Okay, so it clearly meant something to Eshek. It must be the code that makes the treasure map make sense."

"The last entry says there is a second scroll that contains more descriptions and measurements. Maybe that's all it contains. Those two bits."

"Antonia? Five, one?"

"Yep."

She screwed up her face thinking. "A cryptogram?"

"C equals N, that sort of thing? Don't the clues have to be the same length? Vale of Achor has eleven letters. Antonia Fortress has fifteen."

"In English," she said.

He thought about it. Shook his head. "They don't match in Hebrew or Aramaic either. Or Greek."

"What about the numbers? Five, one? What's the first location again?"

"We could check. I mean, the scroll is right up that hill."

She slapped her forehead. "Duh. Come on!"

And they scrambled out of the sea, stumbling on the rocks.

The next few days were spent in a peculiar kind of domestic limbo. They found food the brothers had left behind, although not much of it. The semi-fasted state brought with it moments of great clarity as well as moments of near delirium.

The scroll yielded no secrets, however. They obsessed over the first and fifth locations:

"In the fortress, which is in the Vale of Achor, forty cubits under the steps entering from the east: a money chest, seventeen talents."

And:

"In the ascent of the staircase of Refuge, in the left-hand side, three cubits up from the floor: forty talents of silver."

But they could make no sense of the clues. Every few hours, one of them would bounce around another theory and they would return to the scroll, partially unfurled on a table in the reading room. But nothing seemed to stick.

In the meantime, they talked.

Rabbit learned more about Helen's childhood. How she had held her widowed father's admiration without trying, while Olympia strove after it bitterly, imitating anything in which he expressed interest. Olympia became a historian, poring over her father's books while Helen was constantly in motion. Olympia formed a deep-seated resentment for her sister that hurt and surprised Helen, but which she eventually came to accept.

"Do you see him much, your dad?"

She shook her head. They were perched on the roof of the Yahad compound, looking out over the Dead Sea. "He's dead."

"I'm sorry."

"You didn't kill him." She said it as a joke, but it fell very flat. "He died when I was nineteen. Pancreatic cancer."

Rabbit remembered her frosty reception to his earlier sympathy, so he kept it to himself.

"Where did you grow up?" he asked instead.

"New Haven."

"No shit. Your dad taught at Yale? That's big-league history."

"I suppose your parents were faculty, too."

He shook his head. "Dad was an air traffic controller at Detroit Metro. My mom did administrative stuff for a bunch of little companies. They're both retired now." His own parents were in their late seventies. He didn't see them very often but took it for granted they would always be there. Inwardly, he resolved to fly out to Michigan after this job was wrapped up.

Rabbit told her about his silly nickname and how he'd come by it. He described the remote and chilly atmosphere of his home, never violent or cruel or loud, just missing in action somehow. He relayed his dating history, a string of short-term flings that fizzled out before they got started. How he had been described once as "emotionally unavailable, but not in the good way."

"That's horrible!" she exclaimed, taking his hand as she did. Rabbit didn't say anything, just enjoyed the feeling of her fingers interlaced with his.

He told her how he had once and only once gotten into a brief and steamy tryst with a woman in ancient Greece while on a mission, how he didn't think of it as real, since he was playing a character. It had felt more like a very realistic game of make-believe.

She was cagey about her professional life. She had worked in Ukraine, then in Turkey, both times for major manufacturing companies, but when pressed would only say she was in "logistics," whatever that meant.

They spent more time floating in the sea, exchanging ideas about

Eshek and the case, but also about life and history and ethics and everything in between. After one particularly long soak in the brine, they had both developed itchy skin from the salt crust and finally succumbed to the allure of the freshwater mikveh pools. For obvious reasons, they avoided the location of the murder and selected two baths at the far end of the complex, separated by a low stone wall and covered with open-walled thatch roofs.

"Don't fall asleep," her voice chided from the other side of the wall.

"I'm not," Rabbit assured her, sinking into the pleasantly cool water. He rubbed his skin and submerged himself under the surface, scrubbing his hair.

". . . off?" he heard as he surfaced.

"What?"

"I asked if you dropped off."

"No. I don't even feel tired." Truth was, he felt lighter and better than he could ever remember feeling.

"Hnh," she said. Then there was the sound of falling water.

And suddenly, she appeared around the side of the wall, squeezing water from her wet hair, achingly beautiful.

"We're being stupid," she said.

"I don't under—"

She came around the side of the pool, bent low, and kissed him. Her lips were cool and wet and tasted like rain. Her breath was quick.

Rabbit was out of the pool before he realized he was in motion, and she was pressing herself against him, their hands roaming each other as though their bodies contained keys to each other's personal prisons. His head buzzed and his vision telescoped until all he could see was her face.

And then they were on the ground, and he thought she might have knocked him down and she was above him, kneading his chest, pulsing, and lifting with the same mirrored fever of desperation that built in him and had been building since he first saw her in Alexandria. She seemed to contract, tighter and tighter, her body drawing in on itself until she rose off him, body shaking in a long, gasping inhale as though she had surfaced from a dive to the bottom of the ocean, and this was the first breath she had ever drawn.

She unfolded and draped herself across him. She was trembling, her voice shook. "Sorry."

It caught him so off guard he laughed. "Jesus, why?"

"I didn't ask if that was okay."

He wrapped his arms around her.

She was still shuddering. "That was kind of intense. Okay if we take a little pause?"

"We have all the time in the world."

Which is how Rabbit and Helen honeymooned in the abandoned compound of a doomed apocalyptic cult in 68 CE. They didn't do much besides eat what little they could find, make love, float in the Dead Sea, and talk. And, to his surprise, Rabbit, who had never thought he had much to say, turned out to be a bottomless pit of talking. They never saw or heard another person. Their only visitors were birds and tiny lizards that seemed just as excited to explore the once busy human hive as Rabbit and Helen were.

One morning, she went for a run around the broad flat plain to the west of the compound, her robes flapping. As he watched her small figure at the edge of the plain running along in a steady, even pace, Rabbit spotted a thin plume of smoke over the distant hills, black against the blue sky.

"Time to go," he said when she returned, breathing heavily and drenched in sweat. She followed his pointing finger to the mountains. "Romans."

They packed up makeshift containers of water and headed out before noon. Her decay point wouldn't activate until the following day, and Rabbit felt robbed. They were quiet while they packed, neither saying anything that wasn't germane to the task at hand.

Despite telling himself he wouldn't, Rabbit looked over his shoulder at the compound one more time before they rounded the ridge, feeling the loss acutely.

Helen took his hand.

They reached the valley in plenty of time, made camp, and waited. After so much talking, suddenly neither of them had much to say. Or rather, Rabbit had plenty to say, but was afraid to say it. The spell of Qumran was broken, and he was wary of telling her the truth. The whole truth.

That he had come here to help her.

And to rob her.

That he had been lying from the beginning.

That none of that changed the way he felt about her. That he was terrified it would ruin everything and this would be yet another failed attempt at intimacy for Doctor Rabbit Ward.

No, that wasn't quite right. He had never attempted intimacy before. That's precisely what the women he had dated had detected was off about him. He had never trusted anyone enough to peel back his layers of armor. Now that he had, he was afraid the relationship was about to go up in smoke.

"What are you thinking about?" he asked her. It was a stupid question. Middle-school-crush stupid.

"Spatial displacement."

Her answer caught him off guard. "What?"

"Spatial displacement," she repeated, as though that explained everything. Then continued. "I was just thinking, okay, maybe there is a second scroll that decodes all the locations on the first scroll. If there is, Eshek is going to have to do another fucking mission to get that scroll, right?"

"Sure, I guess so."

"But he didn't. He didn't come back again. Olympia's boss hired me because Eshek made off with the treasure after this mission." She was getting excited.

As Rabbit was processing that, she popped to her feet and started to pace the shady little grove they had settled in to wait.

"Which means whatever he needed, he got it from Antipas and Tuvia in that interrogation."

"So, it can't have been that complicated," he agreed.

"Right! The code must be just a couple of goddamn words that cast the treasure map in a new light. One way to do that is—"

"Spatial displacement," he finished.

"Exactly. The relative positions of all the locations are accurate, but not the absolute positions."

He was on his feet, too. "So, you could find all the cache locations if you knew where to find the first one."

"That's what Antipas told him. Where the map starts."

They both stood there in silence for a moment.

Suddenly, she snatched up a stick from under the tree, walked into the sun, and plunged it into the sand where it cast a shadow.

"It's about time," she said. "Come on."

He looked at the primitive sundial she had just made, shaking his head in admiration.

She led him to a wadi that fed the valley, just a narrow cut in the rock but wide enough to admit a panel van, which of course was exactly how she had gotten there.

Helen marched over to a ring of stones.

"I'm going to get him, Rabbit. I'm going to get my sister back."

Rabbit was standing on the edge of the ring, grinning as wide as she was.

"And you're going to help."

Without warning, she reached out and jerked him forward into her arms.

"What . . ." The lights winked out.

JERUSALEM

2015 CE

. . . are you doing?" he finished in the time machine. They were standing on the dilator pad. Helen's sister, whom he now knew by the name Olympia, stared at them, mouth open. Thankfully, there was only her and the technicians in the van. The mercenaries he would encounter with them in 2018 must have been later additions to the crew.

Helen hopped off the platform and hugged her sister. "Hey, girl. I have a lot to tell you."

Olympia was still staring at Rabbit from behind the round rims of her glasses.

"Who is that?" she asked

"I found him outside," Helen chirped. "Can I keep him?"

Rabbit could hear them shouting through the wall. They were almost loud enough for him to pick out the words. He was sitting at a card table that served as the administrative hub of a tiny factory in an industrial park near the jump point. Judging from the boxes and disorganized paperwork, the place was called Uni-Co and appeared to make nothing but peculiarly shaped plastic valves. Olympia had stowed him in the bleak office so she and her sister could verbally eviscerate each other in peace. Rabbit could have walked out, no one appeared to be armed, but to what end? Where would he go?

A motorcycle-themed wall calendar mounted with a thumbtack

above the card table told him it was November 2015. He was in his own past, which meant he couldn't contact anyone he knew. He had no money or identification. Helen had trapped him more effectively than even she could know.

Olympia hadn't recognized him but, once she found out who he was, her shock turned to rage. Rabbit represented lawful chrono archaeology. To bring him into the inner sanctum of the organization was unforgivable. Knowing what he did about Olympia, Rabbit suspected some of her anger was independent of the organizational risk. He represented not just legal time travel but the Smithsonian, the organization that had rejected her. There was plenty of fuel behind the argument taking place next door.

Helen had put Rabbit in a hell of a bind. How was he supposed to get back to 2019? He couldn't stay here, obviously. What was he supposed to do, lay low for four years and then step back into his regular life once he caught up with his own timeline? Jesus, what a mess.

They were still shouting.

A red Solo cup was sitting on the card table, empty but for a ring of brown crust in the bottom. Curiosity got the better of him. He held the cup against the wall and pressed his ear to its base. The voices on the opposite wall were muffled, but audible.

"Are you mad at me, or are you scared of your boss?" Helen hissed. "Can't you see how fucked-up this whole thing is?"

"The only fucked-up thing here is you. I don't know why he wanted you anyway," Olympia spat back.

There was a little pause. Helen's reply was quieter, Rabbit had to strain to hear it.

"I thought you recommended me."

"What, after you threw it in my face last time that you were too good for this?"

"I said *you* were too good for this, and I meant it. When are you gonna get it through your skull, I was never competing with you?"

Her sister's response was icy. "Well, you never had to, did you?"

A door slammed closed.

"Did you seriously just lock me in? Olympia? Fuck!"

No one returned for over an hour. When the door to Rabbit's office-cell finally opened, Olympia was holding a blocky little 9-millimeter pistol in her hand. She was aiming the muzzle at the floor away from her feet and looked distinctly uncomfortable carrying it. So, when she used it to gesture Rabbit out of the office, he got pretty nervous, too.

"Would you mind not waving that directly at me?" Rabbit asked. "You don't want to kill me, and I don't want to be dead."

"You don't know what I want." It sounded petulant. Rabbit wondered how she developed the slick confidence she wore when he would meet her next in 2018.

She led him into the next room where he rejoined Helen, who popped up from a grimy couch. Rabbit sat next to her, but not too close. He didn't want to give away their intimacy.

Olympia remained at the door. Her next words were a bad performance. She sounded every bit a subordinate pretending to be the one in charge. She was following orders; Rabbit would have bet his life on it.

"I've given it some thought. The top priority hasn't changed. You need to find the thief and bring him to me."

"Why didn't you just say so?" said Helen. "We know who he is and how to get him already."

She was a hell of a lot better liar than Olympia.

"Really?" The word was smeared with disbelief.

"Sure. We need a change of clothes. We're going to Atlanta."

In record time, they boarded a plane to the US. Two first-class seats on El Al Air, no layovers. Rabbit was sitting on a well-made fake passport bearing the name "Kent Meloy," the same name Olympia would use again in three years to shuttle Rabbit overseas.

Helen was dressed in black slacks, boots, and a soft grey sweater. Her hair was in a ponytail with a few loose, curling locks framing her face. Rabbit had never seen her outside of their missions to the past, and her modern appearance looked like a costume to him. Rabbit was wearing uncomfortably new black jeans and a blue button-down shirt. Helen said the color made his eyes pop, which sounded like a bad thing but she assured him was not. At least the new clothes beat the ill-fitting ones he had been handed by Olympia at the factory. Smelled less like cigarettes, too.

"That was a dangerous stunt you pulled back there," Rabbit said. It was the first moment he'd had alone with her since she pulled him into her timeline.

"Not really," she said, buckling in. "I figured you'd either come back with me or you wouldn't. What did I have to lose?"

"Why, though?"

She raised her eyebrows in disbelief. "You think I was going to turn you loose on Eshek without me? Hell, no. You're staying right here where I can keep an eye on you."

Rabbit couldn't tell her what she had to lose without giving something away. Many theories of time travel said a person could not occupy the same time as their past self. No one seemed to have much of a concept of what the outcome would be, and the single rat study that had been performed was inconclusive. Still, it didn't seem like a great idea. Pointing out the risk she had taken would open up a whole can of questions, however. He had to think of this as a mission. Traveling to the ancient past of 2015.

And then it occurred to him what she had just said. *Turn you loose on Eshek.* "What makes you think—"

"Let me stop you before you perjure yourself. The Book of Esther was found and secured in two days, you didn't need a twenty-day mission to get it. I make no bones about my disdain for your employer, but I don't think the people at the Smithsonian are dumb. So, if you didn't have a whole mission for the Book, I ask myself, why did you really go to Jerusalem with me? Why did you spend days putting yourself in danger? It wasn't for the Copper Scroll. Which leaves me with one option. You came back for Eshek, just like me. Tell me I'm wrong," she said.

"I'm not—"

"Tell me I'm wrong."

Rabbit sighed. "You're not wrong."

"I know," she said, sliding the plastic screen down over her window, "but thanks for admitting it."

"When did you know?"

"I was pretty sure when you made a big show of walking off toward Qumran right after we met."

"Seriously?"

"Yeah, for someone who makes a living at this, I thought you'd be better at manipulating people."

"Great. Thanks."

"Don't take it too hard. If you were better at it, I might not have clocked you, but I also wouldn't like you as much. Plus, I appreciated the help."

A flight attendant came by and offered them mimosas. Helen accepted. Rabbit asked for coffee. No time like the present to renew a favorite addiction.

The moment the solicitous young man left, Rabbit turned back to Helen, wanting to touch her hand but afraid to.

"Listen. About this. Yes, I was after Eshek, too. But that doesn't take away from . . . well, the last few weeks in Qumran. Not for me, anyway. I hope not for you."

"For a smart guy, you're awfully stupid sometimes," she said. Then chirped, "Thanks!" over his shoulder and accepted the mimosa. Rabbit took his coffee.

"Cream? Sugar?"

"Just the coffee, thanks," Rabbit said. The man went on to the next row.

Helen sipped her drink and sighed.

"So that means . . ." Rabbit asked.

"Doctor Ward. We're competing for the same prize. I'm going to get him before you. Plain and simple. I don't see why that has to get in the way of us being us," she said. "If you don't."

"I don't," he said.

"Well, then." She clinked her champagne glass against his coffee cup. "Game on, handsome."

Somewhere over the Atlantic, Rabbit woke up from a nap he hadn't intended to take.

"Why are we going to Atlanta?" he asked, drawing her attention away from the clouds outside.

"Good morning. Good sleep?"

"Planes knock me out. Atlanta?"

"You know how many Einar Esheks there are in the United States?"

Rabbit shrugged.

"Zero. Which means he changed his name. If we're very, very lucky, Eshek is the name on his birth certificate but he's traveling under a new legal identity. If we're unlucky, Eshek is a pseudonym. We're going to see if we can find out who he really is."

"Huh. Okay."

"So, what do we know about him that would help?"

Rabbit started cataloguing. "He's from the South but has unlearned most of his accent. That implies time spent elsewhere in his formative years but doesn't guarantee it."

"I feel like there's a bigger differentiator." At his blank glance, she said, "He's a goddamned psychotic murderer?"

"Well, yes. I suppose that's more of a standout."

"So, I wonder, what are the odds he was able to keep his psychosis under wraps until he happened to get his first trip to the past?"

"You think he's killed people in the present? His past. You know what I mean."

"Well, he wasn't caught if he did, or he'd be in jail. Still, nobody just wakes up one day and decides 'I think I'll kill some people today,' right? That shit takes time to simmer. I wonder if there were earlier signs that might have landed him in trouble. Something that would have left a trail."

"Violent behavior, killing animals, that sort of thing."

"That sort of thing, yeah. If he ever did time, we might be able to find records on him. I searched the BoP's database before we left Israel. No Esheks."

"Which means?" he asked.

"Well, we can still rule out—"

"No, what does BoP mean?"

"Federal Bureau of Prisons."

"Gotcha." He sighed. "Well, that's it, then."

She stared at him, a theatrically disbelieving look on her face.

"What?" he asked.

"After what we just accomplished in Jerusalem, you throw in the towel that easily?"

"No," he said gruffly and looked away. He glared at the back of the seat in front of him for a while before beginning again. "I know how to operate in the ancient world. I didn't even know you could search the FoP."

"BoP," she corrected. "The *F* is silent."

"I don't know how to navigate the modern world. Oh, I can schedule flights and dig through digital archives, but I don't have the first idea how to find Eshek, or whatever his name really is."

"Oh, is that all?"

He glared at her. Realized she wasn't joking.

"Don't worry about it. I'll teach you." She continued in the same matter-of-fact tone as before. "I've got a guy searching the state prison records, so we can pursue or rule that out by the time we land. The pseudonym might be harder to track depending on how he did it."

"Why?"

"It'll basically go one of three directions, depending on why and when he changed his name. If he legally changed it, we'll pick that up, easy. If he's traveling under a pseudonym, he'll have sprinkled the name Eshek all over immigration and the airlines. The worst scenario is if he uses his legal name for everything except his dealings with the organization."

"Because he won't have left a digital trail we can follow."

"Right."

"But how do you even follow a digital trail? I get the concept but what's the execution?"

She leaned forward and kissed him.

"A girl has to keep some secrets."

When she turned on her phone, a text message awaited her. None of the state prisons had a record of Eshek, either.

"Well, fuck," she said, drawing a look from the prim woman and her teenage daughter standing up in front of their seats waiting to disembark. Rabbit never understood why people did that. He steadfastly refused to rise until there was an opportunity to move. "Maybe I'm wrong. Maybe he doesn't have a record after all." This she said more quietly at least.

The teenage girl was staring at Rabbit. She leaned over and whispered to her mother, who glanced at him while trying to appear as though she was checking the crowd behind them in the plane.

Being a time-traveling archaeologist didn't draw the kind of attention entertainers were subjected to, but every once in a while, Rabbit would run into this sort of thing. He smiled politely but said nothing.

Still, the teenager kept glancing back at him until her mother noticed and turned her around by the shoulder. She leaned forward and said to Rabbit in quiet tones laced with a refined Israeli accent, "I'm sorry. She thinks she saw you deplaning in Tel Aviv just before our flight took off. Imagination." The woman shrugged, while the teenager slumped forward, trying to sink into the floor.

2015. Rabbit had done a job in Tel Aviv in November of 2015.

He pulled out his ticket and looked at the date.

November 16, 2015. He must have just missed himself.

"Whatcha doing?" asked Helen.

Rabbit shook his head in mock amusement at himself. "Checking baggage claim. Like we have any baggage."

She pointed him forward, where the front rows were filing off the plane.

The teenage girl turned for one more look at Rabbit, glaring as though he had gotten her in trouble. It was amazing how quickly teenagers could turn from adorable kids into truly frightening people . . .

Frightening people.

"Juvie," Rabbit said.

"What?" Helen was arranging the contents of a fashionably tiny backpack.

"Eshek might be too smart to get caught for crimes as an adult, but everybody has a past. What about juvenile detention?"

Helen zipped closed the top of the bag. "Welcome back, Doctor Ward."

HUNTSVILLE, ALABAMA, USA

2015 CE

Ten days of calling and searching turned up eleven false leads, three sexually suggestive comments from wardens, nineteen stops at local diners, drives to Florida, Mississippi, and South Carolina, and zero leads about Einar Eshek.

"We have no record of that name in our files," said the clerk at the latest facility, the Adams-Rind Center for Children in Huntsville, Alabama.

Rabbit didn't ask how Helen managed to get such ready access to the records from these facilities. She would make a few calls and, by the time they arrived, the staff would be waiting with open arms. He could only assume some palms were being greased, and he didn't really want to know.

"Can you search by crimes committed between 1990 and 2005? I'm looking for things like animal torture, assault, violent crimes."

"It'll be a long list."

"We've got time," she said.

Rabbit and Helen knew this drill by now. The clerk would give them a printout, pages and pages of names, convictions, and sentences; everything that was public record. They would be given some place to sit and go through the pages. After a few hours of reading, they would admit defeat. Even Rabbit, who was no stranger to tedious research, was weary of it.

The clerk completed her search and was about to print the records when she paused. "How old is the man you're looking for?"

"Late twenties, early thirties," Rabbit said.

"You might have more luck talking to Doctor Fortner. He was the warden here forever. They don't use that title anymore. Retired last year but he still lives in town. He's as sharp as a tack and has a great memory. I'll give you his phone number if you like."

And so, two hours later, Rabbit and Helen sat down across the table from Alan Fortner at the Cozy Cow, a cute local coffee and sandwich place overlooking Big Spring Park.

"I shouldn't have this," Fortner said of his pastry. "High blood sugar." He sighed. "But I suppose something gets us all in the end. If I had to choose, I'd take death by pastry over getting hit by a car."

"Thanks for meeting with us, Doctor Fortner."

Rabbit expected the gent to correct Helen, ask her to use his first name, but he just smiled and nodded, making his white Prince Valiant haircut bob like a living thing. Fortner was rail thin and tall, with hollow cheeks, wide blue eyes, and a soul patch under his bottom lip that looked like an aging caterpillar. He wore a faded oxford shirt with a hole in one elbow, jeans, and cowboy boots.

"So, tell me more about this person you're trying to locate. I must say, I'm always sad to hear when one of my kids turns out for the worse. I was at Adams-Rind for thirty-two years and worked with a lot of young people. Most of them turned out all right, I'm proud to say. Not that I take credit for their success, but it comforts me to know I helped some of them onto a stable base from which to proceed into their lives."

"If this young man was under your care, I think you're going to be very disappointed," said Rabbit.

"He goes by the name Einar Eshek, but we think that's a pseudonym," Helen said, cradling her steaming cappuccino in both hands. "We haven't been able to find any trace of him under that name."

"What has he done?"

"He murdered seven people . . . that we know about."

Fortner looked sad rather than horrified. "I don't really want to know, but tortured how? Murdered how? It's not morbid curiosity; the details might narrow down the list."

Rabbit described the careful, methodical method by which Eshek killed.

Fortner looked grim. "How has this not made the news?"

"The murders were committed thousands of years ago," Rabbit said, then explained what he meant.

The retired warden leaned back in his chair and closed his eyes as he listened. His pastry sat untouched. When Rabbit and Helen were done, he stayed silent for a few moments, then rocked forward abruptly, letting the front feet of his chair whack the floor.

"So, we're dealing with someone who uses heinous methods to get what he wants. He has figured out a way to perform these actions such that he does not get caught, and may, I stress *may*, console himself that there is nothing immoral about his actions due to the context in which they are performed. He has extensive knowledge of anatomy and language and enough history to get by in these societies, which suggests intellectual capacity and significant ability to focus his attention. How old did you say he is now?"

"Early thirties, by the look of him," Rabbit said.

The psychologist picked up his pastry and took a big bite. He chewed it slowly, thinking, then pronounced, "Leroy Bonneau."

"You . . . you think you know someone who fits that description?" Helen asked, sounding as surprised as Rabbit felt.

"I want to be very clear; I am not accusing anyone. But the only person from my acquaintance with the potential for developing the capabilities you describe is Leroy Bonneau. Leroy came to Adams-Rind in 1994. He was eleven at the time."

"What was he convicted of?" Helen asked.

"He wasn't."

"I'm confused," said Rabbit.

"Leroy had been charged with and admitted to killing his mother and her boyfriend in their sleep. His attorneys made the case that due to the extreme nature of the abuse to which he had been subjected, the murders should be considered self-defense. In the end, the jury agreed. However, Leroy was so obviously disturbed that the judge felt he would be safer in a structured environment and made a dispensation for him to continue his stay at Adams-Rind until his legal majority."

"He must have really freaked out that judge," Helen concluded.

"Yes and no. Leroy wouldn't have scared anyone to look at him. His growth was stunted from malnutrition, and he displayed much of the affect we associate with severe autism. He avoided eye contact, spoke in a quiet monotone, and was prone to soothe himself through rocking. PTSD was assumed."

"Jesus, what did they do to him?"

"Evidence at the home suggested long-term incarceration. In a dog kennel. Leroy had vanished from school two years before; his mother reported to the school that he had gone to live with his biological father, the factuality of which no one bothered to confirm."

"Two years?" Rabbit felt sick.

"Two years. It took a while, but he began to show signs of improvement while he was at the center. Leroy was remarkably intelligent. He had an eidetic memory and a remarkable affinity for languages and music. His occupational therapist told me a story that underlines the point. She played the boy a piece of Bach, excluding the last stanza. Mind you, Leroy had never heard chamber music before. A week later, she asked him if he remembered the piece. He said he did, and proceeded to hum the melody, while tapping out the percussive rhythms on the desk. And he completed the piece." He paused for effect. "Including the last stanza, which he had never heard.

"He became fluent in Spanish solely by listening to other boys at the center. I say solely because he didn't engage with the other boys directly. They all knew to leave him alone. Well, most of them. There was once a new boy who decided Leroy, being so small and frail, would be an easy victim. This boy verbally harassed him for weeks, despite repeated warnings from other boys and admonitions from the staff. Leroy never retaliated, never objected, never uttered a word of complaint to anyone. Then one day the boy took a book Leroy was reading in the library and refused to give it back. The next day the boy complained of feeling ill and was taken to the nurse with blood in his stool. Someone had slipped a handful of fine metal shavings into his meal, which had horribly lacerated the boy's digestive system. He was shipped to a hospital, and we didn't see him again. There was an investigation, but it revealed nothing."

"Did you suspect Leroy?"

"I like to assume the best of the boys, but I'll admit he was the one with the clearest motive. I asked him how he felt about it. He looked at me like I'd asked him the riddle of the sphinx. You know what he answered?" Fortner adopted a thick accent as he imitated the boy. "'He et metal, en now he's gawn.' Calm as that."

"What kind of psychological treatment did he receive?"

"We focused on getting him physically healthy, rebuilding his sense of self and self-esteem. By the time he left Adams-Rind at eighteen, anyone would say he was a model of success. He got his GED and had taken enough online credits for a junior college degree. He came out of his shell. Interpersonally, he appeared to be competent, self-assured, calm, and intelligent."

"But . . ." prompted Helen.

"Well, I never got past the feeling that it was a persona he had constructed. He never opened up about the pain of his experiences, he just became this new person day by day."

Something clicked in Rabbit.

"Where are you from, Doctor Fortner?"

"Houston, Texas."

"You don't have much of an accent."

"The South Texas accent is subtler than most people realize. Also, I grew up in the fairly insular community around Clear Lake." His brows knitted. "Why do you ask?"

"Well, I spoke with Eshek a few times and it just occurred to me who he sounds like."

Fortner pointed to himself in query.

Rabbit nodded. "And it's not just the accent. There's something about it I can't quite name. Cadence, maybe." Rabbit searched for a word.

Helen and Fortner spoke in unison.

"Affect?" he asked.

"Energy?" she offered.

"I wonder how much he modeled his external persona on you."

Fortner sat back and pondered that for a moment, a tight frown making his soul patch stick straight out.

"Sorry, I don't even know if that's relevant," Rabbit said. "It just occurred to me."

Helen broke the silence. "Is there any chance you have a picture of Leroy Bonneau?"

Fortner shook his head. "I wouldn't be able to share that if we do. But I don't need to. His picture was in the papers when he was arrested."

"Hello, Einar," Rabbit said. He and Helen were pressed together in front of a microfiche reader at the local library. They had found some newspaper archives online, but nothing from 1994, so they had gone back to basics.

The *Huntsville Times* front page, November 11, 1994, featured the salacious story of the boy who murdered his caretakers. There were two photographs accompanying the story, one of a double bed, its sheets soaked with blood in the rough shapes of two people. The other a picture of a terrified, emaciated boy pinioned between two police officers, his wide eyes looking up at the camera from a downturned face. It was the exact expression you might expect to see on a chastened hound.

"That's him, all right," said Helen. "Seeing him like this, I almost feel sorry for him."

"I pity how he got this way, but that doesn't make me sympathetic for the person he became," said Rabbit. "So, what now?"

"Now we find him."

She sicced her mysterious friend on the case and within a day turned up several things.

"After Adams-Rind, he applied to Auburn but was turned down." She was summarizing for Rabbit as she speed-read her phone screen over breakfast in a local café. "So, he enlisted in the army and got selected for the Green Berets straight out of basic."

"I guess we know how he learned to fight like that," Rabbit said, feeling a little better about the ass-kickings he received from the man.

"He spent eight years with Special Forces and then, nothing."

"What do you mean 'nothing'?"

"No job history since 2011."

"Was he working for your sister that whole time?"

"Maybe. Olympia hasn't given much to go on."

"Where does he live?"

Helen glanced at the phone. "He has an apartment in DC."

"Great," Rabbit growled.

WASHINGTON, DC, USA

2015 CE

Rabbit was on edge the moment they entered the city limits. Every second they spent in DC was one in which he might be recognized. He recalled a discussion he had once had with Rick Chang, one of the godfathers of time travel research. Chang was a surprisingly poetic man who preferred to speak in metaphors to anyone who didn't understand the mathematical poetry that truly underpinned time.

"Think of time like a tapestry, yeah?" he had said, weaving his fingers together for effect. "Go waaaaaay up to the top and break one little thread, can you tell at the bottom of the tapestry?"

"No?" Rabbit guessed, hoping he was right.

"Of course not! Buuut, if you break the same little thread two knots above the bottom, what happens? It frays, yeah? That's what time is like."

Which explained why time travel wasn't permitted by law to recent destinations. The odds of creating splinters were exponentially larger the closer you got to the present. Exactly the opposite of the Butterfly Effect, which attributed increasing magnitude of relevance to every action the further back you went.

So, as Rabbit walked the streets of the city he called home, he was on edge.

Of course, Helen was too observant to miss it. "What's the matter with you? Do you owe a loan shark or something?"

"Or something," he conceded.

She huffed as they parked outside a towering brick of an apartment building in Arlington. Wedged between Richmond Highway and Reagan National Airport, the strip of medium- to high-rise residences called Crystal City was about as convenient for frequent travelers as you could get in the DC area.

An airplane roared overhead, making Rabbit wince. It was also one of the loudest.

"Not what I expected," admitted Rabbit, looking up at the '90s vintage apartment building. The neighborhood was clean and attractive, with the aesthetics of a quality shopping mall. Eshek/Bonneau's building had a quaint little plaza outside its front door ringed with restaurants and shops. Rabbit had a hard time picturing the sadistic murderer shopping for something at the Victoria's Secret tucked pinkly in the corner of his residence. Then again, what did he know about murderers?

"What were you picturing? A *Silence of the Lambs* house of horrors?"

"Basically, yes," he replied.

They waited in the plaza, Rabbit sipping black coffee, Helen some liquid confection that required entirely too many words to describe.

When a rideshare dropped off a young, fashionably dressed couple, Rabbit and Helen rose without a word and proceeded like flocking birds, falling in behind them while Helen described a scene from a popular play with flamboyant excitement.

Social pressure is a wonderful tool, thought Rabbit.

The couple used a key card to enter through the glass doors into the lobby with Rabbit and Helen right on their heels. Rabbit fished around in his back pocket until the couple politely held the door for them.

Moments later, the elevator deposited the couple on the fourth floor, leaving the car to Rabbit and Helen.

They bumped fists.

At Eshek's door, Helen pulled a long, black leather wallet out of her back pocket. The wallet contained a set of metal rods that looked like tools a dentist might use. One glance at the lock and she picked out a few of them and set to work.

What do you do for a living?

Although it felt like an eternity, the click of the tumblers came less than a minute later.

"All right, Leroy. Let's see what you're hiding."

She pushed the door open and Rabbit followed.

"So, I'm getting less *Silence of the Lambs* and more *American Psycho*," she said.

"Never saw it," Rabbit admitted, "but I get the idea."

The one-bedroom apartment was exceptionally clean and spare. Minimalist, charcoal-grey and white furnishings made the small space feel expansive. A black and stainless steel kitchen opened onto the living and dining area. The only decorations were shields. Oxidized Greek aspides and Roman scuta hanging on the wall like paintings. A bronze buckler sat like a centerpiece on the round dining table.

Rabbit didn't want to admit it, but it reminded him of his own place.

"It's like a model home," she said.

"What do you mean?"

She opened the refrigerator. It was spotless and smelled of lemon cleanser. The only things in it were an empty butter dish and a half-empty bottle of very nice Modena vinegar.

"Four plates, four sets of silverware." She was opening drawers and cabinets. "Everything looks brand-new. Did this guy really even live here?"

More searching turned up a cleaning closet, which, unlike the rest of the place, was chock-full of supplies. A low, queen-size bed, desk, and nightstand were the sole occupants of the bedroom. Even the desk had nothing in it but a few pens.

Rabbit stared around the place as Helen continued to search. He breathed in the air and looked at the furnishings. He thought about Eshek's face when he was finished butchering Antipas and his son. Splattered with blood, ecstatic, rapturous, free. Was it sexual? Not exactly, but it wasn't far off. It was a release. And release implied containment.

In that light, he saw this apartment differently. One could easily see Zen simplicity in the space but, through another lens, it looked like a crucible. The calm Einar Eshek working so hard to maintain his veneer of civility, not just for the world but for himself, while underneath seethed the animal urges of his childhood. Rabbit was curious about and repelled by whatever happened in young Leroy's house to cultivate this urge in him. Like anything denied, it would build until it had to be released. And the man had architected a life in which those urges could be released in ways that were, if not socially sanctioned, at least not legally prohibited.

"Like masturbation," he mumbled.

Helen stuck her head out from the bathroom. "Excuse me?"

Rabbit shook his head. "Sorry, I was just thinking about something you said in Jerusalem about how masturbation releases tension."

"I mean, ballpark, but okay. What about it?"

"This place looks so . . . normal, right?"

She nodded. "Creepy normal."

"I imagine Leroy trying so hard to be someone else, imitating his old warden who he probably admired, living in all this clean austerity, ramming his true self down as hard as he can into the basement of his psyche, hoping if he packs it down hard enough, he can extinguish it."

"Maybe," she said. "What does this have to do with what he's doing?"

"Maybe nothing, but that's what got me thinking about masturbation."

She shook her head in confusion. "Throw me a rope here."

Rabbit walked into the bathroom. Like the rest of the apartment, it was clean and white, with dark grey towels folded precisely on the bar.

"The act of release. Of letting go." He opened the vanity cabinet under the sink. More cleaning supplies. "What other act does that sound like?"

"Using the toilet?" she asked. Rabbit was staring at the porcelain bowl.

"That's what I was thinking, yeah. Maybe there's some kind of safe space connection there. One place you can . . ." He lifted the lid off the water tank. "Let go."

A black notebook was secured to the inside of the lid with two meticulously attached Velcro straps. Rabbit removed it and smiled at Helen.

"Wild speculation, undeniable results," she admitted.

"I just became a felon for this?" Rabbit asked no one in particular. They were sitting in a little park a few blocks away from Eshek's place, thumbing through the journal.

"'Felon' is a strong word."

"I hoped we'd find his notes. Or maybe some crazy confessional of his crimes. What does this even mean?"

The book was filled with numbers. Neat, precise columns of numbers with no written information to say what they meant. Some pages had just a couple of entries, while others had dozens.

"Maybe it's a code," Helen offered.

"Maybe it's useless," Rabbit huffed.

She took the book from him.

"What's the pattern? Each page has a single number at the top. That's the top-level category for whatever he's describing, right?"

"Sure. But they're just a sequence. One, two, three . . . it might not mean anything."

She ignored him. "The second-tier information are all lists. A number, a comma, and second number."

Despite his frustration, he started playing. "The whole part of every number is either thirty-one or thirty-five. Then you have this long decimal string." The pattern started to tickle something in Rabbit's brain. *Two numbers with a comma. Two numbers with a comma.*

"Latitude and longitude!" he said.

She stared at the book, then at him. "They're geocodes?"

Rabbit snatched back the book and started flipping through the pages. "There are sixty-four pages with entries." Rabbit slapped the book on his palm. "This is his geocoded map of the Copper Scroll treasures."

Helen snatched it back. Stared at the first page she flipped to. "These must be his best guesses on the locations of the caches. He's got a couple for some of them, and a lot for others."

"Go to page four."

"Tons of entries."

"I think that's Kohlit. Nobody knows where the city was located. So, he's just speculating on that one, though he may have cracked it while he was there. I wonder why he didn't take this with him to Jerusalem."

"He probably entered it all into an app on his phone."

"Right." Rabbit stared at the book. "You realize what this means?"

"It means we know every place he might go."

Rabbit nodded. "It means we've got him."

JERUSALEM, ISRAEL

2015 CE

Rabbit and Helen camped out at some of the likeliest locations from Eshek's list that he might visit to pillage, while Olympia's people camped out at others. But as the days passed, their hope passed with them. There was no sign of him. It was as if, having discovered the final piece of the puzzle, Einar Eshek had abandoned his quest and evaporated.

"Maybe he already took everything he intends to. Maybe we're too late," sighed Helen, flopping back on their bed. The two of them were staying in a studio apartment across the street from the Mahane Yehuda Market. Olympia had produced a 1978 Yamaha three-cylinder motorcycle with a leaky gas tank and weak rear shocks for them to get around town.

"I don't know. Every site we've visited would be damn near impossible to loot. We know there have been no excavations at any of the sites, so he didn't fly under the official radar and take the finds." Rabbit pulled the pot of shakshuka he'd made them for late dinner out of the compact oven. The stew of spiced vegetables and chickpeas topped with poached eggs filled the little apartment with the smell of cumin and hot peppers. "Maybe he's trying to engineer something and it just hasn't come to fruition."

The weeks in America and Israel had been some of the best of Rabbit's life. Sure, the work was frustrating, but they were in it together and that made all the difference. Rabbit had always viewed couples in the early blush of romance with a healthy dose of skepticism. The model he grew up with had convinced him that reality would eventually drop a cold, wet blanket on every relationship. Which made all that cooing sweetness nothing more than limerence. A joke of the endocrine system to coax you into reproducing, nothing more. And then you have a few decades of distance and barely concealed contempt to enjoy before you die.

But now he had to admit, corny is only corny when it's happening to someone else.

He spooned up a bite from the pot and carried it over to her, warding off drips with his other hand. Helen sat up and sipped the proffered spoon.

"Needs more harissa."

He scowled, popped the rest of the bite into his own mouth, and felt the heat prickle his tongue. "Woman, you could smelt lead in that mouth."

"It's all the fuckin' swearing that does it." She grimaced, looking out the window. "I don't know, maybe you're right. I'm just so impatient."

She wasn't the only one. Despite the relative bliss he had felt since Qumran, Rabbit was increasingly worried. While they were in America, he had sniffed out the details of his 2015 time travel expedition. His past self would be returning to 2015 in two days, and Rabbit knew he should be gone before that happened. Not that he knew how he was going to make that happen.

"That's the real time dilation, isn't it? Nothing changes your perception . . . of . . ."

Rabbit was staring into the pot of shakshuka.

"Are you okay?"

He had been pushing the spoon into the center of the thick vegetable stew and noticed the poached eggs slide away from each other in response.

"Five, one," he mumbled.

Helen came to his side, concerned. "What's going on?"

Rabbit tore open the laptop sitting on the two-person table by the kitchen window, hunching over the machine as it sprang to life.

"Hey, clue me in," she said.

"Five, one," he repeated. He opened up the spreadsheet they had populated with the geocodes from Eshek's journal and typed in a quick field calculation. "Antipas wasn't referring to the first and fifth clues. It's a proportional ratio. Five-to-one."

He loaded the results into the geocoding software they were using and a bunch of pin icons appeared on the map of Israel. "These are the locations Eshek identified in his journal before he spoke to Antipas. But if you change the scale to one-fifth the distance between the markers, it looks like this." The pins all relocated themselves into a much tighter pattern around Qumran.

Helen stared at the screen, mouth open. "Most of these locations are just scattered around the desert."

"Which might explain why we haven't seen Eshek. We're looking in the wrong places. Think how much easier it would have been to bury this stuff out in the desert. And why no one's found it."

"Yeah," she said, "but look at that one. It's right in the middle of the Jordan."

"Now, sure. But rivers change course all the time."

She grunted in a very Rabbit-ish way. Pointed at the screen. "Why is that one in the middle of Highway 1? That's the same road we took between Qumran and Jerusalem."

"It's . . . well, maybe Eshek got that one wrong."

"That one's in the Dead Sea."

Rabbit felt his excitement melting away. "Yeah."

"You want to try something?"

"Sure."

"Scoot over." She slid into the seat beside him and pulled the laptop in front of her. "Antipas said, 'Not Achor. Antonia,' right?"

"Yes, but that doesn't—"

She shifted back to the spreadsheet. "The first location is the fortress in the Vale of Achor, right?"

"Yeah."

"So, what if we just shifted the whole map over, making the Antonia Fortress the first location instead of the Vale of Achor."

"Save that before . . ." He reached across her for the keyboard, but she slapped his hand.

"I duplicated the tab. So, if we adjust the starting point, keep everything else in the same relative locations at a scale of five-to-one . . ." She plugged the data into the mapping software.

"Huh," Rabbit said, staring at the screen.

"Yeah. Huh."

The pins were now tightly clustered around Jerusalem. The farthest locations were in the hills surrounding the old city.

They spent the next few hours painstakingly comparing the treasure locations with the sites of current archaeological or industrial digs. Once that was exhausted, they compared the locations against the layout of the city, looking for any spots that might be promising. Morning light was spilling through the window when they scrolled the close-up of the map for the fiftieth time and Rabbit sat up straight.

"That one."

"That? It's just the old Damascus Gate. No way are they digging there."

"They don't need to. Herod did it for them."

She looked from him to the map and back again.

"Zedekiah's Cave is right there under the city. An old stone mine. It's where Herod got a lot of the blocks for his building projects. For a while it was called King Solomon's Quarries. The thing is sprawling. Acres of underground caves. What's the cache that's supposed to be there?"

"According to this, sixty-five bars of gold."

"Yeah, I think that's it."

"Why?"

"Remember I told you about meeting Nazarian? He said, 'The cave was empty,' or something like that. What if something is about to happen in that cave that causes him to go back to 68?"

"Are the mines open to the public?"

"They use it as a concert venue."

"You're shitting me."

"Here," he said, turning the computer so she could see it clearly. "Somebody named Nitai Odah is playing there tonight."

"Whoa, really?" Her expression was starstruck.

"You know who this is?"

"Uh, yeah, he came in ninth in Eurovision this year." *Obviously,* her tone implied.

Rabbit stared at her.

"A lot of people thought he should have done better."

Rabbit continued to stare at her.

"So, are we getting scalped tickets, or what?"

"People really pay this kind of money to see a concert these days?" Rabbit asked as they stood in line that night. They had managed to score two tickets for the standing-room-only at the Cave for what Rabbit considered an extortionate price.

She leaned over, kissed him on the cheek, and rested her chin on his shoulder. "You're a time traveler and that is officially the oldest thing I've ever heard you say. It's kinda geriatrically sexy."

"Like that? You're going to love my opinions on social media."

"Not in public, handsome!"

She glanced around at the crowd, excited. The musician's fan base was clearly younger than the two of them. Well, Helen could pass, but he felt every bit as old as she accused him of being.

After waiting around for an hour or so, the crowd began to slowly shuffle forward beside the ancient stone wall toward the mouth of the cave system, funneling toward a gated entrance no bigger than a double fire door at its base. A couple of hard-looking soldiers scanned everyone entering the space for weapons while an eager dog just inside the entrance panted and sniffed the passing fans, presumably for explosives.

The narrow path leading down into the cavern was lit with blue and pink floor lamps that threw elongated shadows of the crowd onto the ceiling. Rabbit wasn't a big fan of crowds. Packing them into an underground tunnel didn't help the irritation that crawled over his skin. It eased somewhat when the cave yawned open around them and he could see the geometric divots in the ceiling where great slabs of limestone had been removed for the construction of the ancient city. Helen's mood was as ebullient as ever. She bobbed in time to the recorded music thudding through the caves.

At every branching tunnel of the cave, soldiers stood by to steer the crowd down the right path. Unlike American security, which tended to rely on the intimidation factor of individual mass, the Israeli security detachment was made mostly of wiry young people. The submachine guns they held at the ready were a more serious deterrent, anyway.

Freemasons Hall opened up before them like a band shell, a stone dome overhead that rose and spread toward the crowd. At the far wall, an elevated stage groaned under the weight of speaker towers and banks of lights flashing and spinning, transforming the two-thousand-year-old mine into a rave. No one had taken the stage yet, but the crowd was already dancing like there was no tomorrow.

Helen tugged on Rabbit's sleeve. Her mouth moved, but he couldn't hear a word. He pointed at his ear and shook his head.

She pulled him close and shouted, "How's he going to get it out of here?"

He shouted back, "I don't know, but it's probably not pleasant. Come on, let's try to get free of the crowd."

As if he'd cued it, the lights went black and a single, dramatic note droned through the space. Her hand tightened on his.

The light sprang back to life, all focused on the stage where a young man, presumably Nitai Odah, stood with mic in hand, looking down at his feet. The crowd went bananas. Odah slowly raised his head and lifted the mic to his lips. Slowly, everyone went quiet and he began to sing.

> Come on in, the water's fine
> Come on in, on in, on in.

The music was surprisingly simple, just a regular bouncing rhythm Rabbit associated with Klezmer. It was also very, very loud. Rabbit could feel the bass in his chest.

He gestured to Helen, who looked disappointed but followed him through the crowd.

They wove through the tightly packed mass undulating to Nitai's happy, deafening tune while eyeing the security stationed at the offshoots from the main cavern. They had studied the map that day and had a good sense of the shape the caves took, but it hadn't prepared Rabbit for the reality of the scene. The volume, the flashing lights, the hordes of young people packing Freemasons Hall made it difficult to orient oneself.

Soldiers guarding the many offshoot passages from the big cave appeared to be just as interested in the music as the audience. Rabbit could see them craning for a view of the stage in between clench-jawed scans of the crowd.

It might have been possible to slip past them, but that was risky. In Rabbit's experience, it was safer to draw and release the attention in situations like this. They approached a young-looking soldier at one of the side tributaries. Once his attention was on them, he was all business. But Rabbit got just close enough to be heard and shouted in English, "Bathroom?"

The young man pointed back toward the exit. "You must exit the cave. They won't let you back in."

Rabbit gave him a thumbs-up. "Thank you!"

Four steps toward the exit and they doubled back, seeing the young man's attention was diverted to the crowd in front of him. Draw and release. Rabbit and Helen walked right past him into the darkened cave offshoot.

After the first bend, the strobing lights from Freemasons Hall did little to penetrate the darkness of the cave. If anything, the contrast made the deeper parts of the natural cavities expanded by human industry darker.

While the light didn't penetrate the deeper caves, the sound certainly did. Rabbit had once heard it said that sound traveled more like water than light. It flowed through any opening, pounded through solid surfaces by converting them into resonating accomplices. That's what made soundproofing a room damn near impossible. It was unnerving to have one's vision starved of input after so much stimulation, while the assault to the ears went unabated.

> Move your feet and clear your senses
> Drop those insecure defenses
> Come in, come in.

Helen's phone flashlight popped on, casting a weak cone of white that illuminated a few feet of rocky path ahead but fell short of the ceiling.

The cavern twisted and turned, giving up its secrets begrudgingly and with little warning. Rabbit wasn't sure exactly what he was looking for. Signs of digging, maybe? He certainly wasn't prepared for it when the cave floor descended steeply into a black pool of water in which Einar Eshek was standing knee-deep.

He looked up at them, his round eyes reflecting the flashlight glare like a wolf.

No. Not his eyes. He was wearing something on his head, working in complete darkness. Night vision. He was wearing night vision goggles. Eshek threw up his hand to shield himself from the sudden glare.

"Keep the light on him," Rabbit shouted.

Helen shouted something back, but he didn't hear it. Rabbit had already launched himself at the pool.

Eshek's right hand slipped into his rubber coveralls.

Rabbit reached the pool's edge, and his boots hit the slippery surface and skidded. To keep from falling on his ass, he softened his knees, dropped into a squat, and slid into the pool.

The fall saved Rabbit's life. Eshek whipped out a pistol. The muzzle flashed, but Rabbit couldn't hear the gun over the sound of the pounding music.

Put it down to breathing lessons
Open up, class is in session.

Rabbit thought of Helen in Constantinople, dying from a gunshot wound. So much like this.

Not again.

He slid into Eshek's legs. Took them out from under him. Eshek went down over Rabbit's shoulder.

There was a hole at the bottom of the pool. Rabbit dropped into it, feeling the lurch in his belly as he splashed to hip depth. His fingers finding purchase on Eshek's slippery coveralls.

Try those fancy kicks in here, you sonofabitch.

Something hard hit him on the shoulder. Too hard for a hand. The gun butt.

The light caught a flash of Eshek flailing with his other hand for his night vision goggles. He was blind. Good.

Rabbit had spent much of his adult life practicing grappling skills. He didn't need to see anything to know where every part of Eshek was in relation to himself.

The butt landed again, and his left arm went numb.

With his right, Rabbit grabbed Eshek by the testicles and gave them a squeeze. He felt Eshek's body convulse with pain and shock. Rabbit got his feet under him, planted them, and shot upward. The back of his skull collided with something hard. He hoped it was a face.

They both stumbled through the water, tangled up together, and fell in the shallower part of the water.

There was no light in the cave anymore.

Rabbit found Eshek's neck.

> You check my mask, I'll check your purchase
> Laughing underneath the surface
> Careful, now, this idol burns
> And once you buy, there's no returns.

He slipped his arm around Eshek's throat, closed his forearm, and flexed his biceps, squeezing shut the man's carotid artery.

Eshek's hand found Rabbit's face, his fingers digging for his eyes. He might destroy one of them before the choke rendered the man unconscious. Rabbit thought that was a fair trade.

Then something occurred to him.

What happens if you win?

Say you render him unconscious. You and Helen take him back to Olympia's boss. Eshek is subjected to the same cruelty he inflicts upon others until he confirms the locations of the treasures. And then he is killed.

Eshek dies.

And in Rabbit's 2019, Eshek is no longer available for Rabbit to find.

Without the help that Eshek might offer, Helen goes to prison.

Help Helen now or help her later.

You can't do both.

Eshek's fingernails were digging at Rabbit's eyelid.

Rabbit released the choke.

Eshek slithered free and instantly lashed out with his elbow, catching Rabbit on the side of the head, ringing his bell.

A boot came down on his midsection.

A light flashed again.

Eshek stood over him holding a flashing gold brick in his hand, raised overhead.

A muzzle flash from the edge of the cave.

Splashing, and Eshek was gone.

Broke my heart in Tel Aviv
Call her up before you leave.

Helen at his side, shouting near his head. "Are you okay?"

Coughing on mineral-heavy water. He shouted back, "I'm fine. I'm okay. I lost him."

"It's okay. Later. We'll get him later."

"He might still be armed. We ought to get out of here," Rabbit said.

They managed to slip out along with the rest of the crowd as the concert ended. If the soldiers manning the cave noticed the two drenched fans, they didn't say anything.

Helen's phone was nonfunctional from the water, and they weren't able to report in to Olympia for hours after they escaped Zedekiah's Cave.

Helen paced around the apartment taking in whatever Olympia was dishing out, saying nothing, then finally hung up.

She sat on the edge of the bed where Rabbit was still lying.

"The police found a tunnel from the cave to a storm sewer line. They think someone was digging it with a jackhammer during concerts to cover the noise of the tools. Of course, they don't know who was digging. Or why."

"The police might not, but the Israeli Historical Authority figures it out. They're about to send Yeshua Nazarian to 68."

Helen nodded.

"What about the gold?" Rabbit asked.

"Gone."

"Did you fire a gun in the cave?"

She nodded again. "Eshek's. I picked it up after he dropped it. How's your eye?"

"Hurts," he said, "but I can see. Why, does it look bad?"

He got up on one elbow and looked at his reflection in the bathroom mirror across the room. *Bad* was an understatement. The skin around the eye was bruised purple and channeled with welts. The white of the eye was deep red with bruising.

Helen was staring at the floor, lost in her own thoughts.

"I'm sorry," he said.

"We did our best," she said. Somehow, her forgiveness made his guilt worse.

"We'll try again," he said.

She shook her head. "It's over. Olympia's boss said he's done. Eshek might turn up later, but I'm not to waste any more time on him."

"What are you going to do?"

She took a deep breath, let it go.

"They have another job for me."

She seemed so small. So lost. "You don't have to—"

"Yes, I do," she said. "I do have to. I shouldn't ask this. It's not fair. But do you think you and I . . ."

She let it trail off. Rabbit had never seen her like this. Hurting like this. He didn't know what to say. How could he promise anything to her? He wasn't even supposed to be here. He couldn't stay. And he couldn't tell her.

"Don't worry about you and me," he said, hating himself for it. He took her hand. "We'll figure it out."

At noon he stood before Olympia. He had managed to lie away his absence from Helen and seek out her sister for a one-on-one. She was sitting in the crappy little office in the industrial park, Rabbit standing before her like a penitent.

"I need you to send me back."

Her eyebrows shot up above her glasses. "I know this is an obvious question, but why should I?"

"I'm not from this timeline."

She looked confused.

"I mean, I am, but for me this is history. I'm from 2019. When your sister brought me back, she assumed we were contemporaries. We're not."

"I can't send you to the future."

"I know. I want you to send me back to 68. I'm hoping I can catch my own decay point back to 2019."

Olympia, putting the pieces together, smiled. She leaned back in the metal folding chair like it was a throne and sipped her latte.

"Same question. Why should I?"

"Because the version of me that was supposed to be here returns in a few hours and I don't know what happens if he does and I'm still here."

"You might die?"

"I might."

She pondered that for a long moment, then said something that took him by surprise. "Love is pain."

Rabbit knitted his brow in confusion.

Olympia went on. "Helen never understood that because she never truly loved the way I do. Love strips away your armor, makes you vulnerable." She tightened her lips. "Love always lets you down. So, maybe I should do nothing with you. Let time take its course. She'd get over you eventually, but it would hurt her." She lapsed into silence, relishing the idea.

He couldn't believe what he was about to say. For a moment, he contemplated walking out of the room, letting time take its course as she suggested. Yes, it would hurt if he died, but Helen was resilient, and they hadn't truly known each other that long. She'd recover. What he proposed instead was worse.

"Send me back."

That drew Olympia out of her reverie.

"Helen won't understand. She'll feel betrayed. She might even seek me out in present day but I won't know her face because this version of me hasn't met her yet. I'll treat her like a crazy stranger, and I won't even remember it. Maybe she'll figure it out, maybe she won't. But for years she will wonder what she did wrong, how I could leave her when she needed me most. She'll hate me, and one day you can use that hate, turn her against me. Kill me today and she'll be sad. Save me and she will truly suffer."

Olympia took that in quietly. Let it sit in her mind a moment.

"You must really think I'm some kind of monster." She sounded shocked and offended.

Rabbit said nothing.

"I'm not a monster. And I'm not a murderer. I only want what's best for my sister."

She nodded earnestly.

"I'll send you back."

How she had the fuel source ready, Rabbit didn't ask. But within the hour, they had driven the portable time machine away from the industrial park into the desert.

Rabbit stood on the dilator pad. He was dressed again in his historically appropriate clothing, although Olympia had conspicuously withheld his knife.

The technicians never said a word to him. Never asked why they were sending this strange man back in time again. They didn't speak to Olympia either, for that matter. Fun place to work.

Olympia studied Rabbit as he arranged himself on the dilator pad.

He could have stayed silent, too. He didn't owe her anything. He couldn't, though.

"You're wrong, you know," Rabbit said. "About your sister. She has been in love before."

Olympia's face screwed up. Her lips formed a ring to say the word *who*, but Rabbit never heard it.

He was standing on the sandy floor of a desert valley in 68 CE.

"She loves you, idiot."

The following morning, Rabbit ventured close enough to the city to ask an olive farmer the date. Olympia had nailed it. He only had a day left before his own return point decayed. His location marker was securely in place. Everything had gone to plan.

Some plan.

He was sick about what he'd done to Helen. He kept playing out scenes of her finding out he had abandoned her. He racked his brain, trying to remember if she had ever approached him before he met her in Alexandria. If he'd been a jerk. He probably had been.

As the hours ticked down, however, he shifted his thoughts. If there was a time to make it up to her, this was it.

He was about to return to 2019. He knew Einar Eshek / Leroy Bonneau better than he would have liked to. So, the question remained, *why did she send you after him in the first place?*

Helen had been accused of being a client of Alexi Misherenko's illegal time travel ring, which was obvious bullshit. She had all the access to time travel she could ever want. Which meant someone was framing her. Misherenko? Maybe, but Rabbit doubted it. Misherenko seemed like a front. Helen sent Rabbit after Eshek for a reason. He had taken sixty-five bars of gold from Jerusalem under the nose of her powerful employer. Sure, he could have just wanted to be rich, but that didn't connect the dots.

And then, sitting under the shade of the tree in his decay point, it all clicked.

JERUSALEM, ISRAEL

2019 CE

The crew in the time machine went silent.

PJ spun around, still holding Rabbit's duffel bag in her hand, mouth agape. The two junior techs were staring at their boss in horror. Ian waved his hands in the air with terribly mimed surprise. His improv skills may have been lacking, but he had come through for Rabbit. Only a few seconds had passed since they had sent him through.

Then the moment of stunned silence exploded into chaos, and everyone seemed to be shouting at everyone else.

"PJ, Ian!" Rabbit boomed. His voice rebounded around the little metal room, silencing everyone. "I need to talk to you. Now."

"Don't worry about the Energy Authority," Rabbit said. "I've got something to offer them that will more than compensate for a thirty-second brownout."

Claire and Trey had been released from the explosive, leaving Rabbit alone with PJ and Ian in the dilator. Rabbit was leaning on the control console while PJ stood beside Ian's seat on the other side of it, glaring ice daggers at him.

PJ pulled a disdainful face. "Oh really, what exactly do you—"

"The Copper Scroll treasure. Well, sans a cache or two."

She blinked.

"Anyway, that's not important right now."

"Not important?" she said, flabbergasted.

"Would you just . . ." Rabbit calmed his tone. "I have some things to tell you, and I need you to listen."

She planted her fists firmly on her hips. "Oh, now you have something to say?"

"Shut up! I'm trying to apologize."

She looked like he'd slapped her. Ian stared at PJ with eyes like saucers. Rabbit doubted anyone had ever spoken to her like that in her life.

He sighed. "I'm sorry. I've been a shitty friend to you both. I've been lying to you because, well, I guess the smaller reason is that I didn't trust you to be able to handle the truth."

"*A Few Good Men*," Ian whispered. Rabbit and PJ ignored him.

"During the menorah job, I struck up a . . . let's just say a friendship with the stringer who robbed us in Alexandria. We worked together to get out of there alive and we've been working together since then. We partnered up on the last few jobs. Since Constantinople, she never went after my scores, and I never went after hers."

"You could be arrested for that," PJ said quietly.

"I know that. That's another reason I haven't told you. If I had, I'd have made accomplices of you both. But the biggest reason is I didn't want you to talk me out of it. I knew you'd try."

"More than try; I would have—"

"PJ," Rabbit said firmly, holding up his hand to silence her. "Let me finish, then we can talk about what comes next, all right?"

She scowled but stayed silent.

"When the stringer didn't show up for the Claudian scrolls job, I knew something was wrong. And then I found out she was one of the suspects in the Misherenko time travel ring."

PJ's eyes widened, but Rabbit held up a preemptive hand again.

"The Italian police had a photograph of her in their lineup. And no, I didn't admit to knowing her. It's a bullshit charge. There's no way she would be involved."

"How do you know that?" Ian asked.

"I'll get to that. Anyway, when I started digging through my text messages built up during the trip, I found one from her asking me to find a man named Einar Eshek in 68 CE Qumran."

PJ couldn't resist. "I knew it! You made up a reason to get there! There was no Book of Esther, was there!"

"I mean, sure, I made it up, but I still got the Book. I'll give you the coordinates when we're done." He continued. "Helen made it clear she needed me to find this guy ASAP. So, I made Ian promise to bring me back immediately after the jump."

PJ glared at Ian, who couldn't meet her gaze.

"Well, did you find him?" Ian asked, trying to shift the subject.

"I found him. Turns out I had already met him. He was the murderer I ran into in 64, on the Claudian scrolls job. By the time I caught up with him in 68, he had killed at least six more people and tried to make me the seventh a few times. He was the chrono-archaeologist for the stringer organization before . . . my friend joined it. They sent him back to uncover the Copper Scroll treasures. But when he returned, he disappeared and made off with at least one of the major treasure caches. She and I figured out how he did it and almost had him in 2015."

"What?" PJ's confusion overrode her anger.

"Oh, yeah. For a few weeks, I went back to 2015 with Helen. We were in Jerusalem and for a while in America, trying to catch the sonofabitch."

PJ's eyes widened. "Do you remember?"

Ian nodded and explained to Rabbit, "That 2015 trip PJ swore she saw you in the Old City while you were supposed to be in the past. I told her she must have imagined it. We argued about it for days."

"And I was right!"

"And you were right," Ian conceded, dryly. "Continue, please."

"We dug up a lot of information about Eshek. His real name is Leroy Bonneau. He's ex–Special Forces, present psychopath. When

I first encountered him, I thought he might be a client of Misherenko's, remember? A serial killer who had figured out a way to murder people legally. Well, I was in the ballpark, but I missed the main points. One, he didn't just kill people to get his rocks off, although I'm sure that's part of it. He tortured people to get information about the Copper Scroll. Two, he's not Misherenko's client. Misherenko is his."

"I don't understand," said PJ.

"Eshek took sixty-five bars of gold from Zedekiah's Cave in 2015. For all I know, he may have gotten more of the treasures, too. I'm convinced he used it to buy himself a time machine and was running the illegal ring. Misherenko might have been his majordomo, or he might have just been a client. Either way, I'm confident that he scared Misherenko into claiming the top spot. If the Russian knows him at all, he'd be plenty scared of him."

"What does your stringer 'friend' have to do with it?" PJ asked.

"I suspect Misherenko was instructed to implicate both real clients and people Eshek wanted to get rid of. Helen and her organization were competition for Eshek and he might have had an ax to grind with her dating back to 2015 when we pursued him."

"I asked you this morning," Ian began. "Well, a few months ago for you. Do you have feelings for this woman?"

Rabbit paused for a moment. He hadn't even said it to Helen yet. "I'm in love with her."

Ian made what could only be described as an "aww" face. PJ frowned.

"What if she's using you?" PJ demanded.

"She might be. The way I left things, she'd have every right to. But I don't believe it."

PJ was silent, thinking.

Rabbit continued. "I'm sorry for putting you both through this. I should have trusted you enough to tell you the truth before. And now I'm asking for your help because I can't do this by myself."

"Can't do what?" Ian asked.

"Catch Einar Eshek."

As Rabbit had promised, the Israeli government graciously forgave the team for the incident with the electrical grid after Rabbit offered them the key to the Copper Scroll treasures. But it still left him wondering how to pin down Eshek.

"How do you catch a man who can go anywhere, any time?" he said to PJ and Ian over a drink that night at a chic little watering hole in Tel Aviv. "I thought I might intercept him at one of the Jerusalem digs. But now that the government is onto the locations, they'll protect the hell out of them. One whiff of that kind of military backing and Eshek will drift into the wind."

"Well, he can't really, can he? Go anywhere?" Ian asked.

"Why not? He still has a dilator."

"Oh sure, but with all the pressure over this Misherenko fuckery, no one is going to sell him a power source to use it. He's stuck here."

"Unless he still has power," PJ said. They both looked at her. "That actor who was implicated."

"Ethan Davies?" Rabbit said.

She nodded. "He was the one who rolled over on Misherenko. Or Eshek, I guess. He went to the police before he made the jump, not after. Apparently, he grew a conscience at the eleventh hour."

"So, if Davies never made his jump, then Eshek still has at least one portable power source."

She nodded.

They all sipped their drinks in unison.

Ian broke the silence. "If you could go back in time one last time, where would you go?" he asked his companions.

PJ exhaled slowly. "That's easy. I'd get Savanah diagnosed earlier. It was too late by the time the doctors caught the cancer." Savanah was PJ's eldest daughter, who had died over a decade ago.

"You?" Ian asked Rabbit.

"Qumran. 68 CE." Rabbit smiled to himself. "What about you?"

Ian thought about that for a moment. "I guess I'd go tell my sweet little fifteen-year-old self it was gonna be okay. That all that worrying I was doing about being who I am was just wasting fear on people who didn't deserve it." Rabbit and PJ toasted him as Ian took a long swig. "So, where would Einar Eshek go?"

Slowly, Rabbit smiled.

HUNTSVILLE, ALABAMA, USA

1994 CE

There was no way to get the clearances they needed. The specifics of the mission compounded the illegality of the whole operation, and they all knew it. Ian hadn't been that hard to convince. PJ had fought him for days, but Rabbit wore her down eventually.

"The risk is all on me. If it comes to it, you both deny you knew anything about it."

"I wouldn't trust that woman with your loose change let alone your life." They were talking, of course, about Olympia.

"I feel like we were just here," Helen's sister said, smiling.

She had met him in a park downtown close to the café where Helen and Rabbit had interviewed Bonneau's old warden. She was dressed beautifully as always.

"New glasses?" he asked.

She adjusted them, a little self-consciously.

"Look, we could debate this, but what's the point? I want Eshek and so do you. His testimony is the only sure bet of keeping Helen out of prison where she could say who knows what. And something tells me your boss wouldn't mind Eshek being behind bars where he can reach out and touch him any time he wants. So, can we skip the part where you pretend you hold all the cards and I'm here begging for aid and just accept the fact that, this time, our interests align?"

"Even if I agreed with you, what makes you think I have the power core to run this mission?"

"Because if you didn't, you wouldn't have met me here."

She huffed.

"I'll have to check with—"

Rabbit shook his head. "Your boss already approved this before you came. But, before you drop the stalling and agree, there is something else."

"I'm all ears."

"My team is running the jump."

Which is how, forty-eight hours later, Rabbit, PJ, Ian, Olympia, and two of her technicians found themselves in a portable time machine in the middle of the Alabama countryside.

It felt surreal to be standing on a dilator pad wearing modern street clothing. The gun in his belt holster felt even stranger.

"I hate guns," Rabbit had protested.

"I don't care," PJ had insisted. "If this man is half as dangerous as you say, you need to be prepared." The gun was hers, a compact .38 pocket pistol with a curved polymer grip that felt too small for Rabbit's palm.

Ian was in the zone, talking through the jump process as if it were Trey and Claire beside him instead of two strangers. They had left the other two Smithsonian techs out of this. No reason to ruin their careers, too, if everything went sideways.

Olympia and PJ ignored each other coldly.

"Good hunting," PJ said to him. Rabbit's heart swelled at the old familiar phrase.

He nodded once and disappeared.

Rabbit was standing on the same rock ledge where the team had parked the truck. The same waterfall bubbled down the rocks. But here, in

1994, he would have sworn the trees seemed deeper green, the area more remote.

He marked his decay point and set off at a watchful jog.

It had taken him some digging to find the old property lines of Leroy's home. His mother had moved in with her boyfriend Rand Boyce a few years before Leroy took both their lives. Boyce had a big piece of land, over fifty acres, that had been left to him by his family. Most of it was woodland. Boyce was a big hunter; Rabbit had found a picture of him kneeling next to the glassy-eyed corpse of a twelve-point buck that had made the local paper.

Happily, it wasn't deer season.

As Rabbit approached the center of the property, he slowed his pace. When the clearing came into sight, he parked himself on high ground and waited for nightfall.

The long double track driveway that wound its way to the center of the property from the county road ended at a sad patch of earth. The modest, two-story farmhouse had been amateurishly re-sided with cheap vinyl, faded and curled at the edges. The asphalt shingle roof was missing more than a few pieces, and Rabbit swore he could smell the mold in the attic from his perch on the hill.

There was a clear patch in front of the house, presumably for Boyce's rig, and a loop for circling it back to the driveway. A garden fence tilted drunkenly against the trunks of scrub trees, enclosing a thicket of the same weeds that choked the rest of the yard. Near the edge of the clearing, where the baby trees merged into the towering oaks and sycamores, the front half of a faded yellow school bus poked up from a mass of kudzu vines like a giant insect emerging from its burrow.

And scattered throughout the yard, nearly everywhere he looked, were oversized representations of flowers. Faded paintings on plywood cutouts festooned the bus. Flowers hammered out of tin cans and stop signs were nailed to the trees and leaned against the house. He wondered if there was a time when they added cheer to this dismal place. When Rabbit looked at the spread petals, all he could see were the open body cavities of Eshek's victims.

Darkness settled. A light flicked on inside the house, but Rabbit didn't approach. Not yet.

An hour later, a rumbling engine slowly approached through the woods and two headlights swept into the yard at the head of Rand Boyce's rig. It stopped in front of the house and the diesel engine coughed to silence with what sounded like an emphysemic death rattle. The darkened figure of the driver got out, withdrew a duffel bag, and walked into the house.

Slowly and quietly, Rabbit crept down the hill.

The windows at the back of the house were open. The sounds of movement floated up the ridge through screens that were more hole than mesh. The Boyce manse smelled of mildew, convenience-store canned stew, and excrement.

Rabbit slid into a patch of thick underbrush and looked through the kitchen window. Dirty dishes precariously stacked up in the sink. A Formica kitchen table. Beyond that, the back of a decrepit brown recliner aimed at a tube television the size of a taxi.

The living room wall bristled with mounted deer antlers.

Boyce tossed his duffel bag and a greasy trucker cap on the kitchen table. He was medium height and solidly built with thinning brown hair shaved close to the scalp and a beard-stubbled face that looked like it had never been creased with a smile.

He unzipped his duffel.

"Get your fat ass up, Mona!" he barked.

Almost instantly, a woman stumbled into the kitchen wearing nothing but a long T-shirt. She wasn't fat. In fact, she looked too thin to be healthy. Her blond hair was in disarray. She tried to pat it into place.

"Hey, baby." She awkwardly lunged to kiss him, but he dodged her without even making eye contact. "You're home early."

"Is that why it stinks so bad in here? Is that why you ain't cleaned the kitchen since I left? 'Cause I'm home early?" He spoke in soft tones that promised violence.

She was trembling.

"I'll do it now, baby, I'll get all cleaned up and you and I can party a little bit, okay?"

She clung to his arm as he dug through his duffel. With a casual swipe, he backhanded her across the cheek and she stumbled, covering her face.

"It stinks like the fucking monkey house at the zoo in here. You let the boy shit hisself again, Mona. What did I tell you about that?"

She immediately spun toward the living room and hissed, "Bad boy! I don't know what I'm gonna do with him, baby. He's a bad boy!" She lunged her face toward the object of her vitriol like an animal threatening to bite.

Boyce pulled a big candy bar out of his bag.

"Who wants a treat, boy? You want a treat?" He waved the candy bar in the air by the edge of the wrapper. He opened the front door, took a step outside, and threw the candy. It sailed out into the night.

Boyce went just out of sight beyond the recliner. There was the clatter of metal. "Well, go on, git it!"

A skinny blond boy, hunched over and wearing nothing but a drooping pair of soiled tighty-whities, ran out the front door.

Boyce returned to the kitchen.

"Do you have a treat for Mama, too, baby?"

"I don't know you've done anything to deserve it."

She sidled up to him, stroking herself in a grotesque parody of sexuality. "I know what Daddy needs to feel welcomed home. You just leave it to Mama."

She began to kneel in front of him, but he grabbed her by the elbow, spun her roughly around, and bent her over the Formica tabletop.

Rabbit closed his eyes, feeling unclean. He wished he could close his ears. A few moments of grunting and violent thumping and it was over.

Breathing heavily, Boyce said, "Here."

Rabbit opened his eyes in time to see her catch a small, wadded baggie filled with tan powder.

She tore into it, dipped a finger into the bag, and tasted it with far more erotic energy than she had mimed for the trucker. "Thank you, Daddy."

Mona disappeared into another room while Boyce fished around in his bag. Finally, he kicked off his boots and followed her back to the bedroom.

After a few moments, the house settled into quiet.

Where the hell are you, Eshek? Tonight's the night. I know you're coming.

After some time, the front door opened, and young Leroy reentered the house. He had found the candy bar; there was chocolate melted around his mouth.

He started back toward what Rabbit had to imagine was the dog kennel in which he slept, but then paused. Eyes on the back bedroom, he fearfully inched toward Boyce's duffel. The boy was so skinny, it was hard to see the resemblance to the Special Forces soldier he would become. But the bright blue eyes were unmistakable. Rabbit wondered if he had dyed his hair to fit in in Jerusalem or if his blond locks had darkened with age.

Leroy leaned over the bag, sniffing.

Eyes darting between the bag and the bedroom, he reached a bony hand into the open canvas and pulled out a sheathed hunting knife. He turned it over and over in his hands for a moment, then unsnapped the safety strap. He flinched at the noise, but no one stirred.

Reverently, fearfully, the boy slid the hunting knife from the sheath.

Then he turned his eyes toward the bedroom.

A quiet "tsk" made the boy jump. He covered his mouth with his hand to stifle the little whimper that escaped him.

Einar Eshek silently stepped into the kitchen from a darkened corner, maybe the stairs leading to the second floor. He was wearing black fatigue pants and a tight black T-shirt. A gun was holstered at his hip, but he made no move for it.

"Hi, Leroy. Your name's Leroy, isn't it?" He spoke quietly and kindly.

The young boy Leroy stared back at him, pointing the knife at the newcomer.

Eshek held his hands palms-up to indicate he meant no harm. "That sure is a shiny knife, Leroy. You could do all kinds of things with a knife like that, couldn't you?"

The boy just stared.

"Why, you could whittle a pretty flower with a knife like that. Or carve your name in an old dead tree. I know you'd never cut a live tree, because you wouldn't want to hurt it, would you? But you know your name, and you know your letters. I know you do."

He took a step closer and squatted low to put his head below the level of the boy's.

"What do you think about going back to school? Remember school? Remember Miss Addison, she was so clean and nice, wasn't she?"

The boy nodded.

"Here's the thing, Leroy. I know you love your mama, but she's real sick. And you can't help her. I know you wish you could. You were thinking maybe you could scare Rand real bad with that shiny knife and make him go away, weren't you?"

The boy nodded again.

"I know. You just want to help. But I tell you what. You know where the driveway meets the paved road, way out through the woods? Well, there's a car waiting out there. A blue car. Blue's your favorite color, isn't it? What do you say you walk out to that blue car and wait for me a spell?"

Leroy shrunk back in terror and shook his head.

"It's okay. Rand Boyce don't scare me. I'll talk to him and your mama and get them to understand how you're not going to live with them anymore. You're going to a new place, with a bed, and food and things to learn, where the people are nice. And maybe one day your mama will get better, and she can join you there. What do you say to that? Pretty good?"

Hesitantly, the boy nodded.

"Okay, then. Why don't you head on down to that blue car and I'll have a talk with the folks here? I'll meet you down there before you know it. It's all right. Everybody's going to be just fine. Do you want to leave that knife here on the table? I won't tell anybody you touched it. It'll be our secret. You didn't do no harm."

The boy set the knife down on the Formica, hovered on the edge of decision, then ran through the front door into the night.

Eshek took a deep breath and held it. Shakily exhaled.

"Good boy," he whispered, almost imperceptibly.

He checked his watch, waited a little more. When he appeared satisfied with the time, he picked up the hunting knife and began to whistle softly.

He spun the knife in his hand and headed for the back bedroom.

Rabbit crept out of his hiding spot and made his way quietly around the house to the front door. He gripped the .38 in his shaking hand.

A wire mesh dog kennel sat next to the recliner, lined with soiled blankets. Rabbit's stomach rolled over at the oppressive smell of the place, the low, dark ceiling, the filth. He imagined Eshek's apartment, gleaming white and spotless.

". . . the fuck you think—" came from the bedroom. Followed by a blow, a sharp exhalation, and Mona's bleary cry.

Rabbit slowly crossed the room past the staircase door where Eshek had been hiding. There was a short hall off the kitchen lined with cracked tile leading back to the bedroom. The bedside table lamp was on and Eshek stood in the doorway, framed by the light.

Boyce was sitting on the bed where Eshek had apparently shoved him. Eshek's gun was still holstered on his hip.

"You best get the fuck outta my house before I—"

"Shh," said Eshek. "I've got some things to say to you and you're going to listen. You'll answer when I ask you questions, but you will otherwise be silent." His hand was on the butt of his pistol to emphasize his point. Good. Rabbit knew Eshek would be far superior to him with a gun and didn't want to give him an opportunity to draw it.

Rabbit leaned out of sight of the doorway, pressing his back against the strip of wall between the staircase and the bedroom hallway.

"Mama, you're going to do me a favor and take this"—something thumped on the bed—"and tie that around your boyfriend's wrists, all right?"

There was a sudden scuffle of quick movement inside. A sharp crack of flesh on flesh and the thump of a body hitting the floor.

"You always did take his side," Eshek said.

Mona's whimpers were her only reply.

"Nothing to say, Rand? Aren't you going to defend your woman? No? What a surprise. Grab that brass headboard with both hands." The metal click of a pistol hammer cocking. "Good. Now, this can go easy for you, but if you fight me, it's going to be a lot worse. You understand?"

There was a quiet but heavy clunk. Like the sound of a gun being set down on a dresser.

Rabbit took three breaths as he heard bedsprings creak, then he stepped around the corner, his .38 aimed in front of him.

Eshek had his boot on Rand's chest and was stretching out a wind from a spool of steel wire.

Boyce looked past Eshek at Rabbit, his mouth hanging open. Eshek followed his eyes.

"No," the killer said.

"I'm afraid so," Rabbit replied. Keeping his eyes trained on them, Rabbit took Eshek's gun from the dresser as well.

Mona cowered on the floor between the bed and the wall, blood trickling from her mouth.

"I've waited too long for this," Eshek said, his voice shaking. "I'll go back with you when I'm done. Promise."

He sounded oddly childlike in his offer. Rabbit shook his head. "You already did the important part. At least there's one timeline where Leroy can have some other kind of life. You gave that to him. What's another death to you?"

Eshek shook his head. "You don't understand." He looked desperate.

"He's afraid of you," Rabbit said. "See how he's shaking? He's afraid of *you* now. You won."

Eshek's face twisted. He shook his head and Rabbit could feel it. Despite his physical power and all his skill with violence, the boy Leroy was still in there, and he was still terrified of the man pinioned to the bed. Just like Eshek and others had been trapped inside Rabbit, Eshek had been carrying around Rand Boyce long after the man's death.

"Come on, Leroy. We have somewhere to be."

With a sudden burst of motion, Boyce snatched the wire from Eshek's hand and lashed out with his feet. There was a blur, a tumble, and the wire was around Eshek's throat. Boyce was behind him, his face purple with exertion and rage.

"Let him go!" shouted Rabbit, brandishing the gun.

A bead of blood formed around the wire. Eshek was reaching back to try to claw his way free, but it wasn't going to be enough. Rand would slit his throat before Eshek could stop him.

Rabbit pulled the trigger.

A deafening crack ricocheted around the room. Blood splashed the wall, and the two men flopped over.

Eshek jerked himself free of Boyce and shot to a crouch over him.

The bullet had entered just below the man's hairline and exited in a spray of gore that dripped down the brass headboard and the wall behind it.

Eshek bellowed, "Noooooo!" He grabbed Boyce's shirtfront and shook him, trying to will him back to life. "Wake up! Wake up, motherfucker!" Mona screamed and sobbed from the corner.

Eshek slammed his fist on Boyce's chest in a mockery of first aid, once, twice, panting. Then he rounded on Rabbit. His eyes were alight with a lifetime of impotent rage.

Rabbit backpedaled as Eshek sprang from the bed at him like an animal. The threat of the gun didn't deter him one bit.

"Leroy?" His mother's whimpering voice halted him.

Eshek stood in the doorway, coiled like a spring. Rabbit held both guns, terrified that he would have to kill the man to stop him.

"Leroy?" she said again.

The vibration in Eshek's body appeared to slow down. "That's right, Mama. It's Leroy."

Her eyes blurry with cocaine or heroin, whatever it was, she slowly stood, trembling. "My baby boy?"

"That's right, Mama." Rabbit could swear Eshek's accent had gotten thicker.

Mona took a step toward her son. Leroy cringed back from her touch, but she didn't let it stop her. She took another step forward, glancing at the corpse on the bed with apparent disinterest.

"What's happening, Leroy?"

"I don't know," he said, and his voice shook.

"Rand is hurt."

"Yeah, Mama."

Her face sank. "Oh, oh, oh, my baby. How sad you look."

"I ain't sad, Mama."

"Mama knows when her boy is sad. Come here."

She was clearly high as a kite, nearly insensible of her surroundings.

"You just need a little lovin'. Come here." She pulled at his T-shirt and eased him to her. "That's it." She wrapped her arms around him, and, to Rabbit's surprise, he leaned into her embrace. "Mama's sorry. I been real sick. You know? Mama's been real sick."

"I know, Mama."

She rubbed his back, her stubby fingernails red with chipped polish.

"You're gonna be all right, baby boy. In the morning, I'll make you pancakes. Rand will leave tomorrow for Texas, and I'll make you pancakes."

"Okay, Mama."

"It's just I'm so tired," she said.

"I know. You been sick. Why don't you lie down now?" He gently walked his mother over to the side of the bed and pulled back the coverlet. "You just lie down."

"With maple syrup," she murmured.

"I'd like that a lot," he said softly back, easing her under the cover next to the dead body of her boyfriend.

"That's my boy," she mumbled as she fell asleep.

Eshek smoothed the hair away from her forehead.

"Good night, Mama."

He softly walked to the door and flipped off the light switch.

"All right," he said to Rabbit. "We can go now."

Rabbit's hands trembled all the way back to the decay point. He was sure Eshek would make a break for it; the woods were dark, the trees thick. Rabbit would have no choice but to fire on him if he ran, and Eshek had to know he was needed alive.

The murderer was silent the entire walk. Rabbit was shaken by what he'd just witnessed; he could only imagine the impact it had on the grown-up Leroy.

When the killer did speak, Rabbit wished he would shut up again.

They were standing on the decay point, Rabbit pressing the guns against Eshek's back. His fingers shook on the triggers, so sure he was that Eshek would make one final move. But, true to Eshek, his final move was unexpected.

In a calm, almost friendly tone, he said, "It's easier than you think, isn't it? Killing a man, I mean."

ROME, ITALY

2019 CE

"Our top story. Another surprising turn in what many are calling 'the case for all time' today as a new suspect was arrested by police in Alabama. Huntsville native Leroy Bonneau, who was charged with killing his own mother over two decades ago in this same Southern town, was charged as the ringleader in an illegal time travel operation that spanned four continents. Charges against former suspect Alexi Misherenko have been reduced though not dropped.

"Police say Bonneau, who served in an elite American Special Forces unit for eight years, ran an unlicensed business charging some of the world's richest people over a million dollars a trip to destinations in world history. In addition to the charges of illegal time travel operation and trafficking radioactive material across international borders, Bonneau is also accused of murdering client Wu Bo Cheng, son of shipping magnate Wu Gang, who never returned from his ill-fated trip to China in 300 BC."

"BCE," Rabbit corrected, under his breath.

"Snob," Ian replied.

Rabbit shrugged. "Probably."

"Come on." Ian rose from his seat at the airport bar. "We board in ten minutes."

Eshek had been unsettlingly submissive from the moment the two had left his childhood home all the way until Rabbit turned him over to the police in Huntsville.

The desk sergeant in the Huntsville PD had stared for a moment when Rabbit had explained. "Good evening, Sergeant. I have made a citizen's arrest."

The thick-necked man with the silver crew cut looked amused at first.

"What's he done, exactly?"

"Mainly illegal time travel. But also murder."

The sergeant blinked as he tried to figure out if he was being jerked around. Unsure what to make of Rabbit's level tone, he looked at Eshek, who nodded in the affirmative.

"Well," the man concluded. "Okay, then."

Eshek was arrested on the spot. Rabbit was asked to give a statement as to Eshek's crimes and how he knew about them. It probably would have been smooth sailing, if a reporter hadn't been in the building interviewing a small-time con man for a story in the local paper. The reporter, improbably named Kestrel Keene, had taken Rabbit's picture, then bugged and/or bribed the desk sergeant to give up information on the specifics of Eshek's incarceration. By the time he was home in DC, Rabbit had become part of the story that skyrocketed him, Eshek/Bonneau, and Keene into the international spotlight.

Rabbit had already been the subject of furtive glances in the airport before the story played out on the multiple TVs mounted over the bar. He had repeatedly refused requests for interviews, hoping it would all go away, but that had only added fuel to the fire. Keene had made him out to be some sort of silent hero, the yin to Eshek's brutal yang. Footage of Rabbit was pulled from old Smithsonian press releases and trotted out whenever one of these stories ran. Sure enough, Rabbit's face splashed across the screen. He was wearing a jacket and tie, seen before the façade of the Natural History Museum, the heads of what appeared to be a significant crowd in the foreground. Rabbit remembered that dedication. There had been no more than a dozen people in attendance.

More faces swiveled toward him.

Rabbit dropped some cash on the bar and left with Ian in tow.

"I hate this," Rabbit growled to his friend as they flowed down the Reagan National concourse with the crowd. "I shot a man."

"I know."

"In the face."

"I know."

Having started the trend of truthfulness with his friends, Rabbit had decided to continue it. He had told them everything about the night he had captured Eshek, including his own violent role in what happened. PJ had demanded he see a therapist, had worn him down until she won the fight. To his surprise, it wasn't as bad as he'd feared. As the weeks went by leading up to Eshek's trial, he had engaged in twice-a-week sessions with a wiseass named Paul who challenged every trick in Rabbit's mental shed. It helped. Still, the hero narrative grated on him daily. His only solace was his confidence in the short attention spans of people. A week after Eshek was sentenced, Rabbit would sink happily into obscurity. He was sure of it.

PJ met them in Rome for the first of the trials in which Eshek was accused.

Eshek. Rabbit couldn't quite think of him any other way, although the press referred to him by his legal name.

"Have you heard from her, honey?" she asked as they met on the courthouse steps. PJ was still no Helen fan, but his boss had come to accept how much she meant to Rabbit.

He shook his head. "Not a word."

The trial was being held in Rome's Palace of Justice, a 1910 courthouse built on the Tiber near Hadrian's tomb. The building's sumptuous design led contemporary critics of its ostentation and corruption to call it "the Bad Palace."

Rabbit was called as a witness on the second day of the trial. He was questioned by the prosecuting attorney, but there was no cross-examination; Eshek had waived counsel and elected to represent himself. And what did he do on his own behalf?

Nothing. He asked not a single question, said nary a word except to answer direct questions from the judge.

This, of course, delighted the press. The unorthodox trial only added to the bizarre story that had enraptured the world.

The prosecuting attorney had asked questions of Rabbit in such a way to let him tell his story. The tortures. The murders. None of it admissible, since those crimes weren't relevant to the illegal time travel charges. But there was no one to object and the judge allowed it.

Rabbit wanted to confess how he had secured Eshek from Rand Boyce, but PJ and Ian had convinced him to stay mum on the shooting. It wasn't relevant and it would only incriminate Rabbit in public perception, if not in court.

Eshek noted the obvious omission and grinned at Rabbit, bright blue eyes sparkling. But he didn't say a word. The look in those eyes was worse.

In the second week of the trial, Eshek's clients were questioned, most notably Alexi Misherenko, who described purchasing three trips to the past from Eshek in exchange for providing the power sources needed to run the machine. He said he only claimed responsibility as the ringleader because he was terrified of the real mastermind. However, since he had gladly availed himself of the three journeys, it didn't play well to the jury.

The Russian wouldn't meet Eshek's eye during the entire proceedings.

One by one the other clients were questioned. Each had firsthand knowledge of Eshek and could pick him out in the courtroom. Their own days in court would come, but first they were witnesses in his trial. Rabbit was certain they were cooperating in hopes of lightening their own sentences.

Helen never appeared in court and was never mentioned in the proceedings.

Finally, Eshek himself took the stand.

He answered every question put to him without hesitation and pled guilty to sixteen counts of illegal time travel, transporting radioactive materials across international boundaries, and racketeering. The murder charge would be handled separately in Chinese court. Eshek uttered no complaints or justifications for his actions. When asked why he had carried out the crimes for which he was accused, he said simply, "We all have a few things we'd like to do over, don't we?" His refusal to answer follow-up questions got him slapped with a contempt of court order.

When asked if he would be revealing additional participants in an effort to gain the favorable view of the court, he smiled and said, "The accused who have testified in this court today represent all my former clients."

"All?" the judge prompted.

Rabbit held his breath. If he was going to implicate Helen or him, this was his moment.

"All," he confirmed. Then he swiveled in his chair to stare at Rabbit with that same sparkle in his eyes.

Rabbit exited the court that day feeling more relieved than he had in weeks. Sentencing wouldn't be done until the following day, but Eshek had been found guilty on all counts and the judge had made it clear that the law would fall hard on him.

"You feel like a drink?" PJ asked on the courthouse steps.

"Not tonight. All I want to do is take a shower and sleep for a year."

She hugged him. "It's over. You've earned the rest, honey."

Despite his assertion, however, Rabbit found he wasn't tired. He ate dinner in a little café near the Villa Borghese, walked around the streets, dodged mopeds. He didn't feel like company, but he didn't want to be alone, either.

Finally, he returned to his hotel around midnight.

"Mi scusi, dottore. Una donna ti aspetta nel bar dell'hotel."

"Grazie," Rabbit replied. *A woman at the bar? What is PJ doing here at this hour?*

He went into the little cocktail lounge off the lobby where a pianist was playing "Beyond the Sea" to a seemingly empty room. The bartender pointed to a couple of wingback chairs facing the window.

Rabbit dropped onto the opposite settee as the words "Hey PJ" died on his lips.

"Hi, handsome."

Before he knew what he was doing, Rabbit was on his feet and so was she and they were clinging to each other like life preservers.

"Thank you," she whispered into the side of his neck.

"I'm sorry. I'm so sorry."

She pulled away and laughed, wiping away tears. "For what?"

"I left you. I abandoned you to work for them. I didn't know what else to do—"

She silenced him with a hand on his chest. "I forget this is new for you. I've had time to adjust."

"And your sister?"

She sniffed. "Olympia doesn't want to be saved. That's one thing I've come to realize. I'm done. I told her I was out as soon as they dropped me as a suspect."

Rabbit was speechless for a moment. Then something occurred to him. "What were you going to do if they didn't?"

"Have them send me back somewhere and not come back."

"Oh. Right."

She punched him lightly in the chest. "I would have told you where I was going. Anyway, it doesn't matter now. They dropped it."

"You know, if you're not going to meet me in remote destinations, you might consider letting me know, I don't know, your phone number. Or your last name."

"One step at a time, Boy Scout. One step at a time."

Eshek was sentenced to fifteen years for each instance of illegal time travel. Another twenty for the weapons of mass destruction charge.

Ten for racketeering. A total of 270 years. And that didn't include the time he was facing in China.

He never uttered a word of protest. He held his head high throughout the proceedings and nodded at the judge after the pronouncement was read.

He's going to die.

It hit Rabbit like a truck. He had that look of certainty and acceptance that the truly condemned wear. Rabbit's grandfather wore it during the last stages of his battle with emphysema. The battle was lost and Eshek was laying down his arms.

The court attendees were allowed to process out first, spilling onto the steps of the courthouse. A paddy wagon idled at the curb, waiting to take Eshek to the first of the maximum-security prisons where he would spend the rest of his life.

Cameras went off like machine guns.

Journalists shouted questions.

Eshek was coming down the stairs. Flanked by guards on both sides, the chains holding his wrists and ankles jingling against his orange jumpsuit.

He paused for one moment, looked around at the sky, the buildings, the people, smiling like an angel. Rabbit knew he would see that look for years to come after it was splashed on screens across the world.

Then he nodded to his guards and proceeded into the waiting wagon.

After a moment, the guards exited, closed the armored van door, and signaled the driver, who lurched the vehicle into motion down the Piazza dei Tribunali. At the northwest corner of the building, the car exited the turnaround and lapped back, heading for the Ponte Umberto Primo, the closest bridge across the Tiber.

The crowd lost interest before the van reached the bridge. Even PJ and Ian started talking to each other.

Rabbit didn't. He wasn't even sure why. He just couldn't take his eyes off it.

He was the first to see the van veer off course.

Instead of sharply turning onto the bridge, the van slowly swerved, rocking on its springs and cutting across the opposite lane of traffic amid a squall of horns.

Sonofabitch.

Rabbit was in motion, sprinting across the lawn that separated the palace from the cobbled street. He was ahead of the police, who shouted behind him.

He dodged through the snarl of honking cars to the side of the paddy wagon. It idled at an angle, one front tire up on the curb, the automatic transmission trying doggedly to push the bridge rail out of its path. A crowd was gathering.

Rabbit tried the side door, but it was locked, of course.

He ran to the front and saw exactly what he dreaded. A splash of crimson across the windshield and driver's side window.

The police were trying to get in, too, but none of them had a key. In the end, one of them had to painstakingly jimmy the passenger's side door lock.

When the door finally popped, the police tried to block the view of the onlookers as they opened the panel door. A hundred camera phones were aimed at the door when it slid open at last.

In the courtroom, Eshek had the look of a man who was taking his last breaths. With every fiber of his being, Rabbit expected to see the killer's body lying dead on the van floor, a self-inflicted bullet through his brain.

Instead, he saw a metal disk a few inches thick with a miniaturized control panel nearby.

Einar Eshek had escaped through time.

WASHINGTON, DC, USA

2019 CE

The machine's controls were cleared. Bastard used a damn USB stick to do it. He must have shot the driver before he executed the controls," Rabbit explained to Helen later.

"No witnesses," she said.

Rabbit shook his head. "He could have gone anywhere. They traced the machine down. Some tiny island nation built it for him using their one license. They just shot their chance of ever joining NATO."

The two of them were walking down the National Mall. Helen had traveled to DC to see him. They had a lot to discuss. Rabbit planned to show her some sights around the capital as an attractive background to some hard conversation. But first things first. Rabbit had been summoned to see the secretary this morning. He was mentally preparing for a royal chewing out for all the rule bending he'd done to make Jerusalem happen.

He and Helen walked into the "Castle" together, the Smithsonian administrative building where Martin Friedman, general secretary of the Institution, had his offices.

Rabbit paused. "Do you want to wait in the garden?"

"No, I'll come with you."

"Uh, okay." Until this week, Helen had been like a ghost in Rabbit's world. It was unsettling to have her walking next to him in these hallowed halls. Not bad, just unsettling.

She accompanied him all the way to Friedman's office and, when the door swung wide to greet them, through the door onto the Persian rug.

Rabbit looked at Helen, profoundly confused.

Friedman, all burly six foot two of him packed into a tweed suit, came around his desk, smiling at them.

PJ swiveled in the seat across from Friedman's desk. Nodded at Rabbit.

The secretary beamed.

"Ms. Fletcher!" he said and shook Helen's hand.

Rabbit's head was spinning.

"I see you two have already met," the secretary continued. "So, at the risk of being duplicative, let me introduce you again. Doctor Robert Ward, meet Ms. Helen Fletcher.

"Your new partner."

ACKNOWLEDGMENTS

Writing a series demands a skill set unique and different from working on a single book. I anticipated this, I suppose, but I got the specifics wrong. I thought the hardest part would be keeping track of all the moving parts in the narrative to avoid contradictory plot details. In fact, the real challenge was shifting gears between the various parts of the editorial process. In a single morning, I now make space for drafting one book, responding to edits on another, and engaging in marketing activities for a third. That I not only didn't mind the frequent shifts but actually enjoyed them, I credit to my many years working at Northwestern University, where my job requires me to jump between projects and committees on a roughly thirty-minute cadence. To my colleagues, friends, and mentors past and present from NU, I offer you my heartfelt thanks for the training. You're the best co-workers a fella could ever want. I will always be grateful for the support you showed me as I undertook this creative work. Thanks also to my wonderful team in the writing world: David Hale Smith and Naomi Eisenbeiss at InkWell and all the amazing folks at Minotaur/St. Martin's, especially Kelley Ragland, Michael Homler, Madeline Alsup, Hector DeJean, Sara Eslami, and Amy Carbo. I know these little stories of mine are a minor slice of your pie, but to me, you folks are the whole banquet.

Thank you to my family, who have been so supportive of this work and have generously listened to me rant about it (depending on my level of sleep and caffeination). At least now I have an outlet for these stories, which I hope makes me slightly less annoying at Thanksgiving.

Even the best work is cold comfort without friends to share it with, and I can happily say I have some of the best (sorry, everyone else). Justin and Lauren, Andy and Nicola, Jason, Daryl, Neil and Oksana, Scott, Betsy and David, Kent, Jacob, Harry and Steve, and many, many more. Thanks for making life more fun.

My kids are a constant source of fascination and inspiration to me. Mercurial, talented, beautiful Jo, it continually amazes me how one person can be so good at so many things. I only hope one day you'll be as confident in yourself as I have been in you since the day you were born. And August, little druidic spirit that you are, keep listening to the trees, keep asking if the flowers are happy. You see things none of the rest of us see. Don't ever be convinced to see less.

Tess. How can I begin to thank you for your bottomless support? You celebrated my successes big and small with more passion than I allowed myself. You gave me no quarter to wallow in my doubts or insecurities. You listened to endless passages from the man who can't resist reading aloud and mourned the loss of the passages that ended up on the cutting-room floor. Thank you for firmly nudging me into motion whenever I felt like quitting, for helping me see truths to which I was blind, and for encouraging me to be as big and loud and bright as I want to be. Through your belief, I learned to believe in myself.

You and me.

ABOUT THE AUTHOR

Jeremy Lawson

Andrew Ludington writes transportive adventure stories intended to make you forget your commute. He is the author of *Splinter Effect* and *Double Shadow*. He graduated from Kenyon College with a BA in English Literature and lives in Evanston, Illinois, where he moonlights as a technologist for Northwestern University.